# Emerald

Rev. Larry L. Hintz

*From the Iowa Gem Series*

This book is a work of fiction. Names, characters, places and incidents are either the product of the author's imagination or are used fictitiously, and any resemblance to actual persons, living or dead, events, or locales is entirely coincidental.



**ISBN:** 978-1-9803-9646-8

## The Iowa Gem Series

*Emerald*

*Diamond*

*Pearl*

*Sapphire*

*Agate*

*Onyx*

## DEDICATION

This book is dedicated to the people of my home town. To family, friends, classmates, teachers and everyone who made up the community in which I was raised. The memories and mores that were instilled in all of us and the blessings we experienced and didn't ever realize. May we never take that for granted!

# Chapter 1

*"There was so much blood. How could you lose so much blood and still live? Would she live?"* Jeff sat, head in hands, wondering what was happening. It seemed like she had been in surgery for hours. Was he going to have to face life as a single parent now?

The Fourth of July started with great anticipation of enjoying a day on the lake with friends. It was tradition. They would head out shortly before noon, enjoy sunbathing, talking, snacking, just being with one another. The relationship between the two couples was rock solid, had been for years.

Toward evening they came ashore to pick up the kids, have supper and then head back out to watch the fireworks while lazily floating on the water. That all happened, and it was a great evening. Tonight, their oldest even brought along a date for the first time. Seeing the two of them together, Jeff felt tremendously blessed because of the family he had. Looking at his babe he felt life couldn't get any better.

She was taken back a little when he came from behind and wrapped his arms around her, kissing her on the back of the neck. *"What was that for?"* she inquired.

*"Just wanted to let you know I love you very much,"* he whispered.

She leaned back slightly and felt the security of being loved. *"I love you too."*

The serenity came to an end as they were packing up and getting ready to head home. The boat was docked and while others were pitching in, packing up and getting ice chests and left overs off the pontoon, the girls headed for the restroom.

Minutes later three *"pops"* and then a fourth broke the calm of the evening. It wasn't fireworks and the direction from which they came was where the wives were. Jeff and his friend, Fred, look at one another and immediately take off to investigate.

The smell of gun powder is in the air and in the dim light they see a figure bending over someone on the ground. They are outside the restrooms. Getting closer they are relieved that the town cop was the one kneeling. The door to the restroom is slightly ajar and Jeff pushes it open to see his wife on the floor in a pool of blood.

Now he sits in the waiting room wondering what happened and why. Nothing was making sense. How could a day that started off so well end up this way?

# Part 1

# The Innocence of Youth

# Chapter 2

Fred Lindsay drives a John Deere mower, clipping the moist, dark, green grass outside the school windows. Proceeding over the sidewalks he leaves tire tracks indicating where he has been. No shrubs to mow around so the job goes rather quickly. He will be done before the final bell rings and students exit like freed prisoners. The smell of freshly cut grass ascends through the school windows. It is one of the more pleasant fragrances indicating that spring is in full swing with summer right on its tail.

Jeff and Bernie stand in a hallway, off to the side, eyes locked on one another. The hallway is dimly lit, suiting them fine in their time together. Stolen opportunities to be alone are taken whenever possible. It has always been that way. Communication between the two appears to be serious, but then again, they are just in high school. How serious could it be? What they talk about is anybody's guess. Other students don't even notice them. They have been a *"couple"* for the last four years, and they are a boring couple, at that. They are always together. Every sign points to the probability these two will get married someday, probably sooner than later. Right now, they just want to get through the last weeks of high school, eager to be part of the graduating class of 1971.

Bernie wears a green and white striped jumper, holding her books against her chest. She has always been attractive and could have dated a lot of guys throughout high school. But ever since their freshmen year, Jeff and Bernie have been together exclusively. She is smart, gets good grades, and is popular, but not as popular as she thinks. Somewhat athletic, this tall, 5'9", brunette carries herself well and is well proportioned. Looking at Bernie, you see a person who could go far in life. She could go into politics, be a senator or governor, become a doctor, lawyer or some other professional. But the current culture isn't encouraging that. There is a better chance of her staying right where she is, marrying Jeff, raising a family, being an excellent mother involved in community activities. Along with most of her classmates, she isn't thinking of anything more than that.

She instigated the relationship with Jeff. She saw Jeff as being *"the guy"* to date. That doesn't mean she didn't have feelings for him. She cared for him very much. Their relationship over the years has become very close. But he would give her the life she desired and deserved.

Jeff didn't mind. He liked the attention she gave and having someone as attractive as Bernie was exhilarating as well. And so, they were together for those four years. Jeff was popular all on his own. He had that kind of *"air"* about him. And one thing they had in common was that they were very focused. That helped in a variety of areas.

Jeff, the third of four children, has two older brothers who gave him a lot to live up to. Good-sized and heavily involved in sports, especially football, his brothers left their mark. One graduated high school before Jeff's freshman year. The other was a senior when Jeff started. While not as big as either brother, Jeff is still very good in sports. He is the quarterback for the football team and the captain. He inspires other players and does not have an arrogant bone in his body. The fact he was focused aided him greatly in any endeavor, but especially in sports. He was totally focused on practice and then on the games.

Jeff is an even six-foot and is not muscular per se. But he doesn't have any fat either. He is generally seen in tight jeans and a polo shirt. His short hair is a dirty brown combed down in front. He has never known a pimple, being one of those lucky individuals with a clear complexion.

His family owns the largest of the three grocery stores in town. They aren't rich, but comfortable. Jeff learned from early on what it meant to be in the grocery business. The whole family works in the store. Dad works behind the meat counter and mom is the cashier among many other things. Two checkout lines are used occasionally, but usually business isn't that rushed.

Family members bag groceries, restock shelves, sweep, and do whatever is needed. Jeff's great-grandfather opened the store years ago. It was the first grocery store in town. Actually, it was the first store, period. And it is patronized more than the other two grocery stores.

Jeff's dad has always been involved in the community. He has been on the town council, the school board and a member of the volunteer fire department. He was a good role model for his family.

Jeff's older brothers moved on after high school. They wanted to play pro-football. They were that big and almost that good. Neither of them made the pros. Jeff had no desire to leave town. His eye is on taking over the store just as his father did before him and his father before that. He likes this town, and this is where he wants to live and raise a family. Why go anywhere else!?! In his mind, Bernie is part of his future. Was it mentioned that he was *"focused"*?

# Chapter 3

As students fill the hallway the noise level rises. Lunch break ends and the pleasant aroma of spaghetti fades. Students head toward their lockers, getting books for the next class. Members of the student body come up from two stairwells: one to the west and one to the east. As it starts to get a little loud, the intimate conversation between Jeff and Bernie is interrupted, although neither seem to pay much attention to anyone else. They continue their focus on one another. They are a *"serious"* couple different from other couples walking down the hallway, smiling and talking to those they meet. That is not the case with Jeff and Bernie. It never has been.

One classmate in particular walks down the hall wearing a big smile and approaches the couple with no hesitation. *"Hey, we getting together tonight?"* Fred Kemp gets Jeff's attention. Almost in his face, he gives a friendly slap on the back. Bernie is irritated and doesn't hesitate to let it show, giving him *"the look."* Nothing new to Fred, he doesn't mind. At times, he gets in her face. He has been tight with Jeff a long time, since they were in first grade. He doesn't care much for Bernie and the feeling is mutual. They put up with one another.

Jeff doesn't mind the interruption. It reveals the discussion was not all that important. *"Sure, meet you at the pool hall at seven."* The pool hall was where all the guys met. Females—not allowed, literally.

*"I'll be there."* Fred heads down the hallway smiling, feeling good.

Fred and Jeff grew up together but are different as night and day. Fred is clumsy, shy, has acne and is overweight. He doesn't know the first thing about anything every other teenager seems to know. He is not involved in anything. Fred hasn't dated or gone to a single dance his whole time in high school. He was *"sweet"* on a couple of girls, but nothing materialized. He was relieved to approach his senior year. In fact, he feels pretty good about being a senior. It is really the first time he has ever felt good about anything in high school.

He has no great desire to get out of town or pursue some career. In fact, he doesn't know if he has the *"smarts"* to pursue any kind of career. Other classmates are talking about colleges and universities they might attend, where they might work and ultimately end up in life. Fred feels at a loss. His dad owns Kemp Oil Company in town and has been very successful. Fred has worked at the gas station the same way Jeff has worked at the grocery store. But Fred doesn't see himself in the oil business. He has had enough changing oil, pumping gas and fixing flats. He wants to do something else. What? He hasn't the foggiest.

Fred enjoys being Jeff's best friend. It makes him feel he is part of the *"in"* crowd. Jeff doesn't have any such feelings. He is just Jeff and that is good enough. Their friendship might seem strange to some, but they never give it any thought.

# *Chapter 4*

As Fred heads for class he meets Ginger Price and Anita Olson. They are doing what they always do, whispering to one another. They talk about something personal and then laugh, well, it is more of a mature giggle. You can tell it is personal because they cover their mouths while they talk, trying to withhold whatever is said from the ears of others. They have been friends for a long time. Fred has a *"thing"* for both. Fred has a *"thing"* for a lot of girls but never acts on those feelings. He is way too shy.

Ginger is not as tall as Bernie and her stature is more graceful and slender. She stays fit working on her dad's farm. In the summer she gets a rich tan walking through the bean fields pulling cockleburs and milkweeds. She looks good with her hair pulled back, wearing cutoffs and a tank top. But at school, she, like all the other females, is wearing a dress. That is the norm or at least a blouse and skirt. And while skirts are getting shorter, Ginger's is not—isn't the look she is going for. She is wearing a blue dress with buttons down the front. A thin white belt reveals a trim waist making the look complete. Her figure is modest but appealing.

She is a picture of purity and innocence and a little naïve. She doesn't know it, but she flirts a lot. With a wonderful sense of humor, she does a lot of touching when engaged in conversation with others, male or female. It is a habit she has. No one really minds, especially the guys. Ginger is popular around school and has steadily dated in the past. She might go out with the same guy for a while, but nothing serious has developed. She has a lot of girlfriends but is tight with Anita. You never have to wonder who is going to say something first when meeting Ginger.

Anita is the same height as Ginger but has more delicate features and appears taller. Her long, blonde hair combined with her short skirts demand a lot of attention and get it. Short skirts are in style; she wears them well. Today, Anita is wearing a sleeveless white blouse buttoned down the front along with a yellow and green plaid mini-skirt. Kind of daring apparel for some but on Anita it doesn't look risqué, it looks fashionable and appropriate.

Through high school, Anita dates a lot but never dates any one guy and is never in a *"couple"* situation. Rarely does she go out with the same guy twice—her choice. It doesn't surprise you to see her with someone new on a weekly basis. You wonder who she will be with this week or riding around with the next. And she doesn't seem to mind. Plenty of guys would like to date her on a regular basis but that never happens. She is very popular and a little mysterious. She is also very friendly when you get to know her—all part of her mystique.

One explanation might be, she is not necessarily easy to talk to, not like Ginger. Could be because she is so attractive and... a little shy. Her *"shyness"* could be taken as a snobbish attitude—some may have seen it that way. But all it would take was a simple, *"Hi,"* said in passing and you would realize she wasn't snobbish at all. Some thought she was the way she was because she was so ... eye-catching. Mysterious was definitely the word for her. You had to be the one to break the ice. But when it was broken, that is all it took.

For the last two years Anita has worked part-time at the drug store. It gives her spending money, not that she needs it. Her family is pretty well off. But she enjoys working and being around people. It has helped her come out of her shell in some ways. That is not why she took the job but was one of the *"plusses"* that came with it. When people came into the store she would have a smile that would melt your heart and make you think you were the most important person in the world—at least the guys felt that way.

Neither Anita nor Ginger are good friends with Bernie. Bernie has friends, but in her mind, being her friend is a privilege for ... that other person. She will talk with Anita and Ginger when it is opportune for her to do so but is not really interested in doing that otherwise. They are ... well ... not competition, Bernie doesn't see anyone like that, but definitely rivals when it comes to popularity...at least in her mind.

Anita and Ginger recognize this and since they don't hold a high opinion of Bernie in the first place, it doesn't bother them much. They can take her or leave her. Most of the time they just ignore her. They have a different outlook on life and on other classmates. They are enjoying their *"teen"* years. Not one day goes to waste. They are on the phone quite a bit in the evening and the conversation is basically about *"boys."*

And as far as Jeff is concerned, well, they don't think much about him. He is alright, they assume, but nothing special. He is a nice guy. Why he has chosen Bernie is anybody's guess. But he has and if that is what he likes, more power to him. He has never been a topic of conversation with them or of any interest either.

# Chapter 5

Fred walks down the hallway heading toward class when Ginger gives him a look and a smile as they pass. It is a simple glance for her. She sees him coming and while listening to Anita, Ginger unintentionally flirts looking at Fred. She likes Fred for who he is. She has never spent much time talking to him, but she thinks he is okay and maybe a little ... cute.

It makes Fred's day that their eyes met. He feels good about himself for the next few minutes. For a second, he even thinks of himself as a *"lady's man"* ... yeah, for a second. Maybe Ginger would go out with him if he asked her. *"Was that why she looked at him?"* He had such thoughts and dreams. But going out with Ginger wouldn't happen. He doesn't have the confidence to talk to her let alone ask her out. He stands a little straighter now as he walks to class. He tucks in his shirt. It always seems to be coming out and sucks in his gut.

*"Has he asked you yet?"* Ginger gets close to Anita not wanting others to hear her question. The mower is still running outside and is competition for this intimate conversation.

*"Has 'who' asked me 'what,' yet?"* Anita fakes the need for clarification. She knows what Ginger is asking but plays dumb. She really wants to talk about the guy currently showing interest. She has an interest in him also, well, to begin with. She squints her eyes and bites her lower lip, with redness in her cheeks and a smile waiting for Ginger to continue.

*"Anita! You know who! Has Ben asked you to the prom yet?"*

There are no secrets between these two. They know the love interests of the other. The prom is coming up in just a few weeks. The *"couples"* are all preparing for it and have been for a while. But for those not in that category, a little tension and anxiety is experienced. Anita won't have any problem being asked but sometimes it takes a little while for someone to get up the nerve. That is the case with Ben.

*"Oh, him."* Anita tries to casually reply. *"No, but I think he will. He has been leading up to that, I think. He was waiting at my locker yesterday, well, I thought he was."* Their 5th period class is about to start. They sit together toward the front. "*Then, before I got there, he left."* She continued more quietly and looking around to see if anyone was listening, *"I don't know. He's nice but ... I don't know. Have you got a date yet?"* Anita changed the subject and put the ball in Ginger's court.

Ginger's eyes lit up. *"Ryan asked me. He wasn't my first choice, but he is kind of nice. You went out with him once, didn't you?"* Anita had gone out *"once"* with a lot of guys. Most didn't get a second shot. And this kind of frustrated both Anita and any possible suitors. They just didn't appeal to her.

*"Yeah, he was nice... I guess."* Ben walked in looking Anita's way. She pretended not to notice. As class started she crossed her legs and flipped her hair back on the side where she might want to look in Ben's direction. During class, Anita felt Ben was looking her way occasionally. But then again, maybe she just wanted that to be happening. It was hard not to look Anita's way. She had on that great skirt and wore white knee socks making her legs look enticing. The dynamics of young love can be interesting.

# Chapter 6

A crack of thunder woke Jeff from his latest dream about Bernie. They were together on a country road, listening to the radio and getting very involved in one another's anatomy when... ***BANG***—he woke up. He tried to get back to sleep to drum up that dream again, but it didn't work. Oh, well, that night he wouldn't have to dream about it. He would experience it firsthand. But first he had a whole agonizing day to endure.

Saturday started with skies filled with clouds carrying a deep blue hue, releasing thunder and lightning. A typical spring day. Most fields were planted and so the rain, if it wasn't a *"gulley washer,"* was readily accepted by seeds waiting to poke through the soil searching for the sun. It was the next step in having a good crop. The rain was predicted to stick around till 10:00 a.m. and then move on. It left a little early to the approval of those getting their vehicles prepped for the evening activities.

The Junior/Senior Prom was the last big event of the school year before graduation. Juniors raised money over the year selling magazines, sponsoring car washes, that kind of thing, to finance decorations and hire a band. The gym would be transformed into a magnificent ballroom. The same place that held cheering crowds became a place where romance was foremost. Dim lights provide the right ambiance for people milling around, mingling in hushed tones. It was a great evening but awkward for some, especially those without dates.

The juniors finished decorating the gym on Friday night. The next day helium filled balloons were brought in along with fresh flowers to bring color to the tables. Everything was ready for the recipients to arrive.

This was the first year one guy wore a tux. You would expect him to wear one if anyone was to be so attired. Clint Ashcroft was always a little bolder, a little more formal, a little *"classier."* He had a date, but his date was a girl from a different school, a different town. You expected that from Clint as well. Even though he was probably the most handsome guy at the prom, possibly the best-looking guy in school, he never dated anyone in his class or from the school. Strange! And none of the girls ever talked about him or drooled over him. Some things don't always make sense.

Fred walks into the gym looking for the guys with whom he will spend most of the night. Standing around the punch table, each is holding a glass. An assortment of shapes and sizes, they wear sports coats. They all have ties of course. They sit together for the meal and spend a lot of time looking at the single girls. Before the evening is over a few will pair up, but most won't. The majority that came without a date will leave the same way. Their evening will end riding around together, going to a drive-in and getting something to eat around 3:00 in the morning. You never get home early on prom night. And just for fun they might try to disturb those couples who find a cozy place somewhere out in the country to park.

Tonight, Fred spends a lot of time looking Ginger's way. Earlier he had himself talked in to asking Ginger to the prom. And she probably would have accepted. But he didn't know that. And then, the day he got up the courage, he saw her with her *now* date for the evening. And, of course, she was smiling. She was always smiling. He took that as a signal she was with the love of her life. Had he only known!

Ryan and Ginger enter the gym. Ryan feels pretty good having Ginger on his arm. He has been interested in her for most of the senior year but hasn't gotten close to her for one reason or another. Ginger is happy to be with him but doesn't have the same feelings he does. She is all smiles as they enter. She wears a light green formal, sleeveless with a high collar. Her hair is pinned up and she looks prim and proper—very attractive.

Entering the gym there is a photo-op. The door is decorated according to the theme and a photographer is set up to take your picture—great memento for the evening. The doorway is lit for that purpose but also to showoff what people are wearing—basically, what the formals look like. It is the *"red carpet"* of the day. Couples take advantage of the photos for scrapbook purposes. Some pictures make it into the town paper the following week.

Ryan and Ginger look for people they know to talk with before the program begins. They gravitate towards the punch table but then Ryan sees some of his friends and they move in that direction. Ginger is looking for Anita, but she hasn't arrived yet. Tonight, they won't be sitting together. Ryan and one of his friends have chosen the intimate table at which they will have their meal.

The prom has a tradition that goes with it. You don't want to be the first to enter the gym and appear anxious. You want to make an appearance, an entrance, if you will. Who makes up these rules, no one knows, but everyone seems to know the proper etiquette and what it means.

Bernie knows all about this. She knows how to make an entrance and plays it to the hilt. She always has. Jeff, on the other hand, doesn't have a clue. He is getting a little impatient waiting for Bernie to come down the steps. It is nothing new. He arrived at her place early enough and wasn't particularly happy waiting as long as she was making him wait. But then, this wasn't the first time. Bernie could be a control freak. Jeff knew the routine. He had been in her house dozens if not hundreds of times. This was typical Bernie.

# Chapter 7

Girls without dates are the first to find their seats. Students choose specific places beforehand. The guys are next. Once again, it just happens. Not much mingling between the *"singles"* present has yet to take place. That will happen later, if at all. Lights have dimmed to provide the proper setting to focus on *"love."* The prom is about to start. The spotlight on the door stays the same until all have arrived. Once everyone is seated the evening will begin with dinner served.

Tonight, the menu includes salad, Salisbury steak, mashed potatoes and green beans with cheesecake for dessert. Prepared by the mothers of those in the junior class, it will be served by specially chosen sophomores. It is quite an honor to be picked for this service. All servers are dressed in black and white. This is a formal affair, after all.

Ginger keeps looking for Anita but can't find her. Ryan escorts Ginger over to their table to sit with another couple. Her back is to the door. Hearing a little commotion, Ginger wonders if Anita and Ben have arrived, but, not yet.

Almost everyone is seated when Jeff and Bernie enter. Everyone gets a good look at this premier couple. Bernie enjoys the attention. She looks very attractive wearing an off-white gown, sleeves going just past her elbows with a generous neckline. She does look good, but not as good as she thinks. Still, she is the envy of many females present. Jeff's friends have always been jealous of Jeff's good fortune. All eyes are on this couple. *"Perfect,"* Bernie thinks. It is the way she had it planned. She tries to look sweet and innocent as they head towards their table.

Anita watches the clock. Ben should have been at her place ten minutes ago. *"What has happened?"* Surely, she isn't getting *"stood-up."* The idea would be ridiculous, unthinkable! Such a thing would never happen to Anita. Getting a date with Anita was hard enough the way it was. You didn't want to blow this opportunity. That is the way guys felt. And that was the way Ben, specifically, felt.

Anita wouldn't get stood-up, but car trouble would happen to Ben, of all nights! He washed and waxed his car, cleaned it up inside and out. And then it wouldn't start. Finally, he arrives, but not in his car, his parent's vehicle instead. It is not as clean or as polished, but it will have to do. He apologizes, and she acts like it was nothing. That was Anita.

Everyone else is seated when the very last couple arrives. Ben and Anita come through the doors, entering an exotic place of fantasy and romance. As they enter there is a noticeable gasp. Anita is a little embarrassed by what has happened. She didn't plan it this way but what she is wearing was the most elegant formal ever to grace this room.

She looked like a princess. Her formal is strapless with a sparkly silver material tight around the bodice and flowing blue silk loosely cascading to the floor. She wore a gold necklace and matching earrings. Stunning! Their picture is taken and this one will make the paper. Too bad it wouldn't be in color. Almost every eye is on her as Ben escorts her to their table.

Bernie watches every step they take. Wearing a smile on the outside, Bernie was very irritated on the inside. Anita stole the show. To Bernie, Anita had made the perfect entrance, and everyone was looking at her. Anita didn't have any such thoughts. If anything, Anita felt a little uncomfortable with all the attention!

As Ben and Anita walked by the table where Jeff and Bernie sat,

Bernie watched to see if Jeff noticed Anita. He didn't. Once again that quality of being focused came through. He was devoted to Bernie and their relationship.

As it would happen, Anita and Bernie sat where they could see one another. Anita felt at times that Bernie was giving off vibes that weren't expressing *"happy thoughts."* But it wasn't going to spoil Anita's time at her last prom. Anita's feelings were dead-on. While Bernie usually hadn't thought anything regarding Anita, this night that started to change.

The meal and program are finished, and the clean-up begins in preparation for the dance. Now is the time for couples to talk with other couples but it is more of a time when the females go to the lady's room or congregate in a corner and compliment one another on what they are wearing.

*"You look adorable!"* Ginger finally met up with Anita and whispered, *"You are quite the fox!"* And Ginger wasn't the only one feeling that way. Anita got that look from a wide variety of people along with any number of flattering remarks from other girls and even some chaperones.

*"I love your dress!"* Anita responded—and on and on they went talking about plans for the evening, where they might go, who they might be with and ultimately, how late they would stay out.

It was basically a great night for everyone. But as mentioned before tonight was the beginning of some very definitive negative feelings Bernie would have about Anita. And it wouldn't be long before those feelings would be reciprocated.

# Chapter 8

Clouds of dust ascend as tractors transport the recent harvest to the local elevator. Positioned over the grates, wagons are hoisted to unload the golden bushels and then return to the fields. It is a busy time for farmers. They have prepared for it making sure everything is in working order. Machines have been greased and repairs have been made. Farmers have been waiting for this time since early spring when they were eager to get into the fields. If the fall weather changes, if rain hampers them at all, farmers will even work with seldom used lights into the evening hours. Usually that doesn't happen. The days of harvesting started early this year.

Afternoons can be warm even in September but there are cool temps at night. A hard freeze is not unusual the latter part of September or early October. The trees are beautiful. A few green leaves still hang on, but most have already changed to beautiful shades of red, yellow and orange making the countryside alive with color before the dark, barren days of winter arrive and the white blanket covers the countryside giving the needed rest it longs for.

In some yards, mowers mulch the leaves but in others leaves are raked and burned, giving the lawn a clean appearance. Neighbors leaning on their rakes, watching leaves burn is a familiar sight. These guardians of fire wear light coats or sweaters and talk about politics, the weather and of course, the high school football team and the season they are having. It is the fall custom. The smell of burning leaves is pleasant and wafts through the neighborhoods.

Gardens look sad and bare. In the spring everything was fresh and new matching the hopes of fresh produce. The ground was tilled, and the straight rows were identified by the seed packets attached to twigs at the end of the row. Gardeners looked forward to carrots, radishes, peas and other items on the dinner table. Each was harvested when ready and enjoyed as long as they lasted. Sweet corn was popular. Days would be spent getting the corn off the cob and into small plastic bags to be frozen for *"fresh"* corn during the winter. But now, there isn't much left. Pumpkins reach their prime and are on their way to be carved into scary faces, but most everything else has died and been discarded.

Kids have been back in school and are used to their schedules. The jeans are more comfortable and the new supplies are not so new. Teachers and students have gotten to know each other. Teachers know who the trouble-makers are, and students know what teachers expect. The excitement of interaction in after-school activities is growing. Classmates enjoy the time spent outside of class, where the real social activity takes off!

The new television season just started and is a topic of conversation. *Rowan and Martin's Laugh-In* is still on and more daring than last year. Some phrases shock those not used to such dialogue. Television isn't what it used to be or close to what it will become. *The Brady Bunch* and *The Partridge Family* continue. *The New Dick Van Dyke Show* premiers. There are still just three basic networks. In this town, two of the three come in pretty clear. Cable hasn't been introduced.

The members of last year's graduating class have moved on. Jeff is working in the family business as planned. Bernie left for her first year of higher education with an understanding between the two. Marriage was in their future. They keep in contact and discover writing *"love letters"* can be fun. They even get a little daring in what they put down on paper. They have never done this before and so their creative writing skills stir feelings that have been in place for a while. Who knows what new activities might be realized!

Ginger was off to nursing school, something she has thought about for a long time. She had an aunt that was a nurse and wanted to follow in her footsteps. She was going to be joined by another classmate, Jennifer Schultz, but at the last minute, Jennifer changed careers and attends a different college, focused on teaching. Ginger still does what she planned. She is a little hesitant going without a friend but has always been interested in medicine.

Anita enrolled in a junior college, 30 miles away. She isn't sure what she wants to do, if anything. She lives at home, driving back and forth. She is kind of a *"loner."* She is her own person and feels comfortable with that reality although she wouldn't mind finding the right guy and planning a future together. Maybe she will find him in college! But it seems the guys in junior college are just as intimidated as those in high school were. And she appears to be just as shy.

And Fred, well Fred is growing out of his awkward puberty stage. He starts work at a plant in town and saves his money. His entry is at the grunt level. His job isn't very attractive but is generally where everyone starts that doesn't have special skills. He works at the wash tank. It is filled with solvent used to clean the inside of pipes involved in the construction of hydraulic cylinders. Fred doesn't mind that it is an introductory level job. At least he isn't pumping gas and changing oil. It is a job, a different kind of job. It is a paycheck. And after he puts in his eight hours, he is free. No studying. No pressure. Like a few other graduates, he sticks around town and just enjoys being there. Others looked up to him. And by *"others,"* it is those yet in high school. Fred seems to have it made as far as they are concerned.

Fred feels that way, too. And he spends time with all those peons yet in high school. Sometimes he misses some of his classmates from the past. But soon he will see them all as they come back for homecoming. And besides that, Jeff is always around. Now that Bernie is off to college, Jeff has a little more time to hang out with him. Fred enjoys that.

# *Chapter 9*

One of the places Jeff and Fred can be seen together quite regularly is the pool hall. They are even more regular than before. No *"Bernie"* taking up Jeff's time.

*"Hey, Fred, you got a date for homecoming?"* Jeff kidded knowing Fred never had a date for anything. They are shooting pool, playing a little 8-ball. Fred is ahead for a change. He only must sink 2 striped balls and then the 8-ball to win.

*"Yeah, I'm thinking of taking Bernie out."* Fred has his moments of kidding. But Bernie was not someone Fred even came close to desiring in that way. He was thinking about someone else. In goes one of the two remaining balls Fred has to sink.

*"Oh, really? Does she know that?"*

*"Only in her dreams!"* Fred misses the next shot.

*"Don't you mean, in YOURS?"*

Getting serious, Fred moves close to Jeff. There aren't many guys around, at least they aren't close. *"Hey, I've been thinking about asking Ginger out. What do you think?"* Fred chalks his cue as he talks.

*"Ginger, huh. Don't know. And you won't know unless you give her a try. You really thinking about it?"*

*"Yeah, maybe."* Fred is halfway serious and has almost talked himself into it. He gets his last ball in the corner pocket.

*"I say, 'Go for it!' Bout time you got some lovin'!"* Jeff was always an encourager. Fred takes his last shot trying to sink the 8-ball but scratches and loses the game.

Festivities for homecoming are beginning. Hardly any studying gets done the week before. Storefront windows are painted with pictures revealing how powerful the home team is. Floats are constructed on hayracks that otherwise served their usefulness for the year. A lot of chicken-wire and colorful napkins are used. In school, students vote for this year's Homecoming Queen. It was narrowed down to four senior sweethearts and Friday the final ballots get cast. There is a lot of excitement. The football team practices with greater intensity. Everyone wants the Homecoming Dance to be a victory dance.

# Chapter 10

*"You see anybody yet?"*

*"Nah, probably won't see many before the game tonight."*

*"You going to the dance?"*

*"Sure."*

*"You got a date?"*

*"I never have a date. I think I'll just wait to see who shows up."* And there you have one of those typical conversations during homecoming week.

Some alumni start arriving on Thursday night in time for the pep rally and the snake dance through downtown. Others will come in various times on Friday.

Jeff and Bernie are tight as ever. This weekend finds them together as if they never left one another's side. Jeff got off early to see Bernie who got into town Friday afternoon around 4:30. He hadn't been over to her house since she left in August. It felt good being there again. She didn't make him wait this time—met him at the door. This kiss was the beginning of many more this weekend.

After a few minutes together, they made their way to the football field right next to Bernie's house. Bernie took the lead dragging Jeff around as she talks to her girlfriends. He doesn't mind. He is with her. It has been almost two months of separation, something completely new for these two. They have never been apart for such a lengthy amount of time.

Last year's Homecoming Queen, Ginger, is back to crown the new queen. Ginger loves being reunited with friends. And Fred plans to take advantage of the fact she is around. As of late, Fred has become more confident. His appearance has changed over the last 5 months and he stretches his wings a little. He's lost weight and his complexion has cleared up... somewhat. None of that mattered to Ginger but it mattered a lot to Fred. But his attempt to approach her fails. She gets swept away by friends and his plan goes awry. Well, it wasn't the first time.

*"Maybe next time."* Fred's backup plan is sticking with guys he spent most of his time with through high school. After the game they gravitate toward the pool hall, play a little pool and some cards. Later they drive around, seeing what everyone else is doing and who is parking and where. Going to the dance isn't even considered.

As in high school, Anita has plenty of requests to the homecoming dance. She doesn't accept any. She is going with some of her girlfriends. But, *maybe she'll see them there*! She comes to the dance and dances most of the night but also does a lot of talking.

A half hour into the dance, Ginger is surprised by a tap on her shoulder. *"Hey, how's school?"* Anita finally caught up with her. Ginger had all sorts of responsibilities earlier, so they didn't connect till now. These two had a lot of catching up to do. Writing between them wasn't a high priority. If anything, they might call one another but that didn't happen much either.

*"Anita!"* Ginger gives Anita a big hug. *"How are you doing?"* Without answering the question. Ignoring everyone else they get involved talking with one another and move to an area where the music isn't as loud.

*"I'm doing fine. Nothing has changed much. Have you met any*

*guys yet?"* raising her eyebrows just a little. Even though they hadn't communicated much they could pick up right where they left off.

*"I wish! Well, there are a couple."* Ginger blushes a little as she has had some interested in her but nothing serious... yet. Her *"flirting"* escapades continued into college. She is the same old Ginger and has been getting the same kind of results from the guys.

*"And, might I ask,"* Ginger comes back, *"who have you been seeing lately? Anybody in junior college that looks hot... or thinks you do!"* Ginger was sure that once Anita got out there, a new guy would sweep her off her feet. But nothing like that was happening. There were no prospects at all and to tell the truth, Anita wasn't all that excited about college.

# Chapter 11

Jeff arrives at Bernie's place on Saturday night. Her parents welcome him and there is a little talk about the game the previous night. *"It is good to see you again, Jeff. It has been a while."* Bernie's mom always liked Jeff. Over the last four years Jeff became very comfortable with Bernie's family. It wasn't unusual to see him over at the Becker house. He was a common fixture, seemed to almost be part of the family. Bernie's brother liked Jeff, but Bernie's sister *REALLY* liked him, had a huge crush.

*"Yeah, it has. Good to see you, too."* Jeff spends time chatting with Bernie's mom and continues when Bernie's dad walks in.

Bernie is back to her old habits, keeping him waiting as she prepares for this night together. But Jeff doesn't mind so much. He is just excited that she is back in town. Bernie enters the room ready for a night out. *"Ready to go?"* Jeff wastes no time. They head out the door. Seated in the car they are in an embrace that makes it look like they have been apart for years. But it is early, and they cool it for right now, heading out for a movie and pizza. Bernie sits so close, getting them both excited.

*"How is school going?"* Jeff is curious. He didn't even ask the question the night before. Not a whole lot of *"talking"* went on after the dance. It just felt good being back together. They couldn't get enough of each other. But now was the time to talk more. Passion has its limits.

Bernie didn't talk a lot about school, although she could have.

Even though she had only been there a couple of months, she had a date the very first weekend. She didn't look at it as such, more a time of *"getting to know"* someone new. Bernie was spreading her wings, getting a feel for college. She was still focused on Jeff and becoming his wife, working in the store and having his children. But being away at college, there were times her focus was not as distinct as Jeff's. She started to experience freedom she had never known. It took her by surprise and she played with it all she could. She liked that freedom. And some of the norms from her small-town experience were not so prevalent at college.

Before they went home they found one of their secluded places in the country and continued from where they left off earlier in the evening. In their passionate embrace Jeff could tell that Bernie had changed a little. She seemed more aggressive and not as inhibited. It didn't bother him. In fact, he enjoyed what was happening.

Bernie didn't notice she had changed. This was just a part of who she was. She had a new life, a new life-style. And Jeff was reaping the rewards. At least, he was for now. The night ended too quickly but not without the realization between the two that they were very much in love.

# Chapter 12

Homecoming is a time for reconnecting, but for those in college, when it is over it is back to the books. Bernie returned and to her surprise, it wasn't that difficult leaving Jeff. She spent a lot of time with him and the last night was exceptional, but now it was back to her new surroundings. She would return home for Thanksgiving and Christmas, of course. And Jeff would anticipate that time as well.

Jeff felt the same way about Bernie's leaving, but couldn't figure out why. Had they become so comfortable with one another that this separation was something they could comfortably handle? Was this the new normal for them? Or, was something else going on? Neither knew the other had these thoughts. From the outside, there was no indication anything had changed, but something was brewing.

Ginger is on her way back to nursing school. She has had fun with her friends, especially Anita. The two had always been close and probably would be that way ... forever. Ginger noticed Fred and how much he changed. His physical appearance was quite different. And there was a moment she sensed he was trying to make contact with her. She was hoping he would be at the dance but that didn't happen. If only Fred knew what she was thinking. If only!

The holiday season approaches and the town does a great job decorating. Fred volunteers to help put up wreathes, bows and whatever other decorations the city has bought. Decorations are new this year. They look very festive, adding to the downtown shopping experience.

Fred loved seeing everyone at homecoming but was comfortable with their leaving. Fred felt it was time for them to leave. Well, all but Ginger, of course. He was very possessive of his hometown and he and Jeff, they were going to take care of everything. Their friendship was rock solid. This was their town. They weren't going anywhere. They were both going to be here for the duration.

During the holidays stores have high sales projections with merchandise geared to satisfy the crowds, if you can call them, *"crowds."* Most of the community patronizes local merchants but the city thirty miles east has enticing department stores offering so much more. Still the shop-keepers in this small-town attempt to be competitive.

Jeff is learning more and more about the grocery business. This is his first year in charge of selling Christmas trees. His dad gradually gives him more responsibility. The fact that Jeff can be very focused is a great asset. And so, Christmas trees are his *"baby."* And he is giving everything about them special attention.

All the grocery stores sell Christmas trees. The evergreens are lined up outside in front of the stores. Customers examine trees for color, height, fullness—that kind of thing. You never know what is important to whomever. Children are excited at the mere prospect of buying a tree. Thoughts proceed to setting it up and decorating it as early as possible. It can't happen soon enough for the youngsters. When Jeff sees someone is interested, he grabs his coat, most of the time, and makes his way out to facilitate a sale.

# Chapter 13

*"What do you think of this one?"* Jeff holds up a tree, spinning it around to be seen from every conceivable angle. The *"tree"* decision is never a quick one if the whole family is involved. Everyone has their opinion. Most of the time the kids aren't all that picky. It is much easier when just mom or dad, usually dad, picks one out. Dads are usually very easy to please whether the rest of the family is later happy or not.

Dad gives it a look. The kids think it is perfect. *"I think there is a bare spot over here,"* mom points out. Moms are great at picking out the imperfections. It is what they do. And the fact never changes that you want to always make mom happy.

*"Yeah, but it looks good otherwise."* Dads, on the other hand, can legitimize almost anything. *"That part can be towards the wall."*

But this won't stop the evaluation or the search for the important Christmas import. *"I thought we were going to put it in the front window."* Mom makes the comment not as an *"I thought we were going to do it,"* but more of a *"This is what we ARE going to do!"*

Dad remembers, *"Oh, that's right. Let's look at some others."* The search continues.

Jeff finds himself in many family discussions and decisions. Part of the job! His dad is glad he has turned this over to Jeff. It gives him more experience in public relations.

Finally, Jeff risks an assertive role, *"What do you think of this one?"* Jeff holds a tree up, shakes it so that the old, dry needles fall to the sidewalk.

*"Looks a little dry to me."* Mom sneers lifting her upper lip. *"It isn't tall enough either."*

Dad picks up one way at the end. *"This looks perfect."*

Jeff smiles and says, *"Looks good to me also."*

*"We'll take it."* Dad says before other comments can be made. It is chilly out! A decision has been made and the tree is tied to the top of the car anticipating clearing a place for it somewhere inside very soon.

The December days get colder—great for getting in the spirit. Not so good, health-wise. Jeff is in-and-out a lot. But he enjoys it. He likes helping people. And business is good! Actually, it is good every year at Christmas. People feel more generous and spend a little more than they probably would otherwise. But, hey, it is Christmas and it comes only once a year.

The Christmas season is a busy time for businesses as they take advantage of every day. But sometimes a person gets run down and before you know it, they are sick and in need of special attention. The body can only take so much abuse. It can take a lot but when it is time to shut down a little, it will let you know.

Thursday, Jeff gets a headache. A couple of aspirin make things better. Friday his stomach is giving him problems. Saturday, he doesn't get more than a few feet from the bathroom. By Monday morning, the very week of Christmas, wouldn't you know, he aches all over. Not good. He needs rest. But he also needs something else. The doctor gave him a prescription. Jeff would probably experience a different Christmas from what he anticipated.

# Chapter 14

Looks can be so deceiving. The sky reveals a bright blue canvass seeming to indicate warm temperatures and a time for short sleeves. But opening the door that cold, wintery blast confirms a comfy parka will be more suitable.

Anita is up early enjoying breakfast with mom and dad. She doesn't have to be at work until 9:30. Her dad leaves at 8:00 and could drop her off at the drug store, or, she could drive her own car. But, she decides to walk today. It is crisp and will put a little color in her cheeks. She enjoys the fresh air. She can get a ride home with dad after work.

The morning is semi-busy. Christmas music plays in the background and the store is decorated for Christmas thanks to Anita who wanted to make the work place more festive. The owner didn't mind, actually appreciated the effort. Most had already done their shopping, but the drug store did have some last-minute items some might select, you know, stocking stuffers, that kind of thing.

People outside are not strolling. They are walking very carefully, watching out for ice but also at a brisk pace with hands in pockets or wearing gloves. The wind has picked up just a little, not much. But it hasn't gotten above freezing yet. Anita sees a customer come in but can't identify who the bundled-up creature is.

*"Burr, I think it's getting colder out."* She takes off her gloves and scarf as she enters. The week of Christmas sees a lot of activity in all the stores. It isn't until Christmas Eve that it slows down.

Once unmasked Anita recognizes her. *"Good morning, how are you doing today?"* Anita smiles from behind the counter. Anita wears a blue turtle-neck sweater hiding behind her usual white lab coat. She looks professional but also very attractive with perfect bangs and a little blue eye-shadow with those enticing, squinting eyes.

*"I'm doing great but it sure is chilly!"* Jeff's mom, Bonnie, walks toward the counter. *"How are you doing, Anita?"* You never get right down to business. There is always an exchange of pleasantries. There are a few other customers shopping but no one needs help and so the conversation continues.

*"Just fine, thanks. Are you ready for Christmas?"* That is always a good conversation starter and may even lead to a sale.

*"Pretty much, but I've got other things on my mind."*

*"Really? How can I help?"*

*"Um ... got a prescription that needs to be filled. My boy is a little under the weather."* Bonnie looks a little sad.

*"Jeff's sick?"* Anita expresses concern like she would for anybody. Nothing special.

*"Came down with something. Worst time of the year for this to happen. I guess he just pushed himself too hard. Or, maybe it was something he caught from one of the customers."*

*"Hope it isn't serious."*

*"I don't think it is, but just to be on the safe side, could we get this filled?"* Bonnie was always impressed with Anita, thought she was quite attractive and very nice. Bonnie had been classmates with Anita's mother, Clara, in high school. The two were quite close at one time. They still would be, but it just didn't happen for one reason or another. Bonnie wished at times that Anita and Jeff would *"connect"* but Jeff was always with Bernie. Mothers always have ideas.

The drug store has a pharmacy. The pharmacist, Jeb Blunt, is elderly. He has owned the store for years. He knows everyone in town and what each person needs on a regular basis. In some cases, it is embarrassing for people to get this or that prescription filled. But Jeb, he just smiles and keeps everything confidential. The whole drug store smells like … medicine.

Bonnie handed the prescription to Anita.

*"Well, Mr. Blunt is at lunch right now. He probably could get it filled by um… 2:00 this afternoon."* Anita tried to figure out how much time it would take. *"That soon enough?"*

*"Oh, sure, thanks, dear. I'll be back then."* Bonnie heads for the door.

# Chapter 15

Before Bonnie leaves, Anita comes out from behind the counter. *"Say, ... um."* Bonnie stops and turns around. Anita gets close and looks around hoping no one else will hear. *"Do you know of any job openings in town?"*

Bonnie gives a *"thinking"* look for a moment. *"Hmm, can't say that I do, dear. Why do you ask? You know someone looking for a job?"*

*"Well, it isn't public knowledge yet,"* Anita leaned in a little closer, *"but Mr. Blunt is selling the store at the end of the year and if it all goes through, the new owner won't be needing me. I would like to still work somewhere... and preferably here in town if I can."*

Jeb lost his wife ten years earlier and his only son and family live in southern California. Jeb decided to sell the business and move to that warmer climate. He visited several times and enjoyed the wonderful weather. He didn't care for the price of housing but liked the climate. He had experienced enough snow and ice for one lifetime.

*"Well, dear, I don't know of anything right now, but I will keep my eyes open."* Bonnie smiles but also gives a sympathetic look touching Anita's arm.

*"Thanks! I'd appreciate it. Merry Christmas!"*

*"Merry Christmas to you as well!"*

Everyone comes home for Christmas. Just the right amount of

snow falls giving the ground that white blanket everyone longs to see. The temperature cooperated. It feels good getting into the house, sitting around the tree and getting that great scent provided by the evergreen. Ah, the heat from the furnace warms you up. Fireplaces are rare in town, but if you had one, it was nice both to hear and watch the crackling fire.

Neighborhoods are colorfully decorated. Most homes had outside decorations up right after Thanksgiving. Sometimes houses were outlined with lights. Trees were set up in picture windows to share the joy of the season with those passing by. Shrubbery adorned with blue lights on white snow gives a look of tranquility, just what the season is meant to inspire. Most of the time the decorations were simple, and you might even say, *"Tasteful."* Close to Christmas an evening drive through neighborhoods would get you in the mood.

It was also common to hear carolers make their way through the streets. Some choirs made a practice of walking down sidewalks singing cherished favorites. There were times when they would get invited in to homes for hot chocolate or eggnog along with Christmas candy and/or cookies.

Every church has their own nativity scene. There seemed to be competition between congregations as to which one is best. Each was lit up at night, of course. Some were made of plastic, three dimensional and life-sized. Others were the old style but still looking very nice. The congregation on the highway had a live nativity on selected weekends. One church had a huge star attached to its bell tower. From a distance it appeared to be floating in the night sky waiting for Magi in the area to follow. The countryside looked peaceful. Everything seemed perfect. Well, almost everything.

Jeff continued to hang on to whatever he had, was sick most of the holiday season. He didn't do any caroling. He didn't even get to enjoy the cookies or the candy. He did appreciate the bed however. He and Bernie didn't spend much time together. This kind of perturbed

Bernie, but ... what can you do? When you are sick, you are sick.

And then, as quickly as it came, Christmas was over, and the town got back to normal. It was announced that the drug store was sold and would be under new ownership and management. Townspeople were encouraged to support the new owner and his family, which, of course, they would.

But Anita was out of a job. There were no negative feelings. It was just business. She thought she might have to look out of town for work and had submitted several applications, but her heart wasn't in it. She wanted to stay in town.

# Chapter 16

A new job did present itself shortly after the turning of the calendar. The town got back to normal after Christmas, but Jeff didn't. And Bonnie now needed to take on many of Jeff's responsibilities, and, putting it bluntly, they were short-handed. After a family discussion a decision was made.

Bonnie called Anita's house the first Monday in January. Anita, still in her nice warm pink pajamas hidden under a very bulky beige robe, was drinking coffee and chatting with her mom. She wasn't even thinking about getting dressed and going outside. She was a little depressed not having a job or any prospects. Then the phone rang. *"Anita, this is Bonnie Emerald. How are you doing?"*

*"Oh, just fine, how are you? Did you have a good Christmas?"*

*"Oh, my, yes, it was great. You?"*

*"One of the best."*

*"That's nice."* Time to get down to the reason for the call. *"Say, are you still looking for work?"*

*"Yes, and it isn't looking good. No one is hiring right now. Have you heard anything?"* Anita thinks that maybe an opportunity has opened somewhere in town.

*"Well, as a matter of fact, dear, we need some help. Jeff is still under the weather. Would you be interested in working here?*

If Bonnie could see the expression on Anita's face she would have known the answer immediately. Anita looked at her mom with a look of surprise and excitement. Her eyes lit up as the phone conversation continued. When she hung up she told her mom everything and then phoned her dad to repeat the whole story.

# Chapter 17

*"Daddy, guess what?"* Anita was quick to give the answer before her father could say anything. *"I got a new job."*

*"Really, where?"* Harold Olson always had time for his precious Anita. And he was always the first person she talked to about anything new in her life. Well, almost anything new and almost the very first person.

*"I'll be working just two doors down from you."*

*"At the barber shop?"*

*"No, the other direction!"*

*"Oh ... uh... at the grocery store?"* It took a while to register.

*"Yeah, they need some help. I guess Jeff is sick. So, they asked me! It might only be for a while, but you never know."*

*"They couldn't have made a better choice!"*

There was no question in Anita's mind. She jumped at the opportunity. College was boring, and she was getting tired of the drive back and forth. She quit after the first semester, leaving plenty of time for a full-time job. It seemed perfect. And she was a natural. Her time at the drug store gave her experience in being friendly and helpful to customers. Working the cash register was a breeze. She interacted with more people, chatting with customers she was ringing up. In her mind, hiring her was the best decision Bonnie and her husband could have made. They wouldn't be sorry.

Making a good impression presenting herself was very important to Anita. She was a great asset. Customers appreciated what she added to their shopping experience. She made quite an impact on the grocery store business as 1972 began.

Mid-January, Jeff finally started to feel better. Whatever he had threw him for a loop. He was anxious to get back to work. But with Jeff's return, Anita wondered if her job would be in jeopardy. Would she be needed anymore? Would they want her? She thought she had done a good job. She knew Jeff but didn't know him all that well. Would they get along if she stayed on?

Anita's involvement in the store went beyond what was expected. She pitched in whenever there was a task giving her personal touch to each endeavor. She did more than she got paid for and felt good with each contribution.

Still, with Jeff's return, all kinds of questions cluttered her mind. Her worries could be dismissed. She had become a fixture and there was never a thought of letting her go. She was good at what she did, and they were going to keep her on. How did they get along without her before?

Spending time with someone else enables you to get to know them in ways you never thought. After a few weeks back at work a relationship developed between Jeff and Anita. They had known each other all their lives, but then again, they didn't *really* know each other. Jeff spent most of the last four years with Bernie. Anita, along with most of the girls didn't know what Jeff was actually like. And so, Anita and Jeff were indeed getting to know one another for the first time.

It was easy for this to happen. Just working together can do it. Experiences shared also brings people closer together, memories are produced.

*"Remember the time that display was knocked over and every jar broke? Took forever to clean up! The smell was horrible."*

*"Yeah. And remember when little Jerry Cooper got sick and threw up on all the peaches that were just delivered? Yuck!"*

Jeff and Anita developed a *"professional"* relationship during the first few months of the year. They didn't realize it, of course, but when Bernie came home for the summer, she noticed it immediately. Something was happening. Jeff and Anita had become pretty *"chummy"* in her eyes and Bernie didn't like it. Bernie liked to be in control and this was a sign that she wasn't.

# Chapter 18

Once again, it was all very professional, of course. But a bond between Jeff and Anita had formed. When Bernie found out about it she wanted it all to come to an end ... yesterday. She was suspicious. Her guy was being drawn to another woman, an attractive one at that... *if you liked that type!* The relationship between Bernie and Anita was never positive. Bernie never forgot the prom incident. Bernie knew without a doubt that Anita had planned it. Bernie saw Anita as stuck-up, arrogant, egotistical and conceited.

It started Bernie's first day back from school. The family car was stuffed. Her parents brought her back the day before and she spent part of the morning unpacking. Needing a break, she decided it was time for a little romance. Even though it was the middle of the day, she and Jeff always found a little time for *"lovin'"* even at the store. Entering the store, there was Anita. This was the first time she became aware of Anita's employment. The look on her face made it apparent she was caught completely off guard.

Anita was ringing up Vera Plummer when Bernie entered. Anita welcomed everyone with a great big smile as they walked in. Bernie was no exception, but it started to fade just a smidgeon. Bernie's smile and response were almost identical.

*"How long has* ***she*** *been working here?"* Bernie didn't hesitate to bring up the subject. Jeff could tell she was kind of irritated by their newest employee although she wasn't all that *"new"* anymore. Jeff was working in the back room and glad to see Bernie. He dismissed what he was doing to wrap his arms around her and was about to engage in a

kiss when Bernie made the comment, looking towards the front of the store.

It took him by surprise, *"Who, Anita?"* He gave a questioning look. *"Oh, let's see... she started sometime in ... January... I think. Mom and dad hired her while I was sick. We needed some extra help."* And with that he expected the kiss would take place and starts to pull Bernie close enjoying his arms around her waist. But ... not just yet.

*"Okay, why is she* ***still*** *working?"* Bernie was not letting this go. She kept looking up front. She was sending daggers Anita's way. Anita had no idea this was happening and didn't have the slightest interest in Jeff even though they had gotten to know one another. They just worked together. That is all Anita thought. Jeff felt the same way... totally!

Giving a frustrated look and realizing the time of subdued passion was not going to take place Jeff went on, *"Well, she worked out so well, they decided to keep her on. Gives mom a chance to relax and stay at home some days too."* Jeff really didn't give Anita a second look. And so, he wondered, *"Why all the questions?"* Jeff was confused, *"That a problem?"*

*"I guess not."* At this point Bernie *seemed* convinced Jeff had no interest in Anita and she started a little smile, proceeding to engage in what Jeff had in mind all along. Jeff pulled her as close as he could. Her hands were around his neck as she enjoyed his hands massaging her back and longing for a more intimate time.

Bernie accepted the answer, but it didn't change her outlook. On the other hand, Bernie was involved in things Jeff might question. Bernie attracted her share of guys at college. And there was one in particular she kept company with, Kent Griffin. In fact, she had gone on several dates with him.

Kent was a fourth-year student going to school part-time, had his own apartment. He had Bernie over for dinner several times. And with just the two of them in the apartment there were instances when it got a little heated on the couch. Seeing Jeff and Anita interact as they did, as innocent as it was, Bernie was sure more was going on than either would admit. Could be she felt that way because of her own *"minor"* betrayals? That was Bernie!

As Bernie walked out of the store she ignored Anita who was busy with a customer. Anita saw her leave and while she had no designs on Jeff she wondered what he ever saw in Bernie. A lot of her female classmates felt that way. And many of them had felt the sting of Bernie's meanness over the years. *"Oh, well,"* Anita thought, *"It is his life."*

Then again, she also wondered what it would be like when Jeff and Bernie got married. It was no secret they planned to get hitched at some time. She would worry about that later, if at all. She would probably be married and gone by that time anyway.

# Chapter 19

The freedom summer vacation brings leaves kids unprepared with what to do with their lives. Kids ride their bikes around town with the sound of a flapping noise—a playing card hits the spokes providing a *"cool"* sound. Older kids earn money walking bean fields, pulling weeds. When hay is baled you are always available to go anywhere at any time stretching your muscles making sure bales are stacked properly. There is a fair share of *"nothing"* that also happens during the summer except hanging out with friends.

The summer of 1972 was interesting. Jeff and Bernie continued where they left off. Their romance remained intact along with future plans, but Bernie had her ever-watchful eye on Anita. Then again.... close to the Fourth of July Bernie left for the weekend. She met up with Kent at the nearby lake. She didn't think of it as cheating on Jeff, just meeting up with a college friend. The fact that she didn't mention it to anyone ... well, others really didn't need to know. No one would know about her little rendezvous, except for the fact that Fred and Paul Kemp were there fishing.

Fred chews on a weed he just pulled, looking a little like Tom Sawyer. He had his lucky fishing hat down low shading his eyes, yet high enough he could see what was going on. Not much was happening as he was waiting for some action on his line. Not many people out on the lake. A good time to fish. He looks over at an empty dock and notices a car pull in. He doesn't recognize it but notices who is getting out, at least one of the people. *"Hey, Paul, isn't that Bernie over there."* Paul is almost sleeping. The day hasn't been too productive. He enjoys just being there. Fishing wasn't a high priority with him.

Paul looks up squinting his eyes to get a better look. *"Yeah, I think it is. But who's she with? That doesn't look like Jeff."* They both stare for a minute. They think it is Bernie. It is her form. It is her walk from what they can tell. But they have no idea who the other person is.

Fred concludes, *"Well, it probably isn't Bernie then."* And Fred starts to get in a resting position again. *"Throw me a beer."*

*"You got it."*

People look at life in different ways as time passes. Some see it in milestones. Certain ages mean certain things from getting your driver's license to being able to legally drink alcohol—every stage can be important. In college you look at what year you are in, accumulated hours and how many classes to take before graduation, get that degree and finally be out making money instead of spending it on education.

At a job, you look at promotions or pay raises. Fred looked at his life this way. He wasn't washing pipes anymore. The solvent tank was history. It was now a place for some other *"grunt."* He had advanced. Okay, it wasn't a huge advance, but it did mean a pay raise and new responsibilities. He was upwardly mobile, moving up the ladder. He liked his new status. He liked working at the plant and really got into it. He liked the people he worked with and the job they were doing together, truly a company guy.

He even moved out and now lived on his own in a small, one-bedroom house on a corner lot not far from the plant. He was the envy of his friends. Fred had more friends than he realized. Everyone wanted to help him fill his new home with the necessities needed. An old barn on a deserted farm place was used as a showroom for used furniture. Fred bought some nice stuff here, in his estimation. A fridge, an electric stove, dining room table and some living room furniture—all used stuff except for the couch. The whole layout was very welcoming. His place was where his friends would gather. He felt good about that. Friends were impressed.

They all helped when it came to getting groceries for the first time. Fred and three of his buddies enter Jeff's store, get a cart and go down every aisle. Items were thrown into the cart left and right. A lot of things are needed just starting out. Fred was surprised how fast the cart filled. Of course, Fred would have to pay for it all. The guys made quite a commotion in their shopping spree. Anita wondered what in the world was going on. She would hear some quiet talk and then outrageous laughter. *"They must be having fun."*

Arriving at the cash register Anita was all smiles, ready to ring it up. They enjoyed watching her, but Fred was a little embarrassed when some of the things purchased didn't represent the most sophisticated kind of item.

Anita smiled through it all knowing there were four pairs of eyes assessing her every move. *"Heard you are living on your own."* Anita kept up on things in town and did the expected small talk.

Fred always had a huge crush on Anita and took the opportunity to pursue something with this comment. *"Yeah, just moved in the other day. Getting some of the necessities taken care of. Might have a little get-together when I get settled."* Fred was feeling good about his conversation abilities.

Anita looked up, *"Well, if you do, let me know. I would be glad to come."* She smiled and rang up the last items.

# Chapter 20

Each of Fred's band took a bag as they left the store. *"Whoa! Did you hear that? Anita Olson wants to come to your house for a party. We got to get this planned and I mean right now!"* Fred was excited about what Anita said as well. He began to think he might have a chance with this beauty. It made Fred's day and the whole group thought about little else the rest of the day.

But the party never happened, and the thought of Anita was drowned out by the thought of someone else. Over the summer things had changed for Fred. Ginger started to pay more attention to him—he liked that. She was back on the farm getting that superb tan. In the evenings she drove into town and quite often stopped by Fred's to see what he was up to. No one ever paid so much attention to Fred. And Fred was beside himself, enjoying it. Oh, Ginger used to flirt with Fred in high school, but she flirted with everybody. But now *"everybody"* wasn't around. It was just Fred and Ginger. And Fred looked forward to seeing her car pull up. She even visited him at his place once or twice. They sat in his living room and talked with the television on. He sat in a chair while she on the couch. It wasn't the way he would have wanted but ... Fred still was a little shy.

This all started the first part of June. By the end of June, Fred was determined to take the big step and ask Ginger out. To his surprise, she accepted! His plans for the evening included a movie, dinner and then some cruising so everyone would notice he was with ... Ginger! When he told his friends about his success he got his share of razzing about what the night would be like when he brought Ginger back to his *"love nest."* It would be a lie to say Fred didn't think about that, but it would all just remain in his thoughts.

Things went pretty much as planned. They saw the movie but didn't go out to eat. Neither were all that hungry. They cruised. She sat close to him. He had his arm on the car seat but never around her. For Fred that would have been a huge step. Other cars stopped to talk, and everyone was surprised Ginger was sitting next to Fred? Fred was happy and thought this might be the beginning of one fantastic relationship. At the end of the evening he didn't make the move to kiss her goodnight and felt bad after that. Consequently, that would be their only date that summer although had he asked her again, she would have readily gone. He didn't know that.

Summer months go so quickly. You don't accomplish all the things you want to before it is time to think about going back to school. Plans have to be made in the midst of your relaxing. The fall of the year approaches even as the summer still hangs on. August can be a boring month.

Back at college, Kent came to help Bernie move in. She had a car her second year and loved the freedom. It wasn't new, but it was *"wheels"* and she enjoyed her ability to go and do whatever she wanted, when she wanted. But she was even happier with the fact that she and Kent were back together. She didn't feel guilty about him helping her. In her mind she had a guy at home and had a friend, albeit close friend, at college.

And she wasn't that sure about Jeff anymore. She hated the fact Anita worked in the store. She always thought that *SHE* would be working the cash register. She thought Anita was one big flirt out to steal Jeff. She thought to herself, *"Anita isn't fooling anybody trying to look sweet and innocent. She is so disgusting and manipulative!"* Who knows whether Bernie's personality was starting to show through in her actions and general demeanor? Changes were happening though. A little bit here and a little bit there, things weren't quite right.

# *Chapter 21*

Letters went back and forth between Jeff and Bernie and sometimes they got a little snippy from Bernie's end. There were times Jeff felt he had enough and let it be known as well. That can happen with letters. When it comes to *love-letters*, it is easy to read something into them regardless of whether it was intended or not. Most of the time it is okay, sometimes it is not. Jeff and Bernie's relationship was going through a turbulent time.

Bernie was changing her whole second year. She got more involved with Kent and it had an impact on her relationship with Jeff. Jeff knew nothing about Bernie's college escapades. By the spring of 1973 the Bernie/Jeff relationship was on the rocks. Both knew it. Bernie knew why, where Jeff was still in the dark.

The *"ever-focused"* Jeff thought he would take care of everything and get their love life back on track by surprising Bernie with a personal visit. He would get things back to the way they used to be. He drove up on Friday intending to take her to dinner. He checked everything out. One of his brothers had gone to school there, so Jeff knew the area. He made reservations at a very nice restaurant. He didn't share any details but told Bernie not to plan anything for that night. He had a surprise in store. She thought he was just going to phone and talk for a while. He did that a lot at first. She had no idea he was planning to see her. He had never done that before... ever!

He pulls onto campus, excited about what the night will be like. He has no trouble finding her dorm. He's got on a coat and tie as he heads for her room. *"Should he have gotten flowers?"* Too late now.

Not that important. Just being together is the important thing. At 7:00 he knocks on her door. She answers wearing an extremely tight, little, black dress leaving little to the imagination. Sleeveless, it came down to just above the knee with a slit in the back. Very low cut, revealing a sinful amount of cleavage. Seeing her like this Jeff immediately got excited! *"This was going to be better than he thought... at first!"*

*"Well, hello ... Jeff? What in the world are you doing here?"* He could tell Bernie was very surprised.

At this response, Jeff looked a little startled. *"Wow! You look good! Remember, I told you to leave tonight open. Uh, how did you know we...?"* And then, then he realized Bernie was not dressed up for him. It was obvious she had other plans. *"What's going on?"* Jeff had a confused look in his eyes.

Before Bernie could answer, Kent popped in. He was just a few feet behind Jeff. *"Hi, babe! Ready to go? Wow! You look sensational!"* Kent got between Jeff and Bernie and kissed her on the lips patting Jeff on the shoulder and moving into the room with a package and a bouquet of assorted flowers.

Jeff looked at Kent and then at Bernie, not saying a word. She could tell he was stunned and shocked. He just turned and walked away. He looked like a puppy-dog that had been hit with a rolled-up newspaper. Her first instinct was to explain. For a moment she felt bad about what happened. But that feeling didn't last.

*"Jeff,"* she called out. But he just kept walking. There was nothing she could say.

Kent innocently asked, *"Who was that?"* Bernie never told him about Jeff.

Rejected, betrayed and disheartened, Jeff got in his car. He just sat there at first, looking out the window resting his chin on his fist. After a while he put his face in his hands and cried. He couldn't believe it. He just couldn't believe it. He went through all kinds of emotions. He was angry. He was confused. He replayed it through his mind dozens of times. He didn't know what to think. And then he started driving. He just wanted to get away from there. Getting to the city limits around midnight, he wasn't going home yet. Instead he went to the pool hall.

*"Hey, man, you look terrible. What happened?"* Fred saw his pal walk in. Jeff had loosened his tie and was looking a little sloppy.

*"Not a good night, Fred, not a good night at all. I need some beer."*

*"I'll see if Hank will get us some. Feel like talking?"*

*"Yeah, I feel like talking ... and drinking. Better get at least a couple of six packs."*

# Chapter 22

Bernie handled things differently. After the initial shock of Jeff knocking at the door, she was going to explain what was happening. She was good at explaining. There was an explanation for anything and everything. And then Kent came... and Jeff left.

In her mind, she would explain everything to Jeff ... later. She would make something up. Kent grabbed Bernie around the waist and gave her a tender kiss. She put her arms around his neck and they stood there together for a few minutes. *"Well, what do you think of my new outfit?"* Bernie pushed him away, so he could see the complete package.

Kent gave her the once over that produced a huge smile and gave the tired old line, *"That is a beautiful dress! Can I talk you out of it?"* Tired and old, still Bernie hadn't heard it before and blushed when she did. The two went off and had a great evening. Dinner and a movie and then back to the apartment for some very heavy necking. Jeff wasn't even an afterthought at that point. Actually, Jeff wasn't thought about a whole lot since the beginning of the school year. The idea of Kent being her new guy was very much fixed in place, now more than ever.

In the spring of the year birds build their nests and eggs are laid. As time goes on you hear the chirping of baby birds with empty stomachs wanting to be fed. Springtime songs by birds almost go unnoticed unless you are thinking about them and intentionally listening for them. When you do, it seems they bring new life to the world.

Saturday morning Jeff gets to the store and looks *"like death warmed over,"* no *"new life"* present here as far as he is concerned. He's had about three hours sleep and it wasn't good sleep. It was the kind that comes when too much alcohol has been consumed. He is not in the best mood and doesn't care who knows it. Co-workers notice something is wrong and give him a wide berth. They know any kind of greeting is not going to be appreciated. It takes a while for him to get in the right frame of mind, but eventually, he does. And soon, even though he is tired and a little hung-over, he starts to deal with life and with people more positively.

Anita's night was very different. She had her second date, a rarity for her, with a guy she met from her brief college days, Parker Boone. They had a class together and he was dating someone else at the time. When they broke up, he hunted Anita down and they seemed to get along pretty well. Anita started to think she found someone she could spend her life with. She also had been out pretty late, but her mood was the complete opposite of Jeff's.

Anita walks through the door around 8:30. She started at 10:00 during the week, but Saturday's are different. It is busier and so she comes in earlier. Of course, she has a beautiful smile, induced a little from the previous evening's activities. The spring morning makes you feel wonderful. Life is great. Birds are serenading passersby. Life is fresh and new in Anita's mind.

*"Morning!"* Anita lights up any room she enters. She heads for the cash register with a different attitude from Jeff's. Her walk indicates she enjoys being a woman. She notices Jeff looks like he hasn't gotten much sleep. *"Short night?"* She says looking over at Jeff with kind of a smirk and putting her purse under the counter.

He says, *"I guess. Don't want to talk about it."* And he moves on.

Okay, whatever—she doesn't pursue it. She doesn't pry into his personal life. They don't have that kind of relationship. But Anita, she is ready for the day! She has a spring in her step to be sure. And as she walks down the aisle she has enough hip action to make anyone appreciate just watching. She is in a really good mood!

Around noon things slowed down and Anita breaks for lunch. Bonnie takes over at the register. On Saturdays, Anita has a practice of going over to the café for lunch. She did it to treat herself on the last workday of the week. She grabbed her purse and headed towards the door. At the last minute she decided to see if Jeff wanted to join her. She is feeling good. She might even share a little about the new love of her life if Jeff wants to listen. *"Hey, Jeff, I'm going to the café for lunch, want to join me?"* This was the first time she ever invited him to join her for lunch.

He didn't know why she did it. He was totally surprised. Who knows, it might help get him out of the *"dumps."* And so, for Jeff, the invitation was something magical. It was at that point Jeff took notice of Anita for the first time in a different way. Why? He doesn't know, doesn't have the foggiest idea. But he does.

It was like he had never seen her before or looked at her the way he was now. Her hair was pulled back into a ponytail and she wore a hot-pink tank top with a denim miniskirt, very attractive. She tilted her head as she offered the invitation. He thought she gave a sincere look of concern and that just added to the image of what was before him.

# Chapter 23

"Y*eah. Yeah, you know, maybe I will."* He thought to himself, *"I could use a little female companionship right now."* Jeff said, *"Sure. But only if I can buy. Deal?"*

*"Deal."* Anita smiled thinking she could help Jeff get in a better mood and maybe get his opinion on her new romance at the same time. All very innocent. Besides, the whole atmosphere at the store needed some uplifting. It was no fun working when others were down. It brought everyone down.

The café was crowded, and they had to wait a few minutes before a booth was available. But not very long. Saturdays were big days in town. A lot of shopping took place as people got ready for the weekend. When a booth opened, they immediately slid in. At the café they each ordered a hamburger basket: a hamburger with a generous portion of fries and pop—very popular on the menu. The total cost for the two comes to a little over $6.

*"How did your date with Bernie go last night?"* Anita asked, not knowing what the response would be. It was just small talk. And after he responded maybe she could share a little about her date.

*"Not good."* Jeff looked irritated. *"She looked good, but I found out it was not for me. Sometimes I feel like such a fool."* He pursed his lips. He was past the *"hurt"* stage, he was angry.

*"Why? What happened?"* Anita didn't know if he wanted to continue or not. Fortunately, right after she asked, the waitress came with their drinks. She also knew she wouldn't be talking about her date

with Parker any time soon.

*"She was ready to go out with another guy."* Jeff unwrapped his straw.

*"Are you sure?"* Anita did the same thing.

*"Yeah, I'm sure... I met him."*

*"Oh, oh!"* Anita raised her eyebrows and looked away taking a sip. Now she didn't know if she should ask any more questions or not. Maybe asking Jeff to join her for lunch was not such a good idea. It could be a long lunch break. She didn't have to wonder whether she should ask anything more. Jeff was eager to talk about the disastrous night.

*"Yeah, he was right behind me. And by the kiss he gave, I could tell it wasn't the first time it happened."*

Their orders came, and they paused and started to eat before the conversation continued. Between bites Anita was going to find out more about Bernie and Jeff's relationship than she wanted to know.

*"I thought you and Bernie were tight. You were always together. Weren't you going to get married or something after she graduated?"* Anita looked confused.

*"That was the plan. Guess I didn't get the memo."* Jeff starts to think, *"Anita, what ... um... in high school, what kind of opinion did you have of Bernie?"* Jeff looked at her with a side glance—showing an inquisitive look. He wanted an objective answer. Jeff really didn't have a clue as to how other females looked at Bernie or what they thought of her.

Anita wasn't expecting that. *"What do you mean?"* She tried to buy time, thinking of a good answer. She didn't know if she should tell the truth or tell him what he wanted to hear. As she thought about it, she didn't know *"what"* he wanted to hear.

*"Well, did you like her, not like her... how did you feel about her?"* Jeff explained further. He got the idea Anita was being a little evasive, which is what she was.

# Chapter 24

*"Oh, I don't know. I guess I didn't think about her much. We never ran in the same circles."* In reality Anita didn't care for her at all but didn't think she needed to say that at this point. This was probably just a lover's spat, nothing more. *"Are you having second thoughts about her? Don't get me wrong, I can see why you would. But you two were together for so long."* At this point Anita was scrambling for something to say.

*"I don't know what to think anymore."* Jeff looked down shaking his head.

*"Maybe it was all just a misunderstanding. Are you going to phone her to find out what happened?"* Anita looked for something positive to say.

*"I hope she'll phone me."* To Jeff, it was all up to Bernie. He would wait to see what she was going to do.

Anita listened with a sympathetic ear. She tried to console him, but it didn't seem to do much good. He was still bewildered, baffled by Bernie's actions.

*"I'm really sorry about what happened. Everything will probably turn out okay."* Anita felt she needed to say more. *"But, if you ever want to talk more ... just let me know."*

*"Thanks. I appreciate it. Hey. Uh, I'll be right back."* Jeff wiped his mouth, threw the napkin into the empty basket and headed for the restroom.

Anita picked up her glass and finished her soda. She felt she helped Jeff with his *"Bernie"* problem. It wasn't the lunch time conversation she envisioned. She didn't get a chance to share anything about her date with Parker. That was okay, though. Sitting there she daydreamed about how good last night was for her.

On his way back, Jeff noticed Anita. She was sitting there, looking around with her chin in her hand, and a far off look in her eyes. Her shapely legs were crossed, one leg slightly swinging—she was feeling pretty good about life. *"Hmm, not bad. How had I missed this before?"* Or, he thought, maybe this was just a natural reaction from being scorned by Bernie? *"Still, not bad, not bad at all!"* Jeff started to have thoughts. Jeff was always a focused person. When he was tight with Bernie he was focused on her and her alone. Now, that *"tightness"* was loosening. His focus could be going in other directions.

# Chapter 25

The alarm doesn't go off quite as early Sunday morning. Jeff is used to getting up at the same time every day and he is awake, looking out the window to get an indication what the day is going to be like. The last couple of days have been unsettling for him. He liked to be focused in his life but right now his outlook on life was a little hazy. For years, his future with Bernie was crystal clear but now his relationship glasses were getting foggy. He wasn't sure what he was seeing. And then when he had lunch with Anita, another vision was introduced. Jeff's focus was out of whack!

Still, Jeff thought Bernie would call but no call came. Maybe she would write—that week, no letter came. There was no explanation forthcoming and after a week of no contact whatsoever he couldn't take it anymore. He decided to call, find out what was going on, where they stood. He was going to be very blunt asking for an explanation. He felt he deserved it.

Well, she was never in. Her roommate said she was out. Never said where or with whom, she was just ...out. No calls got returned. And through all that, Jeff felt he got his answer. It was over. After four years of being together constantly, it was over. In some ways, he couldn't believe it. All those nights together. The passion. The kisses! He thought their relationship was stronger than that. Evidently, it wasn't. He was so focused on her and he thought she was focused on him. And even now, if she would come back, give an explanation, say something, say anything, he was willing to continue with this person who had been the love of his life. But that wasn't about to happen. Once again, he felt, deep down it was over. Painful as it was, it was time to move on.

Bernie felt the same way. It just took this episode with Jeff surprising her as he did to make this a reality in her life. She felt relieved in a way. Now all her attention could be on her new life, the life she would have with Kent.

On Saturday, April 14th, Bernie and Kent went out on the town. Starting with drinks at one of the local hot spots, they met friends and went bar-hopping. They blew off reservations at a swanky club on the outskirts of town to stay with the people they met. Appetizers and more drinks did them just fine. By 11:00 they felt pretty good but weren't in any condition to be on the road anymore. They all decided to go back to Kent's apartment. The party continued. But it lasted only about an hour before Kent and Bernie were alone.

*"Well, I guess I better get back to the dorm."* Bernie slurred her words ... slightly. Her eyes were a little glazed over as well. She was feeling pretty good.

*"You don't have to go just yet. You know it is kind of chilly out there."* Kent pulled Bernie close. With his arms around her waist he gave her a couple of soft kisses and let his hands move down even further.

She put her arms around Kent's neck. *"It's not going to get any warmer."* Bernie knew exactly what Kent had in mind and was eager to play along to see where the night might take them.

*"Well, it could get warmer in here."*

*"Why Kent, what **are** you suggesting?"* Bernie playfully slapped his chest.

*"Oh, I don't know. We could go over to the couch and talk about it."* Bernie raised her eyebrows looking in that direction and led the way holding his hand, slightly pulling him.

They went to the couch but didn't do much talking. They stayed there the whole night. It really wasn't a surprise. Their relationship had been leading up to this. Kent pursued her, and she enjoyed it. She thought he was classy and would make the perfect spouse. He thought she was sexy and ready for their relationship to go to the next step.

The sheers in front of the window swayed back and forth as the early morning breeze teased them. The sun had made its appearance but only briefly. Clouds moved in to deliver a brief shower to begin the day. First one drop and then another. Soon the gentle rain was accompanied by a little rumbling as the front made its way across the area.

She woke up before he did and looked at his unshaven face for a while. She pulled the blanket up close to her naked body. This was the first time she ever slept completely naked. The rain made it a little chilly—the blanket—very much appreciated. She was sleeping next to another naked body, a male one. She snuggled up close putting her head and hand on his chest, unintentionally waking him.

Opening his eyes, he realized what the night had brought forth. He smiled and pulled her close feeling her breasts against his chest.

*"You hungry?"* Kent asked making no attempt to get up or wake up any more. His eyes were half open and it looked like he could go back to sleep at any time.

*"Depends on what you have in mind."* She smiled back and then softly kissed him. This got his attention and he opened his eyes and smiled back. They started to caress one another, and both became very awake.

# Chapter 26

Twenty minutes later they got dressed, went out to breakfast. Bernie felt she had found the man of her dreams, the one with whom she would spend the rest of her life. He was older, more mature and perfect in every way. She saw an opportunity for something better... and grabbed it. Kent was the new love of her life.

Jeff was her man for a while but now Jeff and the whole *"small-town scene"* were distant and unsophisticated. Jeff was *"small potatoes."* Bernie saw herself destined for something better, something greater, something Kent could offer.

Bernie and Kent dated for the next few months. He wanted to meet Bernie's family. She didn't want that to happen. It meant she would have to take him back to where she grew up and she wanted to stay as far away from there as possible. That place was where the *"old Bernie"* was from. She wanted Kent to only know the *"new Bernie."* She felt different. She acted different. And, she started to look different. She looked at herself in a different way as well. But, eventually, she did take him home as embarrassing as that was.

Shortly after their night together, Bernie moved in with Kent and they started to chart their future. A wedding which would take place in the college town, not back home, was in the planning stages. She wanted nothing to do with the past. Life was good. Her future looked bright and promising. Her college days were numbered as she looked forward to being Mrs. Kent Griffin.

Then, one Sunday afternoon, Bernie was relaxing in the

apartment, watching television and reading a magazine, off and on. Kent was at the library doing research as he worked on his master's degree. There was a knock at the door. Florence Kincade was looking for Kent. When Bernie opened the door, Florence was very surprised by who answered.

*"Oh, I'm sorry, I was looking for Kent Griffin. Has he moved?"*

*"No, this is his apartment,"* Bernie replied with a smile to indicate she was the lady of the house. *"Can I help you?"*

*"Well ... um ... I need to talk to him, is he here?"* Florence didn't know what to say or how to handle the situation. She was a cute little red head dressed very casual wearing a green blouse and jeans.

*"Not, now, but he should be back soon. Do you want to come in and wait?"* Bernie felt sure of herself as the conversation continued. Then she offered more information. *"I'm his fiancé."*

*"His fiancé?!"* Florence was taken back a little. *"Uh ... how long have you been engaged?"*

*"About three months. Why?"* Bernie started to wonder what was up.

*"Maybe we do need to talk. I guess I better come in."*

*"Okay...."* Florence came in and they sat down in the living room. Bernie inquired, *"So, what do* ***we*** *need to talk about?"*

Florence just found out she was pregnant with Kent's child. Bernie didn't know it, but Kent had been seeing Florence for the last year, along with yet another woman neither knew about. That would be found out later. Needless to say, when Kent got home, he was quite surprised to see two of his *"lovers"* sitting on the couch. Neither had a good expression on their face.

Bernie's relationship with the perfect guy came to an end.

Bernie went into a tailspin after that. She felt she had burned bridges regarding Jeff and anything associated with back home. She fell off the radar as far as those friends were concerned. No one knew anything about her after that... for a while. There were times when she considered getting back together with Jeff but before that could happen she found herself with this guy or in a relationship with yet another person. It didn't happen... yet. But she always was thinking of him in the back of her mind.

# Chapter 27

Frank B. Emerald was looking for adventure. He was tired of living in Pennsylvania. He was tired of the family business. He was restless and wanted out from under his father's thumb. Yes, life was good for him to a certain extent, but it was also boring. To spice up his life he decided to find a girl and get married. That did it for a while, but after a year or two, it was not enough. Oh, he loved his wife very much, but he didn't like where he was. He was restless and wanted to do something different. He wanted to go out and farm. Farming seemed to be the thing to do. He wanted to get his own piece of land and till the ground. He wanted something that was going to be his.

So, one bright morning he joined fourteen other pioneer families and off they went. Frank and his wife didn't go far. They got to the Midwest, at the time you wouldn't have called it that, but it is that now. Frank found himself 80 acres of good farm land, he thought. This would be more than enough to take care of him and his future family. His beautiful bride agreed. Okay, it was out in the middle of nowhere, but that is what he wanted. And that is what they got.

Frank B. Emerald was a terrible farmer, one of the worst this country has ever seen. He didn't know the first thing about farming. The land he chose was the worst, rocky and unproductive. He didn't know anything about horses or livestock and it was a lot tougher than he anticipated. He didn't know what to plant. Other settlers seemed to be doing just fine, but not Frank. He felt like a fool and a failure. He didn't know what to do. He decided to pack up and head back home with his tail between his legs, before he and his wife starved to death.

He was formulating all these plans when one day he heard from his parents. His father was very proud of Frank for taking such a bold move in leaving home and going out to some unknown territory to build a new life. Not just anyone could do that. His father wanted him to know everything was fine back east, but he and Frank's mother were about to call it a life, so to speak. They sold the business and decided to send a portion of what they received to Frank and his wife. Maybe they could use it on the farm. His dad even said they might come to see him if their health permitted.

What they sent was a small fortune as far as Frank and his wife were concerned. But they weren't going to invest in the farm. They were going to invest in something else. They were going to invest in what Frank knew best and what they really needed in their present location. They were going to invest it in something Frank knew very well, kind of the family business, a general store. They built it right next to their house. It was a lot closer than the county seat and farmers living close by soon patronized Frank's General Store on a regular basis.

Before long a livery stable was built. Next, a place to eat and a hotel. And that is just the beginning of the story of how the town of Emerald came into being. Since that time, the family name of *"Emerald"* has always been heard in that small town. They have owned the largest and oldest grocery store since the founding of the town.

Jeff Emerald was proud of his heritage as well he should be. But he didn't gloat about it. It just was what it was. After his romance with Bernie fell through, he started to have thoughts about Anita. She was available, or so it seemed. And he couldn't get those gorgeous legs out of his mind. The long blonde hair didn't hurt either. He didn't know Anita was seeing a guy from college. She didn't share a lot of personal information. But, even if she wasn't dating anyone else, that didn't mean she would have thoughts about him.

While they had a good working relationship, a social one might be questionable. He hadn't asked anybody out in years. He spent all that time with Bernie. A lot of the angst his friends had, he never experienced... until now. Now he had all the anxieties others faced on a regular basis when it came to the opposite sex. One question loomed in his mind: *"What if she says, 'No'."* Every guy faces that thought and it has stopped many would-be relationships. Rejection hurts. It isn't usually fatal, but it feels like it could be.

As it turned out, the relationship Anita thought might blossom didn't materialize. He lasted for five dates however. That was longer than most guys. Most didn't get beyond two. But it ended, and both felt it should. They went their separate ways.

It took Jeff a long time before he got up the nerve to ask Anita out. He talked about it with Fred in the pool hall or whenever they were together. He also had times when he found himself looking at Anita and thinking about how to approach her and if he should even give it a try. Most of the time she didn't notice but there were a couple times she looked up unexpectedly and saw he was watching her. His face got red and he looked away ... and walked away. She would get a puzzled look and check to make sure something wasn't wrong with her apparel.

# Chapter 28

The pool hall smelled like it always did. Cigarette smoke left a little haze in the air. A *"ding"* on the pizza oven indicated somebody's order was ready. The two snooker tables were in use and a couple guys were starting to play 8-ball. This establishment was doing pretty well tonight. Saturday nights were usually good nights. Jeff looked for Fred and finally found him engaged in playing Buck Euchre with three other guys. One guy was a barfly and a little older. The other two were about Fred's age. Fred was winning as usual. This was Fred's game. Jeff pulled up a chair and sat behind his buddy. The game lasted longer than anyone thought it would.

Jeff watched the game as he watched the other patrons as well. He didn't have to work Saturday nights so much. The store wasn't that busy. And now he felt restless. He didn't want to spend the whole night there but didn't know what else to do.

Finally, the game is over. *"Time to pay up guys!"* Fred enjoyed saying that. No one liked to keep score, so Fred always did—he didn't mind. And they jokingly kidded him because he won so often. They played for money: Nickle a set/dime a game. It wasn't big money, but it made things more interesting.

The players got up and their chairs were immediately occupied by another group of card sharks. *"Let's get out of here."* Jeff was eager to leave.

*"What do you want to do?"* Fred put his winnings in his pocket.

*"Aah, let's just drive around for a while, see what's going on. I'll*

*drive."* They bought some chips and beef jerky to eat along with a soda and went cruising in Jeff's car. Over the next forty-five minutes they met up with another car with three guys doing the same thing. They talked for a while and then each went their separate way. This is the way it worked in Emerald and probably a lot of other small towns. Guys cruising, listening to music, maybe doing a little drinking and talking about ... girls mostly. Ultimately that was the main topic in Jeff's car.

*"Well, how are you doing with Anita these days? Asked her out yet?"* Fred knew what was on Jeff's mind.

Jeff was waiting for Fred to bring up Anita. *"Not yet. Anyway, what makes you think I should or even want to?"*

*"Well, it might be because we have driven by her place like a GAZILLION times tonight!"* Fred didn't miss the fact they drifted towards Anita's section of town repeatedly. Driving by, Jeff wondered if Anita was inside or on a date. If a window upstairs was lit, he wondered if that was her room. By the end of the night he always convinced himself she probably had a date, every weekend. Nevertheless, he drove by and would think of her.

Fred was the encourager Jeff needed. *"Why don't you just ask her and get it over with. I bet she is just waiting for you to take her out. Just do it?"* This was the normal conversation that would take place with Fred and his other pals as they encouraged one another. It worked most of the time.

*"You think I should?"*

*"Would you rather spend every Saturday night moping around with me?"* Fred had a point. He didn't need to make it. Jeff was fed up with himself. And truth be told, he felt he needed a little lovin'. After four years being with Bernie, he was used to affection and hadn't had any for much too long.

That night was a turning point for Jeff. Things had to change.

When the sun rose Monday morning Jeff hopped out of bed with the determination that today, TODAY was THE day he would ask Anita for a date. The sun was shining. The birds were singing. He felt good about himself. He was really pumped! He felt so good he decided to walk to work. The air was fresh and clean. He had a smile on his face. As he walked by the elevator he waved at the guys running the scales. He crossed the railroad tracks and thought life just couldn't get any better. He had all the confidence in the world.

Jeff watched the clock waiting for the big hand to hit number twelve even as the little hand inched towards ten. Anita came in at 10:00 every morning except Saturday when she came in earlier. Always prompt, never late. But today, she didn't show. Jeff wondered what was going on. No one else seemed to mind or say anything. Finally, he asked, *"Where's Anita today?"*

*"Oh, she had to take her mom to the doctor this morning. She won't be in until noon."*

Well, with that little bit of information, Jeff's enthusiasm and determination deflated. When she did arrive, he had lost his confidence. Tomorrow would be another day. That is what he said on Tuesday as well. Tuesday night he needed another boost from good ol' Fred. When Wednesday arrived, nothing was going to stop him... he thought.

The minutes went by. The hours went by. Jeff was rehearsing something that really didn't need that much rehearsing. Finally, by 4:00 he was ready. The store was void of customers. Dad was in back at the meat counter. Mom had gone home early. It was just him and Anita. She was at the cash register. He was at the end of the aisle watching her, confident she didn't see him. His breathing gets faster. He feels his heart beating. Finally, in a bold move he walks down the aisle.

# Chapter 29

*"Anita, uh ... would you like to go out sometime."* She seemed to hesitate at the proposition, it appeared that way, but it was only because she was adding some figures in her head. This worried Jeff at first and he got more anxious with each passing second. He hated the feeling of uncertainty, not knowing. It was killing him!

Then, as casual as she could be, she broke the tension looking up to respond, *"Umm... sure. When did you have in mind?"* She was very *"cool, calm and collective"* in her reply to Jeff's nervous request. Looking directly into his eyes she smiled and waited for more details. He was melting inside as he soaked up every aspect of her gaze.

Taking a deep breath but trying not to make it evident he said, *"How about Friday night?"* Jeff was relieved! *"That wasn't so bad,"* he thought.

*"Okay. Sounds good."* Jeff wondered how she could be so unaffected by his inquiry when he was so nervous! Since his freshman year he never had to even think about what he would be doing on any given weekend. Being with Bernie was a *"given!"*

He thought his nervousness was over just with the *"asking"* part but found he was just as nervous figuring out what to do or where to go. They never talked about likes and dislikes in that area of life. If they had, he hadn't remembered any of it. Finally, he decided.

Jeff was on auto-pilot Friday morning. He could only think of one thing and that was his coming date with Anita. He had never been so nervous in all his life. He played football games where the last play would determine who would win. He threw any number of winning touchdowns passes without this much anxiety. He had been at the free throw line with seconds to go and he felt calmer than he did today.

He watched Anita during the day to see if she exhibited any of the same feelings and couldn't see that today was any different from any other day. As far as Anita was concerned, it wasn't. She had a date with Jeff and wasn't expecting much or even thinking about it a lot.

That night they went out for pizza and then to the lake. The lake had a state park with a shelter house and picnic tables. Sitting on a picnic table, they enjoyed the starry evening. The conversation had centered on work at first which was natural. But it gradually went in other directions.

They shared thoughts and ideas they had about other people and life in general. There was a little laughter here and there and a lot of looking into each other's eyes and smiling. In the quietness of the evening these two started to see each other in a different light. It kind of took them both by surprise—not in a bad way.

They talked for a long time and then it started to get quiet. Jeff feels a little nervous and gets up. *"Time to head back?"* Anita followed Jeff's lead although she didn't want to leave.

*"We could, but ... let's go down and sit on the dock for a while?"* Sitting there they threw pebbles in the lake watching the circles form as each one *"plopped"* into the reflecting pool. Neither wanted the night to come to an end. Without saying anything, after about fifteen minutes they got up and headed back toward the shore. Jeff took Anita's hand helping her up. He didn't let go. *"Thanks for tonight. It has been fun."* Jeff was feeling that the night had been a success... so far.

*"Yeah, this has been great. It's nice to talk, away from work. I'm glad you asked me out!"* Anita smiled, and Jeff totally felt the moment.

They were walking slowly, holding hands. *"Before we go, want to take a walk on the beach?"* Jeff suggested.

*"Yeah, that sounds like fun. I feel like taking my shoes off and walking on the sand."* The evening was extended a little longer. It was the perfect setting for romance.

*"Let's do it!"* Still holding his hand, she removed one shoe and then the other. The water was calm although light waves were softly caressing the shore. It was cool and felt good on their feet.

A full moon looked down on them. Not a cloud in the sky. They were the only two on the beach. Jeff was thinking, *"Should I try to kiss her?"* He wanted to. Anita's lips looked very inviting. He had gone this far... why not...?

The last person Jeff kissed was Bernie. He had four years of kisses with her. Holding Anita's hand, he looked over at her. She was looking down at the sand and the water, hair hanging down on one side providing the perfect backdrop for her cute upturned nose. Her arms were swinging gently as a couple fingers held her shoes. He was working up his nerve. *"Why was he so nervous?"* Well, he knew why.

They stopped. He turned to look at her, *"Anita...."* She lifted her head, tilted it slightly and looked into his eyes. He said nothing more but leaned in to kiss her soft lips. Pulling back, Jeff wondered what her response would be.

She smiled, put her arms around his neck and drew him close, foreheads touching. His arms were around her waist. And then she lifted her face and softly kissed him as well. The two tenderly embraced.

The waves washed on shore—the silhouette of two people starting an intimate relationship was beautiful.

# Part 2

# The Return of Bernie

# Chapter 30

*"Hey, buddy, I hear that there is a little hanky-panky going on at Emerald Grocery these days."*

*"What have you heard, Fred?"*

*"I heard that there was a lot of 'making-out' going on in the back room between two people that work there."* He crossed his arms trying to look serious while at the same time suppressing a smile.

*"Well, you heard wrong,"* Jeff grinned, *"it's not in the back room, it's behind the meat freezer ... but only when dad isn't around."*

Their romance officially began in August of 1973 and it changed the dynamics of everything at Emerald Grocery. Relationships had changed. At least that is the way it was at first. But it didn't take long before there was another feeling that was predominant. Once again, it felt like a *"family"* operation. Even though Anita and Jeff were only dating, they ***were*** dating and the closeness of everyone was apparent. As they didn't even consider letting Anita go when Jeff came back to work months ago, now it seemed like Anita would always be a part of the store.

This was a whole new experience for Anita. Five weeks had been the longest she had ever gone with one guy. She used to wonder how long it would be when she started to truly like someone and fall in love. Maybe her relationship with Jeff before they started dating helped to solidify their time together now. Whatever it was, these two were headed toward the altar.

Jeff and Anita dated six months and in another four they were married. It was a big wedding. After all, an *"Emerald"* was getting married... in Emerald. The whole town seemed to come out. Anita had a lot of friends and consequently a lot of bridesmaids. She had six besides her maid of honor, Ginger. Bridesmaid dresses were blue, off the shoulder. The skirt was mid-calf and tight making it a little difficult to walk but appear very attractive. All the bridesmaids had eye-catching figures. None were blonde. Anita was the only one. And she looked stunning.

Anita's wedding gown looked like it was sown on, very form-fitting. It made her breasts look larger than they were and seemed to indicate her waist was almost non-existent. As she walked down the aisle, holding *"daddy's"* arm, her gown hugged her hips so tightly it was impossible for her to walk very quickly. She didn't need to. The wedding veil gave the appearance of a virgin about to be given to her man. And she was a virgin. Truth be known she looked exactly like her mother when Clara took her vows. Anita was a vision of loveliness.

Champagne was plentiful, and the reception included an open bar. Anita's dad took care of all the expenses. She was his pride and joy. No expense was too great for this event. Fred was the best man. He and Ginger took advantage of the opportunity to be dressed up and thrown together in this party atmosphere. Before the night was over they were walking with arms around each other. *Love* was in the air. And they were experiencing every bit of it.

Jeff and Anita splurged on a honeymoon that took them to Chicago. They spent the week doing what honeymooners do. After that, back to Emerald. Life was good for this new couple. Her parents gave them a monetary gift large enough to make a down payment on a house. As luck would have it, they found one in the south part of town, only three blocks from where Anita grew up. It was a two story of modest proportions with two old apple trees in the big backyard. It was perfect!

Jeff's older brothers were proud of their sister-in-law and a little jealous of their brother. They both married college sweethearts but their wives were nothing compared to Anita. They were nice but, well, nothing like Anita. She was the sweetheart of the extended family.

# Chapter 31

One year later, to the day, actually, Jeff and Anita prepare to celebrate their first wedding anniversary in style. It has been a honeymoon year for them. They can't believe just how well they get along. Their squabbles have been few and never lasted overnight. They were very much in love.

*"What are you doing, son?"*

*"We were just getting ready to go out. Why, what's up dad?"* Jeff answered the phone just exiting the shower.

*"Well, could you and Anita come over just for a minute? Your mother and I have something we would like to give you."*

*"Uh, sure, I suppose."* He looked over at Anita and then the clock. *"We'll be over in about ten minutes. That okay?"*

*"Sure, son. See you then."*

*"What was that all about?"* Anita was getting dressed, putting on her earrings.

*"Dad wants us to come over. He's got something for us?"*

*"Doesn't he know this is our first anniversary? I'm sure I told your mom we were going out tonight."*

*"It will be okay we still have plenty of time."*

On their first anniversary, Jeff and Anita were blown away as the family had a surprise party in their honor. His brothers even came in from out of state to make it an even bigger surprise. It was great to have everyone together. The whole family loved these times.

Jeff and Anita's plans for the evening changed. They were going to get out of town for a few hours, eat at a fancy restaurant and then come back, eat the top of their wedding cake they had saved for the last year, have a little champagne and then.... But this took precedent.

*"We're really happy for you two. Hope we didn't spoil things for you tonight. Were you surprised?"*

*"You guys are great."*

*"Yeah, thanks, we wouldn't want to spend this day in any other way."*

That night they wouldn't be eating any year-old wedding cake. The champagne being chilled in the refrigerator would wait as well. No sooner had Jeff and Anita gotten home than the phone rang. While talking with Jeff's older brothers, Jeff's dad gasped and grabbed his chest, almost collapsing to the ground. Jeff's big brothers kept that from happening as Bonnie called 9-1-1. The paramedics arrived to take him to the hospital, but it didn't look good. The same people Jeff's dad joined whenever the siren went off were now at his side.

On the way to the hospital he died. Funny, in a certain sense, how it worked out. The whole family was together for a celebration and in just a few days they would be together for a much more somber event. Three days later the funeral would take place. And after that the family would sit down to make some decisions about the family business, what its future would be.

With Jeff, there was never a question as far as the family business was concerned. He was focused. This was where he saw his future. And with that in mind, the decision was made. Jeff's view of the future was very positive. He mourned his dad's death but also was willing to take on the new responsibility.

He would have even more responsibilities. Four days after that, Anita got news she was pregnant with their first child.

# Chapter 32

Fred continues at the plant giving it his all. He really got into this business, more than he thought he would, and before long he gets a surprise: a promotion to foreman. It seemed to be what he was waiting for because he really took off after this. Added responsibilities meant added opportunities to make a difference. He spent almost as much time in the office as he did on the shop floor encouraging those he supervised. It was hard *NOT* to see Fred's enthusiasm which led to his landing a permanent office job. Turns out he was a natural for the company. The owner took a real *"liking"* to Fred. His advance came as he made some very beneficial suggestions. It was reflected in his paycheck and he was starting to accumulate a little nest egg, one he wanted to share.

But the plant's success and Fred's outlook didn't match what was happening in the community. Emerald was going the way of most Midwest towns. The rural economy wasn't fairing too well. You could sense it looking across the farming landscape. Some farmers had to sell and leave the area. And that hurt every business. Churches were affected as was the school. The only bright spot about the situation was that Emerald didn't decline quite as much as other towns. The population stayed about the same and most merchants survived.

One of Emerald's taverns did close. Funny how it happened. An alcoholic bought it thinking if beer was always around he would lose his taste for it. It was. He didn't. The town didn't need three taverns anyway. It was one of the first empty buildings in town and that never looks good. One of the grocery stores also closed. Too much competition and not enough customers. Fortunately, the building didn't stand empty for long. The town library moved to this larger facility, a much better location.

Three gas stations closed the same year. A new convenience store was built on the outskirts of town, selling gas at lower prices along with snacks and food items. It was hard to compete.

The big surprise was when the bank built a new facility and moved ... just down the block from its original location. What was wrong with the old one? *"Well, it didn't look modern enough."* That was about it. That was the excuse made.

At least the old bank looked like a bank. It was big and solid, made of stone. A bank should look that way. The new one looked more like one of those temporary classrooms schools bring in at times. It just didn't match the rest of downtown. The old bank building stood empty for several years. But there was talk of renovating it and using it for something else.

# *Chapter 33*

Class reunions can be a lot of fun. Class reunions can be a lot of work. Class reunions can be a pain. Class reunions can be all those things. The class members living in town are responsible for organizing, planning and scheduling everything. That is just the way it works. If it weren't for their effort, it probably wouldn't happen.

After some discussion amongst the 1971 graduates, Fred was chosen to head the 10-year reunion. He didn't mind. He wouldn't have to do it alone. His wife, Ginger, would help. And their best friends, Jeff and Anita, would also pitch in with ideas and muscle. Yes, a lot has happened over the last 10 years.

It started at Jeff and Anita's wedding. Fred and Ginger's whirlwind romance took off that evening, growing over the next year. Ginger wanted to finish nursing school before they got married and she did. Her plan was always to graduate and come back to the area to work, possibly at one of the nearby hospitals. She wanted to live near her mom and dad. But instead of a hospital she works at *The Clinic* in Emerald, assisting Dr. Floyd.

Fred has done very well at the plant and is now co-owner. Fred and Ginger purchased an acreage off her dad's farm bordering the south side of Emerald. They were doing quite well. And their place was very impressive. It was the first home people would see coming into town from the south on the highway.

*"What made you decide to get married at the lake?"* Jeff was

curious as the big day approached. The friendship between these two continues to grow.

*"We just wanted to do something different. That is where we really got together for the first time. We have a lot of memories there."*

*"Yeah, that can be kind of a romantic spot."* Jeff thought back to that first night he and Anita were out together. He thought about proposing there but that is another story. *"Hope the weather holds out."*

*"Yeah, you never know. Then again, if it rains, no one will ever forget the day we got married!"* Fred and Jeff were always competing to see who was the most optimistic. Quite often it was a draw. They were good for one another in a lot of ways.

Fred and Ginger honeymooned in New York. They both wanted to visit the Big Apple and so it was ideal. And they did everything! They saw the city from the top of the World Trade Center, went to the Statue of Liberty, toured Ellis Island, took in a couple of Broadway shows and would have seen *Saturday Night Live* but it was July and the show was on hiatus. They even ventured to ride the subway. It wasn't as scary as they thought. It was a great way to start their new life together. But there was no place like home. And they were glad to return.

Fred and Ginger's nuptials brought excitement to the community. And it needed something. It needed a boost in the arm. Hate to say it again, but Emerald really wasn't doing all that well. More businesses were closing. Jeff and Anita's store was now the only grocery store in town. Antique stores were popping up. They were the kind that weren't open on a regular basis. A sign in the front window gave a phone number to call if interested in perusing the vast array of … antiques the store offered. Fred hated to see what was happening to his beloved town and the community in general. It had been good to him and he wanted to repay it. He had ideas. He always had ideas. And that is what got him where he was.

Fred purchased the night spot out at the lake. He renamed it *The Dock*. This eating place was not much more than a dive. Fred saw potential. He gutted the inside and divided it into a lounge and dining room. It used to smell like dead fish and worms—not very appealing. He installed big picture windows overlooking the lake, very classy. Opening night was a great success and it became known as the place to go for excellent cuisine and elegance.

His next project was the old bank building. The café in town closed and there was only one place to eat, located on the highway. It was popular, but Fred thought something nicer was possible. He drew up plans dividing the bank into two stories: a simple restaurant downstairs and something more *"elegant"* upstairs. The interior of the bank was high enough for this to happen. It wouldn't be cheap, but he thought he could finance it without too much trouble. That is how he managed to transform the place at the lake.

It was an attempt to spruce things up, give downtown a face-lift. When demolition and reconstruction started, it didn't look promising... at first. But, after a while, it took shape. The building was across the street from Jeff's grocery store and, on occasion, Jeff would go over and look at what was happening. Seeing Fred and Jeff together, overseeing the whole endeavor, was very common.

# Chapter 34

Back to the reunion. It was planned for the third weekend in June. For those in town by Friday night, the place to meet was *The Dock* which was perfect for drinking, dancing and socializing. Twenty-four people showed and had a great time mingling and enjoying this impressive new place. Fred and Ginger were hosts along with Jeff and Anita. Many were blown away seeing Jeff and Anita together. What happened to Bernie? Some were totally out of the loop.

It was a great beginning. Saturday, everyone would visit on their own until 4:00 p.m. when the school would be opened for a tour—see firsthand how things changed over the last decade.

School hallways smelled the same as years before. Entering the school, it seemed smaller. People located their old lockers, some went on the stage where they performed in dramas and comedies receiving applause from a very appreciative audience. A couple of guys found basketballs and relived past triumphs until a custodian told them to get off the gym floor with street shoes! Some things never change. And the spouses from somewhere else got a good dose of the shenanigans that happened, at least as it was remembered.

After the tour, it was off to Fred and Ginger's for a barbecue. An empty pasture provided the area people could park. A white open-air tent was set up. Underneath it tables and chairs were waiting to be used. A huge sign in dark green letters read, *"Welcome Emerald Eagles of 1971!"* as people drove in. A tapped keg of beer over to the side got instant attention. Red plastic cups were filled and refilled. No one was empty handed. When the caterers arrived the smell of pulled pork and baked beans beckoned everyone towards the tent.

A thunderstorm the day before freshened the air and it was even a little cool for this time of year. A light jacket felt good with a slight breeze and a beautiful blue sky. The sun was going to prevail for a long time yet. The smell of the area was pleasing especially to those who left for more urban areas. This was once home. They didn't mind the smell of cows and hay. Mosquitoes were a different story.

Invitations requested a reply so the committee could get an estimate. Eighty were expected. But a tapped keg reverberates through the community and it is hard to refuse free beer. By the end of the evening, more than 125 were enjoying the festivities.

Name tags were a must. You needed them because of spouses, for one thing, but also because some people had really changed. A couple of guys were taller and slimmed down considerably. They didn't look at all like they did in high school. One of the gals was on her third marriage and from all appearances she seemed ... wild and was probably on her way to her third divorce. She was never that way ... when she lived in Emerald. To be honest, most looked exactly like they did in school down to the way they wore their hair and the way they walked and talked. But there were exceptions. Some of the prime athletes couldn't touch their toes now. And with the guys, what ever happened to all that hair? Some even had a hint of gray. These people weren't even 30 yet!

Three class members were already gone, and a moment of silence reflected their deaths. Gordon died in the military. Clint, Mr. Tuxedo at the prom, died of a drug overdose. And the third to die was killed in a farm accident. Terry turned too sharply carrying a large round bale of hay and the tractor overturned, pinning him to the ground. His little boy wasn't even a year old when it happened. His widow was also a classmate and was present with her new boyfriend.

Jeff, Anita, Fred and Ginger were the perfect hosts. The cost for the feast was very minimal, thanks to a generous donation from Fred and Ginger. To be honest, many were surprised at Fred's great success. He was never one others thought would be the most successful in the class. But he sure looked like it now! Being married to Ginger was also quite a surprise. These two couples seemed to be the pillars of the community.

And then the next guest arrived. *"Who is that?"*

*"I have no idea."*

*"Pretty nice car. Let's see who gets out."*

*"Well, it is a female that is for darn sure!"*

*"Does she look familiar?"*

*"No, but neither do a third of the people here."*

# Chapter 35

Red plastic cups are filled and everyone finds a seat under the tent. A shiny, dark red BMW convertible arrives and parks at the far end of the field—top up. It looks out of place among the other vehicles. All are sitting where cows roamed freely 24 hours earlier. The driver gets out to slowly make her way to where all the action is, careful to avoid spots where Holsteins left their mark.

With the sun as her spotlight, her sunglasses reflect the expressions of wonder of those trying to identify her. Who is this mystery woman? Someone's wife joining her husband at the last minute? She looks familiar but ....

Entering the tent, she pauses for a moment holding a subtle smile before lifting her sunglasses to rest on her shoulder length strawberry blonde hair tucked back behind her ears. Dressed quite well, she looks younger than most of the people present. Her earrings are dangling like wind chimes. She wears tight slacks and a loose halter top.

Who, indeed, was this shapely individual? No one recognizes her although most guys don't hesitate to take a good, long look. She looks over the crowd searching for one person in particular and finds him. Her sultry eyes stare in his direction.

*"I think I know who that is!"* Gloria Pearson was the first to say something. She was ecstatic! *"Bernie is that you!"* Jeff's old girlfriend makes her appearance in typical Bernie fashion. She always liked to make an entrance thriving on being the center of attention.

But Bernie didn't appear the way Bernie used to. She was never overweight, but now she was the size and shape of a model. She enjoyed the attention. Through it all she continued to look over the group and smile, exchanging pleasantries as close friends rushed to greet her and give her a hug.

Anita and Ginger were not two of those *"close friends."* Anita, especially, wondered what to make of Bernie's return. Anita's feelings about her were never positive. And Anita didn't miss the fact that Bernie had looked straight in Jeff's direction.

Jeff hadn't seen Bernie in probably... six years and it didn't bother him a bit. He never thought of her after he started dating Anita. He never imagined what life might have been like with Bernie. He had Anita and that was all that mattered. Memories of Bernie were nothing more than ...nightmares.

Bernie's visits to Emerald were infrequent. When they occurred, it was in-and-out, usually over the course of two days. She never stayed with her parents. After her father suffered a stroke and died, her mother, younger brother and sister moved away. There was no reason for her to return. And she didn't. No one knew what happened to her. She never got an invitation—no one knew her address. How she knew about the reunion was a mystery but, still, here she was in all her glory.

Many watched to see if Jeff would make his way over to Bernie or vice versa. People whispered about the scenario: *"Two long, lost lovers finally reconnecting."* Well, they were under the same roof, but that was it. During the meal nothing happened. And Jeff didn't plan on anything happening! At one time he was very angry and disappointed with Bernie, now he was apathetic, didn't care at all. Her new look might have excited him in the past but his attraction to her was long gone.

As the meal wound down, Fred shared what the rest of the evening held in store. First thing: everyone was invited to briefly talk about their lives over the last decade. What hopes, and dreams were fulfilled... or not. You could say as much or as little as you wanted.

Fred and Ginger started and then, one by one, they went around the tables. It was interesting to hear from people. One person now lived in France with her husband that she met while studying there one summer. Another was teaching English in Hong Kong. How in the world did they ever get there? Most lived somewhere in the states and mainly in larger communities throughout the Midwest.

When it was Bernie's turn, everyone was anxious to get the scoop on her life. They wanted to know where her life had led her especially since she wasn't with Jeff. The two made no secret of their plans when in high school, but obviously, that didn't materialize.

But Bernie was kind of evasive in her comments. She never finished college, but she did get married to a person fifteen years her senior. They didn't have any children and he couldn't come with her to the reunion, but they were happily married and living in Minneapolis. And...that was about it.

*"That was it!"* People wanted details, details! But none would be forthcoming. By the way she was dressed and based on her wheels, they assumed she married into money.

# *Chapter 36*

Jeff and Anita were the last to talk and Jeff did have some explaining to do for those *"out of the loop."* But the story was short and vague enough, he handled it well. Jeff did all the talking and didn't go into a lot of detail. Anita simply looked up at him smiling the whole time. Emerald was their town, the place they were going to live, raise their family. Their family was growing by the way. Two boys already and the baby bump Anita had, well, they hoped it would be a girl.

Anita was watching Jeff and the great love between them was obvious. But Jeff was also being watched by Bernie. She never took her eyes off him. Her smile made you wonder what she was thinking. Her feelings for him were returning with a vengeance even though both were married... to other people.

Ever since her college days and the disappointment with Kent Griffin, Bernie's character changed. Or, maybe it developed into what it always could become. Bernie knew how to manipulate anything and everything. Seeing Jeff again brought back memories capturing her imagination. *"Was some kind of relationship with Jeff again possible?"* His marriage might be a speed bump in her plans but nothing more.

People get up and move around: more mingling, more drinking. Conversations flowing as fast as the beer. A DJ plays music of 1970-71 which everyone enjoyed and remembered. Some songs many hadn't heard for a long time. To do any serious talking you had to get away from the speakers. The music was loud. Funny, didn't seem that loud back then!

Socializing in full swing, Bernie followed her plotted course through the crowd heading for Jeff. Occasionally she was stopped to talk but that didn't stop her from her mission. She had Jeff on her mind bigtime. He is tapping the new keg at the opposite end of the tent from where Anita was cleaning at the food table. A hand softly rubs his shoulder, giving a little squeeze. He smelled perfume from the past and knew exactly who it was.

She bent down close to his ear whispering, *"Hi there!"* Jeff looks up to see Bernie smiling with eyebrows raised, revealing a grand display in her halter top. Jeff wasn't expecting that and found himself staring. Bernie hadn't planned it that way, but it happened, and she felt pretty good about it. They both stood up and were very close to one another. He could smell her breath mint. *"It's been a while. How have you been?"* She waited for a response. These two had been together in the hallways, classrooms, in the back room at the grocery store and ... in Jeff's car. They knew each other's anatomy exceptionally well.

*"Oh, Bernie, hi"* Jeff blushed, a little nervous. He was cordial, *"Good to see you, too. Yeah, I guess It has been quite a while."* He looked into her eyes and had a reaction he wasn't expecting. It brought back memories that had long been buried. While her physique had changed he could sense the old Bernie in there somewhere.

*"Well, don't be so glad to see me."* Bernie pouted. Expecting this kind of reception, she wasn't about to leave their new relationship where she found it. Jeff was looking good in her eyes. He had physically matured—it looked good on him. Shoulders were a little broader and he looked more... mature.

*"No, I'm really glad you came. How have you been?"* Jeff smiled but wasn't quite sure what was going to happen or what they would even talk about. His unexpected nervousness continued.

*"Well, I wouldn't miss this for the world. You have really done a great job here. Oh, and I must say, you've got a cute, little lady there*

*working so hard."* She looked Anita's way. *"Do I see you two have been busy again? My, my, is this your fourth or fifth baby in the making?"* Bernie's comments were slathering with sarcasm as she stood showing off her figure.

*"It's our third."* Jeff smiled looking at Anita. Anita hadn't seen the two together but then noticed as Jeff continued looking her way. She smiled back and subtly blew him a kiss. He looked like he was in a tough spot and didn't know how to get out of it. Right now, he didn't know what kind of spot he was in. With the keg tapped, the first draw was his own. He felt he needed it.

*"Oh, how sweet."* Bernie thought noting the kiss floating his way. Bernie remembered the first time she saw Anita working at the store. She knew that would be trouble. She took the opportunity to look straight at Anita as well. Their eyes met, and Anita felt the challenge.

Anita was a great wife but right now she wasn't feeling too attractive having bouts with morning sickness. Bernie, on the other hand, was the envy of almost every other female present and she knew it. Anita did feel a *"little"* jealous but wasn't about to show it.

# Chapter 37

Looking at Anita, Bernie took Jeff's arm, *"Let's go for a walk and talk a bit. This will be fun."* Off they went. Bernie held him so tight making sure his arm brushed against her breast. She wanted to get him excited and remember the good ol' days. Maybe they could re-live some of the special times.

She led him into the darkness figuratively and literally. A few noticed but didn't think much of it. Those two probably had some *"catching up"* to do. Anita didn't like him being led away by Bernie, but she trusted Jeff. Bernie on the other hand, well.... She wondered about Bernie's motives. She was right to feel that way. *"Bernie was dressed to seduce... somebody,"* Anita thought, *"The tramp!"*

Bernie had nothing she really needed to talk to Jeff about. She just wanted to get him away from the crowd and have the rest of the class know, especially Anita. Bernie had changed and not only physically. She had no qualms about seducing Jeff. Maybe not tonight or tomorrow night, but sometime. Just because they both were married didn't make any difference to Bernie.

Life had been good to her. Her husband's name was Robert. His first wife died after a bout with cancer. Two years later he married Bernie. Robert was a developer and in construction. He met Bernie when she was still in college and he was doing work for the school. He was very wealthy, and Bernie had no problem with his lifestyle or his money.

Personality wise, Bernie was not the same. After the Kent

Griffin fiasco, there were a couple other guys that seemed to be serious, but Bernie felt she was just being used. And she was. So, she started using guys in return. She became very good at it. She became very good getting what she wanted. If she hurt people in the process, that was life. She developed an attitude that wasn't pretty.

But as she and Jeff were taking their stroll, she tried to give the impression she was the same old Bernie from those memorable years in high school. She acted sweet and innocent and they shared some memories. They talked for all of ten minutes, laughed a little, but they never stopped walking. She had hold of his arm and kept pulling him close. She wanted to excite him like in the past and it worked a little although Jeff didn't want to admit it. Sometimes feelings come upon you out of the blue that were never expected or invited. They just come. Getting back to the tent they joined other conversations but not before she gave him a peck on the cheek which stimulated a few conversations by onlookers.

Jeff found his way to Fred none too soon. He looked over at Anita, lifted his eyebrows and shrugged his shoulders. She gave a *"What happened?"* look.

*"What was that all about?"* Fred asked.

*"Frankly, I have absolutely no idea,"* Jeff shrugged watching Bernie walk away... for a moment. *"Uh... What do you think of the "new" Bernie?"*

*"I didn't think much of the old one, quite frankly. Outside of the fact she's got a new bod, well, she never did appeal to me much. Personally, I never knew what you saw in her."* Jeff knew Fred's feelings and had ignored them during high school. At that time Jeff was *"in"* to Bernie and nothing was going to separate them.

When Bernie and Jeff parted, Bernie surveyed the crowd. She was irritated Jeff wasn't more receptive. But, there would be other opportunities, just give it time. More than just their class came--

common with reunions. It was good to see people who were in school at the same time even though not in your class. Scanning the crowd, she saw Scott McClary, a few years older. Scott was 6’3”, weighing 250 lbs. He was not fat, he stayed in good shape working as a farm-hand.

Scott and Bernie talked and then moved off into the shadows. Scott was enjoying himself and before they drifted into the darkness made sure they both had a beer in their hands. Twenty minutes later they came back and were together the rest of the evening. At 11:15 they headed for Bernie’s Bimmer. Anita and Ginger were sitting under the tent talking and could see Scott and Bernie coming their way. Anita and Bernie had a stare down going—both had smiles of course. It was very subtle but there was friction.

Getting into the convertible the first thing Bernie did was put the top down to let in the night sky. Scott thought he was in seventh heaven and was the envy of many guys, both married and single.

About midnight the party slowed down and by 1:00 a.m. almost everyone was gone. The tent would be taken down the next day. Everything else was cleaned up. The reunion was a success. It brought a lot of old friends together. Lives had changed over the last ten years and before the next reunion lives would change even more.

# Chapter 38

Generous people are happy people. The penny-pinchers of the world always seem to carry a scowl on their face. You get an image of *Ebenezer Scrooge* yelling at *Bob Cratchit*. They watch how every cent is spent. Always looking for a deal they never hesitate to ask for a discount. Nothing wrong with watching your money, being thrifty, but don't let your money rule you. Do they really enjoy life? Doubtful.

Fred was a generous individual. He loved the town of Emerald. The plant outside of town had been good to him as he had been good for it. He was co-owner and had a lot to do with its expansion and the hiring of 50 new employees, purchasing new lathes, drill presses and machines demonstrating the latest technology. This was a good move for the town and community. Fred wanted to give back as much as he could, hence, the plan to remodel the old bank building.

Fred's standard question: *"What do you think?"* He looked for second opinions, never afraid to ask. He wanted to do things right. Rarely was he insulted by criticism.

*"I think it looks great, Fred, I can hardly wait until it gets done,"* Anita encouraged. *"It's taking a while."* Even though Anita wanted to be supportive, her heart wasn't into it as much as her husband's. Fred and Jeff were always cooking up something. They did that as kids and now Fred was carrying on the tradition.

*"Yeah, everything takes longer than you expect. Jeff around?"*

*"I think he is in the back."* Anita watched the wheels turn. Fred

stood there for a minute and then quickly turned as if he heard Jeff yelling, *"Help!!"*

Since the café in town closed, Jeff and Anita expanded putting in an area where coffee and a few bakery items were sold. They bought the empty building adjoining them on the north and remodeled it. Jeff cut an opening between the two buildings, put in some booths, a few tables and chairs he picked up when the café closed. Many felt the old café had just moved to a different location.

Retired farmers came in to sit and shoot the breeze, drinking more coffee than they should. They talked about the weather and how the construction was coming along across the street. Of course, they had their own opinions and didn't hesitate to state them, *"Fred should have thought about this project a lot earlier,"* or *"Why is he going to all that trouble? Doesn't make sense to me."* But then again it really wasn't any of *"their"* business. It was Fred's money.

It had been a couple weeks since the reunion. This July day had promises of being a scorcher. Each day seemed to be worse than the one before. It hadn't been cooling off much during the night either. Hot and humid—very sticky. Most people and animals didn't care much for this kind of weather. But farmers didn't mind it in the long run—great for growing corn. And this year, the corn crop was looking good. What were a few hot and humid days when it could mean a profitable harvest?

Jeff turned on the air in the store first thing in the morning. He got the coffee brewing and by 8:00 Anita should be there. This was really a family operation in a lot of ways. They liked working together and had their routine down pat.

Expecting their third child, Anita had been having a difficult pregnancy. Their two boys spent a lot of time with Anita's parents who enjoyed them and spoiled them rotten. Most of the time they were with just Anita's mom, Clara. Anita's dad was still in charge of Olson

Insurance and spent most of his day in the office or out seeing people, checking claims. When the boys got older, Jeff would show them what work was like in the grocery business. He was raising them the same way he was raised.

Everyone expects it, and some set their clocks accordingly. The siren in town goes off at 7:00 a.m. signaling the work day has begun. The huge doors of the grain elevator go up and light pours in sending resident mice for secure spots safe from local felines. Pumps are turned on at gas stations in preparation for the day's sales. Ward Kemp had just driven in to bring his place to life. Almost instantly traffic is on the streets. The air was filled with the noise of hammers and saws—reconstruction in the old bank building continues. Fred was pushing to complete the project by the time school started or at least by homecoming.

Jeff and Anita lived only a few blocks east of her parents. The two boys were sitting in the back seat. They each brought along a toy to play with. They really didn't need to since Grandma and Grandpa had a play box filled to capacity. The drive was very short. Clara was at the front door welcoming her precious little angels to another day of ... well, she had some plans.

# Chapter 39

*"Morning, Mom, how you doing?"* Anita closed the car door behind her. The boys jumped out with their toys. They were about to run right past grandma into the house when they were distracted by a neighborhood cat walking around the corner. Seeing the boys, it stopped dead in its tracks to determine what their next move might be. When they started to move the cat darted to the tree in the front yard to observe their future actions from a higher and safer vantage point.

*"Just fine dear."* It was Clara's first time outside. *"Whew, it's going to be a warm one today. Mind if I take the boys out to the lake?"* Hearing grandma's request the boys forget about the cat. They turn to look at mom, hoping to see a smile of approval.

Anita saw the look in their eyes, *"I think that would be great. Would you like to play in the water?"* She didn't have to ask twice. Little heads bounced with anticipation of what the day was going to be like! The lake was always exciting. Imaginations run wild playing on the beach and in the water.

Anita entered the store at 8:15 a.m. Even though she was starting to show, she still looked very pretty. Her hair was tied back in a ponytail to keep the back of her neck a little cooler. Her maternity top fit loosely. She looked like the perfect wife and mom. Bernie was right in calling her *"a cute little lady."*

By 9:00 the usual crowd was on their way in for morning coffee. Farmers in bib overalls wandered over from the elevator and meandered in. Some talked outside for a while shaking their heads, looking down or over at the bank and doing a little pointing before entering. All had caps tilted at different angles advertising something connected with farming. Most of the caps advertised seed corn but some displayed tractors that had been around since the time of steel wheels. As they walked many looked like they had a limp. It was just a lazy walk. Maybe in some cases it was due to an injury but most of the time it might have just been a little arthritis. They all had a smell about them. Not a bad smell—kind of a smell of the farm and a little grease or oil. No one paid any attention to the way these customers looked or smelled.

*"Morning, Anita, how you feeling today?"* The question was asked every day. It was an excuse to say something to her with the hopes that maybe a more meaningful conversation might continue. It rarely did. Everyone that said it, thought they were unique in their comments and quite the conversationalist. They were sure she appreciated the attention.

Her standard reply always came with a twinkle in her eye and a smile, *"Oh, about the same, thanks for asking."* The response was enough to make you feel you were good making small talk. And you felt you had a meaningful relationship with this attractive young mother. To most, Anita was a much younger woman, more the age of their daughter. In some cases—granddaughter. This was definitely the older crowd.

As the day went on the air got heavier. Those who worked inside appreciated the air conditioning. But even with the air, you still felt uncomfortable. Outside it was very still, nothing was moving. The dogs that snooped around town or chased squirrels were resting in the shade. In the west a growing bank of clouds approached. Looking closely, you might even see a flash of lightning now and then. Some would refer to it as heat lightning. Others thought maybe rain was coming. It had been forecast a 40% chance, but forecasters had been wrong many times before. Still it seemed that 40% grew as the day progressed.  A good thunderstorm might be nice, cool it off a little.  But for some reason it usually doesn't happen that way.  It is hot and sticky. It rains. It storms. Then it gets even hotter and stickier and you go on to the next day.

# *Chapter 40*

Little movement on the streets was an indication that everyone was trying to conserve energy any way possible. Fred was the exception. Born with energy to burn, the heat and humidity didn't have an impact on him. *"Hi, Anita, keeping cool?"* Fred made his daily appearance right on time. Between the plant and this new project, he was on the move.

Anita expected him and the enthusiasm he brought. *"When I'm in here. I'll be glad when this heat and humidity ease up a little. Checking up on things again, Fred?"* As said before, Anita isn't really interested and now seems to really give that impression. She has other things to do.

*"Have to stay on top of it all, you know. Need to talk to Jeff."* He stands for a minute looking across the street, arms crossed and fingers tapping his lips.

*"I think he's sitting in the meat freezer,"* she kidded. Fred wasn't listening at first. Then he looked at her with a serious look and then a great big smile.

*"I think I'll join him,"* Fred headed to the back as if it was an emergency.

Before he got too far, Anita yelled, trying to catch him on his way, *"What do you guys talk about all the time anyway?"*

*"Sorry, top secret!"* he yelled, slightly turning around. *"I could tell you, but then I'd have to kill you."*

Anita rolled her eyes, *"Boys will be boys."*

By 2:00 in the afternoon the sun was hidden. Black and gray clouds looked intense and fierce. The darkness triggered the sensors and street lights came on. Then it got even more still, eerily quiet, nothing—absolutely nothing, was moving. Anita turned on the radio to catch what might be happening. It didn't do much good. The static was unbelievable. Evidently a lightning storm somewhere close by made the radio transmission a loud jumbled mess. She called her mom to see if she heard anything concerning the weather. Clara relayed there was a tornado watch for their county and two counties to the north.

The store had a basement just for that reason. Every house and business had a basement. If necessary, Anita and everyone in the store would head there. Right now, she and Jeff were the only ones in the store. And there weren't many cars downtown. The construction crew was still over in the old bank building but kept a close watch on the sky.

At 3:07 the siren went off. It was a long blast signaling a funnel cloud had been sighted... somewhere! Time to seek shelter. George Meyer watched the clouds closely. They looked threatening and seemed to be rolling. A greenish tint might indicate hail. Then he spotted the churning cloud a few miles northwest of Emerald knowing exactly what it was. He called it in and got his family down the basement. The kids always wanted to stay with dad to join him gazing into the sky, but they were never allowed. He stayed upstairs and watched the movement by himself. The funnel came down in the most perfect fashion. If it weren't so scary to think of the possible damage it would have looked beautiful. It almost touched down, but then went right back up, as if it were stung by something sharp, never to be seen again. That was as much as it was going to do but the warning had been given and no one knew the initial threat was over. The idea of a twister was still prevalent.

Then the wind began to blow, and it blew with tremendous gusts. The stillness was just a memory. The trees whipped back and forth repeatedly. Amazing how far they could bend without snapping. Anita's parents had a huge elm tree in their front yard with low branches. Neighborhood kids had fun climbing it as did cats and squirrels. Kids even tried at one time to build a treehouse in it. It would be the last day of this tree's existence. Six other trees towering into the skies providing beauty and shade would come down this afternoon. Two would inflict tremendous damage. One life would be lost.

Then the rain came. A few sprinkles at first but then it was as if someone opened the faucet to its full force. It pounded the sidewalks. Both Jeff and Anita watched it come down. There is something mesmerizing about a thunderstorm. Thunder and lightning are spectacular. Combined, as they always are, they put on a spectacular aerial display with sound effects.

The rain came down in sheets. It is mind-boggling how the water can come down at various angles sometimes as much as 45 degrees. No one was driving. Windshield wipers couldn't keep up. Those who had been driving pulled over to the side to wait it out.

# Chapter 41

Then the hail started. The dreaded hail. George Meyer was right in his observation. This wasn't good for crops. Hail this time of year could inflict great damage on both the crops and property in general. It started pea size but, in some places, got to marble and even golf ball sized. Some vehicles were dimpled but no windows were broken, not even one was reported. One farmer driving his new car down a country road looked for a place of cover. Seeing an open garage, he drove right in. Luckily the pickup usually housed there was getting an oil change in town.

The hail and the rain started to subside but the thunder and lightning—still strong and getting closer. One storm was following another. When you would see the lightning and almost instantaneously hear the thunder, it wasn't far away.

Then it happened. The flash was blinding like watching a welder at work, looking when you shouldn't, the temptation too great. Lightning hit the siren. It melted into a pile of useless metal and ugly plastic. Another flash came as lightning hit the old bank. An explosion competed with the sound of the thunder. Instantaneously you saw smoke. A fire had broken out that was ready to consume Fred's project.

Siren destroyed, firefighters could not be summoned. Jeff, an eyewitness, jumped into action. He headed out the door yelling to Anita to phone volunteers. He hoped the phone lines were still working. Jeff took off running for two reasons. One was to get things moving to put out the fire and the other was because the fire department was directly behind the old bank. Firetrucks and other equipment were in danger of going up in flames if they didn't get moved, NOW!

Construction workers had taken shelter when they heard the siren the first time, so no one was in the old bank itself. The explosion rearranged the new construction on the second floor. Most of the roof was gone and as the rain had stopped, the fire was growing with nothing to stop it and plenty of oxygen to fuel it. Jeff was able to get both trucks out before the fire had the opportunity to drift in that direction. Ultimately it never did. By the time a dozen firefighters arrived the blaze was intense. The old bank was totally engulfed and the building south of it now on fire.

Directly across from the grocery store, Anita watched it all. She saw the brave volunteers doing what they could. Donned in their yellow jackets and helmets they trained for this activity. There had never been a fire in the business district ever. The hoses blasted water, but it didn't seem to affect the rising flames. It wasn't long before a deafening crash was heard, the newly constructed second floor collapsed, blowing windows out as it came down. Glass flew across the street. Anita was a little taken back by the force of the blast. The battle wasn't over. It was far from over.

Fred got there just in time to experience the crash. It had the same impression on him as it did on Anita. He joined his comrades. Emerald was an old town with old buildings, ripe for a fire. Most were over 50 years old and suitable for being tantalizing tinder. One after the other, store after store, fire went down the line. They fought to save one building and when they saw it was useless, they fought to save the next. Before it was over, only one building was left, the tavern. And they fought hard, so it wasn't destroyed. Everything else was gone. There was nothing but smoldering rubble. Besides the old bank, four of Emerald's main buildings on West Main were gone. They were all empty buildings at the time but in year's past they housed the dime store, a grocery store, furniture store, and drug store. Now—all gone, a complete loss.

Then, the sun came out shedding light on the destruction Mother Nature had initiated. The damage looked even worse. It was hot and humid again, but the feeling was only secondary to the damage done to this once beautiful town.

The ditches along country roads had hail, 3 inches deep in some places. Some farm kids collected the hail in jars and put it in the freezer as evidence of what happened. Corn leaves were sliced. Soybeans looked sad. Those who purchased hail insurance were glad they did, although it wouldn't pay off that much in the end. It seemed it never did. And by the time adjusters got to the field, everything would look nice and green again.

# Chapter 42

The wind blows with tremendous force. One gust after another rolls in indicating determination not to give up until its purpose, whatever that might be, is fulfilled. The wind around Harold and Clara Olson's house was there for one reason.

Anita's parents were in the basement when the big elm came down with a noticeable crash. No damage to the house but the tree wouldn't provide shade any longer. Harold gave the *"all clear"* for everyone to come up. The storm was on its way to the next town to do damage there if it didn't lose its punch on the way. The boys were anxious to see what it looked like outside after the big storm. Their eyes couldn't take it all in. The huge elm cracked and was laying on its side blocking the way to the street. They weren't allowed to get close lest the tree hadn't reached its final resting place before it was cut up and taken away. Another tree came down and blocked a side street missing a house by mere inches.

Ethel Pearson heard the siren go off many times in the past. It was always a false alarm. Emerald had never been hit by a tornado and, truth be told, she liked watching storms. It was a little variety in life that gave her a great deal of joy. Many times, she sat on her front porch to watch rain come down breathing the fresh air, feeling the breeze. Since she broke her hip a few months back she had to use a walker and because the concrete porch might be a little slippery she stayed inside. She was sitting in her favorite chair looking out the window when a tree in her back yard, slightly older than her, cracked and collapsed on her house. The tree and the house were going to die together. Unfortunately, this would also be Ethel's last day. All she heard was a cracking sound and then her world came to an end. Had she been on the porch, it would have missed her completely. She was 84, a lifelong resident who lived alone.

Branches and leaves littered the streets. Lawns were speckled with debris. It would be a while before it all got cleaned up. But almost immediately the cleanup began, at least if there wasn't serious damage. Areas where there was damage, Harold Olson would have to come around, assess the damage and file a claim. He would check everything out to make sure his policy holders were given the consideration they paid for.

The people of Emerald and every other Midwest town or city are used to storms like this. Every summer thunder storms occur on a very regular basis. Most don't do near as much damage or take lives. But this one did, and it would be remembered with sadness.

*The Clinic* suffered no damage. Three mothers and their four toddlers were there when the siren went off. Dr. Floyd, Ginger and the seven visitors all made it to the basement. They didn't take any chances. Like everyone else in town they had no idea of whether the tornado was a reality or not. Ginger knew what this kind of weather could be like and so she wasn't as concerned as Dr. Floyd. Dr. Floyd was always on edge when it came to thunderstorms. He wasn't from the Midwest and whenever that siren went off, he would look out the window and expect to see a tornado with angry eyes searching just for him.

No one came for medical help and there were no calls for the doctor, so it seemed like everything was okay when the wind died down. Ginger had no idea her husband's project had gone up in flames... literally! In all the excitement, Anita didn't think to call her and so it wasn't until Ginger got home that she found out about the catastrophe. Fred was very discouraged.

Everything was insured, of course, but still, his plan to revitalize downtown using the old bank, was over. The building was gone. It didn't look good. That was the story as far as Fred was concerned. And to go a step further, if the downtown area ever needed a boost, it was now!

The storm was not anything to make the news really. Storms are very common. It didn't make anything more than a small story on page 16. It was lucky to just make a paper. Evidently, they had a space that needed to be filled. The storm did make the phone lines. And the recent reunion helped to get the word out, at least between Bernie Becker and Gloria Pearson.

Business meetings were starting to take up more of Bernie's time. Interest in her husband's business intrigued her. She accompanied Robert on a few of his trips and even offered advice on a couple of developments in their finishing stages, advice that was accepted and appreciated. She liked going along. It made her feel important. She had just gotten back in the house when the phone rang.

*"Bernie, you won't believe what happened."* Gloria was filled with grief as to how her grandmother died. Her grandmother raised her, and they were very close. She would call her daily and they ate dinner together every Sunday. Gloria didn't immediately find out about her grandmother's death. She was at work when the storm hit. She was devastated finding out all the details.

Bernie had other things on her mind. Gloria had only one thing and she blurted it all out at once. *"Gloria, is that you? What's wrong?"* Bernie thought she recognized the voice. She had no idea what happened. At first Gloria was hard to understand.

# Chapter 43

Gloria stopped the tears long enough to spit out the words. *"Grandma Ethel is gone."* And then the tears started all over again. It was her first phone call after receiving the news.

*"She died? When? How?"* Bernie had spent a lot of time with *"Grandma Ethel"* growing up. She and Gloria were playmates in their younger years. They didn't live that far apart, and Gloria really didn't have anyone else to play with. Thrown together at first, they got to the point where they liked playing with one another—a friendship grew.

*"Oh, Bernie, she was just sitting watching the storm. I don't think she knew what happened. That tree in the back yard came down and crushed the house."* That tree was the source of a lot of shade and they both remembered playing in the sandbox at its base.

*"I'm so sorry."* And Bernie truly was. *"Do you want me to come down? No, what am I saying? I'll come down as soon as I can. When is the funeral? How can I help? How's the rest of the town?"* Bernie was nice through it all. It even kind of surprised her! She was feeling for her friend.

With all the questions, Gloria calmed down. She took a deep breath and shared what else happened. *"There is a lot of debris all over the place: leaves, trees and branches. And a bunch of buildings on West Main burned down."*

News of the fire got Bernie's attention changing her back into the old Bernie. *"West Main? The grocery store?"* Bernie hoped. Ever since the reunion when she saw Jeff and Anita together and how happy they were with their little family and all, Bernie wasn't happy.

Gloria wasn't even thinking about what happened from that perspective. *"No, the other side of the street,"* she said innocently. She was still focused on her grandmother.

Still, Gloria knew all about Jeff through their high school years. Bernie told Gloria almost all the romantic details. But when Bernie left for college, Bernie didn't share with her what her new life was like. She said absolutely nothing about Kent. And then, when the romance between Jeff and Anita started, Gloria wondered what was going on.

Gloria really didn't care much for Anita. They rubbed one another the wrong way. To be honest, there was a lot of envy on Gloria's part. The difference in appearance and personality was so apparent. She saw Anita as taking advantage of the situation while Bernie was away. And she was miffed at Jeff also. She thought of him as being two-faced. As you might expect, she didn't do a lot of shopping at Emerald Grocery.

Ethel's funeral took place the next Monday. It was well attended because of the circumstances. The church was packed. Ethel had been involved in a variety of activities including the Altar Guild, Ladies Aid and choir. She had been baptized in this church, confirmed and married here. She walked behind her husband's casket when he died and now she was going to rest beside him in the cemetery. As the casket was carried out, the bell tolled 84 times, once for every year of life. It was tradition.

The hearse was driven through town and cars on the streets pulled to the side. Evidence of the storm that took this life was still present everywhere. The storm sucked the life out of the town at this point as well.

There were two cemeteries in this community. One was owned by St. Mary's, the Catholic Church, and the other was a public cemetery. Ethel was Lutheran and would be buried next to her husband who died the same year as Jeff's father. In fact, their plots were close to one another.

The grave had been prepared and was waiting for the casket. Chairs were set up and a small tent shielded a few mourners, the immediate family, from the sun. The flag at the entrance to the cemetery was being whipped by a breeze that ceased by the time it made it to ground level. The heat and humidity of a few days ago was gone. Sitting and listening to the Pastor read through the rite of committal, Bernie watched the crowd. To the side she noticed Jeff and Anita holding hands. No one could tell where Bernie was looking and so she just dwelt on this sight which angered her the more she stared. She couldn't help herself.

Fred and Ginger were with Jeff and Anita. The casket was lowered, and the first handful of dirt thrown. The crowd thinned out. Jeff and Anita took a moment at his father's grave. Most everyone else went back to church for the luncheon that followed.

The funeral was over along with the stress accompanying it. Now is a time to just sit and relax, tell stories about the deceased and laugh a little to relieve tension. It is an important part of the grieving process and a part of the small-town experience.

# Chapter 44

The aroma of coffee was predominant. Jell-O salads and sandwiches covered two long tables outside the kitchen. Walking through the line and getting your drink at the end was the custom they all knew very well. The older ones always wondered if they would be attending the next one or not. Ethel had organized and set up many such luncheons over the years.

Before leaving, Jeff and Anita expressed their sympathy to Gloria. Bernie and Gloria were sitting together at a table close to the front. Bernie was dressed very elegantly, better than anyone else. She wore black, of course, but the dress was very classy—her jewelry, equally so. Bernie was sitting at the end of the table at kind of an angle with legs crossed and her foot playing with her shoe as Jeff and his *"honey"* got close. Bernie looked at Anita in a belittling way, as usual, and then at Jeff in a provocative way, hoping Anita would notice. Gloria accepted their comments with fake sincerity and the Emeralds were off.

Gloria and Bernie immediately started talking about them in whispering tones, none of which was good. The luncheon over, Gloria invited Bernie to her house. Bernie planned on staying in the area for a few days hoping to reconnect with Scott McClary but also thinking about Jeff. She planned to stay at a motel, but Gloria convinced her to stay with her. Gloria would enjoy the company.

Bernie drove her BMW through the streets of Emerald, looking at the town in which she was raised. Bernie liked Gloria and did a fair share of gossiping the night before, but now needed some space. The temperature was pleasant. She got a can of pop, put on her sunglasses, rolled the windows down and went cruising. Her favorite radio station from high school days changed to talk radio so she searched for something else but decided to be alone with her thoughts. She hadn't spent much time here during the reunion. She just drove down that Saturday and returned the next day. This was her time to reminisce.

*"Hmm. This place sure hasn't changed much, still the same old town. School hasn't changed... wait, I guess they are building something. Well, the backstop looks new. It needed to be replaced."* She drove on, talking to herself as she drove by her old house next to the football field/city park. *"Wonder why they put a gate up in front of the park."* She couldn't figure that out. *"Let's see what the country looks like."* She slowly took off down a gravel road careful not to drive too fast and mess up the paint on her convertible.

Bernie never viewed the country landscape as especially attractive. To her it looked barren, empty and ... boring. Even when crops were growing, and everything was green and lush she had the same opinion. She saw herself as destined for the *"city"* life. At one time she would have been happy with Emerald as being her *"city."* That was when Jeff was in the picture and she saw her future as Mrs. Jeff Emerald, working side by side with her husband in Emerald Grocery. But that was a long time ago, that was history. She still had feelings for Jeff, however, and they were growing. But, of course, he was married and had a family. SO?!?!? That wasn't going to stop Bernie in her scheming. Wife and family were merely obstacles she had to get around, to deal with...especially, *"the wife."* But Bernie thought she knew Jeff well enough, maybe she could get him to remember how things were ... before. She hadn't given up.

Out in the country she recognized places where they spent some very intimate time. They had favorite spots where they knew they wouldn't be disturbed. She thought about those times and got a little excited. Closing her eyes, she remembered the last time, on that homecoming weekend. Their favorite place was behind an old corn crib out in a field on the Gutz farm. They were never bothered there. In her mind, Jeff needed to be reminded of those times and long for them once again the way she did.

Back in town, she drove down West Main to view the destruction. A good portion had been destroyed. The clean-up hadn't started yet. It looked pretty much like it did last Tuesday with half-burnt lumber, singed shingles laying around and broken glass. Caution tape secured the area. She parked her Bimmer deciding to get a slow firsthand look at this decaying little town, walking down the sidewalk.

The BMW was a strange sight in Emerald. Most vehicles were old, dirty pickups dented in a few places, a car here and there. None were as new or as clean as Bernie's. And none of the few people downtown had the *"look"* Bernie had. Most of the farm wives looked like ... farm wives in Bernie's arrogant way of looking at them. *"They might clean up pretty good,"* she thought, *"but...."*

It was 10:30 in the morning and Bernie had seen about all that was to be seen. It didn't take that long to tour the whole town and a little of the countryside. Time to get a little exercise. She wouldn't go unnoticed. She parked a few stores down from Emerald Grocery. Getting out of her car she noticed the grass was a little long. Dandelions were in abundance. *"Well, let's see what's going on in Mayberry."* She strolled down the cracked sidewalk taking her sweet time. She wasn't in any hurry.

She stopped in front of an old hardware store. The calendar inside marked the year it closed. Shelves stood, waiting to be filled with nails and screws or wrenches and hammers. But they would never see any of those materials again. The front window provided Bernie with a mirror for her to check herself out. Hair was perfect and her top a little tight—perfect for the image she wanted to portray. She had a nice figure and filled out her shorts in a way that made you want to linger on the image as she might just stand and talk with a friend. In all honesty, Bernie did look better than she ever had before. She moved on down the sidewalk.

# Chapter 45

Anita saw her coming and thought to herself, *"Keep on walking."* Bernie did keep walking although she looked through the huge storefront window hoping to see Jeff inside. Anita pretended not to notice turning away to fix something on a shelf. Anita was having a pretty good day until she saw Bernie. *"What is she doing around here? Why hasn't she left?"*

Sitting in the chair, Archie was looking out the window when Bernie walked by. *"Who's that pretty young thing?"* He interrupted Ben trimming the area around Archie's ear talking about the recent Twins game. Then he said, *"Ouch!"* as the barber unintentionally pulled a hair when Archie turned his head to follow Bernie down the sidewalk.

*"I don't know but if you don't sit still I will be cutting more than hair,"* Ben quipped. Bernie made an impression walking past the barber shop. Some inside pretended not to see her holding up a newspaper. When she got out of sight, they continued turning pages. But the image of Bernie was stuck in their minds.

Still before noon, only a few people were in the pool hall, but Rusty, the bartender/owner, took a second look as Bernie made her way past, casually swinging her purse. A cigarette hung out of his mouth and he had one foot on a chair leaning on that leg. Bernie was in no hurry and he was happy she took her time. A farmer driving toward the elevator saw Bernie and decided it was time to see what the news was in Rusty's.

*"Hey, Carl, look. Who the ...? Wonder where she came from?"*

She stopped all the conversations when she walked by the implement store. No one knew who she was but liked what they saw.

It was a short walk. The business district wasn't that big. She just turned the corner and was at the south end of West Main, walking north, when Jeff came from the north, made a U-turn and parked in front of the store. Jeff got out and carried supplies into the store, not noticing Bernie rounding the corner.

*"Ah, Jeff, I need to talk to Jeff."* She was going to get in her car, but now her plans changed. With the same thoughts she had driving through the country, she remembered visiting Jeff in the store. They enjoyed the privacy the back room offered. Maybe she could remind Jeff of those times. She unbuttoned the top two buttons on her blouse allowing a better view.

Anita just started a fresh pot of coffee and wiped off the counter when she heard, *"Good morning."* It was a voice she didn't want to hear, didn't need to hear. She thought she had seen the last of Bernie—hoped she had, but, here she was.

*"Oh! Hi Bernie. Saw you walking around. Looking at all that has happened?"* Anita wasn't necessarily the jealous type and didn't need to be... then, on the other hand, sometimes she was. She never doubted Jeff's love. But her dislike for Bernie was growing. She noticed Bernie's blouse and wondered what that was all about.

*"Yeah, it sure is a mess."* Bernie didn't waste any time, *"Is your hubby around?"* She knew perfectly well he was. For a moment Anita thought of saying he wasn't, but she didn't.

*"Yeah, he's in the back room taking care of some inventory, I think."* And with that Bernie started down the aisle. Anita couldn't follow but thought to herself, *"Keep your hands off my man!"* She watched Bernie walk and thought to herself Bernie was really pushing it. Who did she think she was?

Jeff was surprised to see Bernie and the *"button factor"* was very apparent. She knew he noticed. *"Hi Jeff."*

Jeff smiled as he lifted a box off the floor. *"Hi Bernie. What are you up to today?"* He leaned back against a work table.

*"Oh, I was just looking at everything, kind of reminiscing about old times. Took a drive through the country. Not much has changed."* Eye contact was being made and it almost seemed like old times. She walked towards him. They stood only a couple feet apart.

Jeff crossed his arms. *"No, not much has changed, although some things have."*

Bernie did most of the talking and she noticed from time to time that Jeff's eyes were not on her eyes but on her blouse. She thought she had scored a victory. After a few minutes she said, *"Well, I guess I better go."*

*"Yeah, I better get back to work."* Jeff didn't want to, but his eyes kept going toward her cleavage.

She went over to him and gave him a hug. Pulling away she wanted to kiss him thinking he might be receptive. But she didn't. Their cheeks did touch however bringing a tantalizing feeling to both. She did bend down slightly revealing a pleasant departing view. She knew he was looking.

Jeff hated himself, but the memories were still there, and he did get a little excited by Bernie's presence. He shared in the hug and....

# Chapter 46

Even though Jeff wouldn't take the bait, that didn't mean she wouldn't try to make Anita think he had. Bernie would like nothing better than to destroy their marriage. Walking up from the back room she gave the appearance her time with Jeff had been very successful. She even made a point of buttoning the buttons she had unbuttoned earlier right in front of Anita, sort of. Anita didn't miss that little show but didn't give Bernie the satisfaction of what she was feeling deep down inside.

Walking past Anita, she said, *"Bye-bye,"* as she put her sunglasses back on and stood there for a moment looking out the glass door.

Anita said, *"Bye-bye,"* and was glad Bernie had finally left. She didn't like the fact that the two of them were in the back room together. She knew what that could mean. Anita had enjoyed being back there with Jeff at various times also when dating. She hated to think about times when he and Bernie were back there. But still, she did. They involuntarily entered her mind.

As she saw Bernie's hourglass figure, Anita felt very fat, and very unattractive, exactly what Bernie hoped. Anita wanted to go back and talk to Jeff, just for reassurance and, well… she didn't know why otherwise, but she didn't. She would wait for him to say something. He never did.

As Bernie walked back to her car a guy from across the street called out. It was Scott. He had just arrived and was going to get a cold one at Ernie's. He had been in the field, didn't look very appealing. He thought Bernie was looking pretty good though. He yelled, *"How long you gonna be around?"*

*"Not sure. What do you have in mind?"* He had a lot in mind. But it started with dinner that night. She accepted.

# Chapter 47

How discouraging life can be. One minute you are on top of the world and the next, the rug is pulled out from under you. It is one thing to get up on the wrong side of the bed and have a bad day, but Fred was having a bad year. Everything seemed to be headed south. It didn't start out bad. In fact, 1981 promised to be a banner year. The wonderful experience with the class reunion started it. In general, he was doing fine. But then came the month of July. With the turning of the calendar everything changed.

His plan to remodel the old bank literally went up in smoke. That was difficult to deal with, but he managed to move on. A couple weeks later, he suffered from something else that came out of nowhere. A long-standing contract with a company Emerald Hydraulics had known and done business with for years, was canceled for no apparent reason. No explanation! The contract was of such magnitude it was devastating to the plant. To keep their heads above water, layoffs had to take place. He hated to do that. It was a last resort, but it had to be done.

The summer can be slow and lazy. Families make this vacation time and survey sights never seen before. That is the normal routine since kids are out of school and you need to get away sometimes. Experiencing a care-free attitude can help to keep your sanity. But a care-free attitude was far from the thoughts of employees of Emerald Hydraulics. The canceling of a major contract prompted rumors to spread like wildfire, some were realized.

The whole shop heard about the layoffs at the same time. Fred tried to be very transparent with his workers and they appreciated it. He told everyone he hoped business would pick up soon but there were no guarantees. The room was quiet.

Many workers were Fred's age or younger. They saw their future with this plant. They counted on it. Now, what were they going to do? Some had just gotten married. Some were starting a family. Some had just purchased houses. There were also older ones, farmers who wanted a little extra cash, who needed a little extra just to get by at times. Arnold Straight was one of them.

The meeting took place in the lunch area. Usually you would hear machines resting during lunch break or a coffee break. They weren't totally turned off, just on *"hold"* so to speak. The shop was known for generally being very noisy. But now everything was still. A bird flew in from the warehouse, looked down on the group and wondered why it was so quiet. What was going on? Then, back to the warehouse and outside again.

Inside, the employees looked at one another wondering who would receive the infamous *"pink slip"* signaling they wouldn't be back Monday. There was some anger but mostly a feeling of hopelessness. There was nothing they could do, nothing anyone could do. Sometimes life deals a bad hand and you just play it as best you can.

In the quietness of the moment, Arnold stood up, *"Fred,"* Arnold has his hands in his pockets and is looking down at the floor but then looks at Fred and around the room. *"Sorry to hear about the layoffs and everything. This is going to hurt a lot of people. I wouldn't want to be in your shoes when it comes to deciding who to keep and who to layoff."* He cleared his throat and looked down again. He wasn't used to speaking in public but doing an outstanding job. *"I'll make it a little easier for you. I volunteer to be the first one you let go. There are a lot of younger guys here who need the job more than I do."* Then he sniffed a little, rubbed his nose and sat down. Once again, silence.

*"Make me the second one,"* another jumped in, *"I can handle a few weeks without a paycheck."*

Sixteen in all volunteered to be laid-off indefinitely. Fred wondered how he got such good workers. Arnold would be one of the first to be rehired when, and if, things got better. When everyone was dismissed, getting ready to leave, Fred looked over at Arnold with a look of thanks. Arnold gave him a wink before he collected his tools.

It was a tough day for Fred but was going to get worse. He left the plant feeling down and headed to see his buddy, Jeff, at the store. Fred needed the encouraging Jeff could give. He drove uptown but didn't see Jeff's car, so he assumed he wasn't in. He thought about heading for the pool hall or Ernie's but knew some employees might be there and thought they might need the time to commiserate together for a while.

# Chapter 48

Fred heads home. Ginger always cheers him up. Walking in the back door feeling depressed he hopes of being snapped out of it by his lovely wife, *"I'm home."* Ginger wasn't in the kitchen where he expected to see her getting supper ready. Her car was in the garage. *"Had she been outside, and he just missed her?"* he wondered. *"Maybe she is planning on going out somewhere. Did they have supper plans this evening?"* Different thoughts cross his mind. He went upstairs to their bedroom, *"Honey, I'm home."* Then he saw her. She was on the bed crying. *"What's wrong?"* He sits down next to her putting his hand on her back.

It took a while for Ginger to compose herself. Sitting up, she blew her nose, took a deep breath and looked directly at Fred with just a few dreaded words, *"We lost the baby."* And then she put her head on his chest and the tears returned.

No one other than Fred knew she was pregnant. Fred and Ginger had been trying to have children since they got married. They built the house hoping to fill it with kids. Ginger had no siblings and Fred had only one brother, Paul, unmarried. Fred and Ginger wanted children.

Dr. Floyd had been helping them. He referred them to specialists and they both went through a variety of tests attempting to find out if there was a problem, medically, with either of them. Ginger was pregnant once before but miscarried then as well. She felt like a failure as a wife.

Fred was also upset but it was just another one of those things out of his hands. He didn't mean to appear cold but what could he do? Ginger went into a deep depression for a while. It was good she had a job. It kept her mind on other things. Dr. Floyd helped a lot as did Anita. Anita and Ginger talked daily the way it was and just talking about anything and everything helped.

On top of all that, Ginger had other concerns. Her parents were still living on the farm. Her dad was getting older, almost at retirement age. The past few years were proving difficult for him. His hands were being crippled by arthritis. He couldn't work like he did and gave up most of the livestock. Chickens and pigs on their farmstead were history.

He still grew corn, soybeans and had a few acres of hay. He would bale the hay and sell it to neighbors. But the price of corn and soybeans had not been good recently and harvests hadn't been what he hoped. He borrowed more than he should and now he was caught in the middle and afraid of losing the farm altogether. The timing was terrible as Ginger just found that out earlier in the week and now she had to deal with her miscarriage as well.

Ginger's dad was like many other farmers in similar situations. It was embarrassing. They were hard workers. They weren't slackers. Most farmers are that way. They give it their all. They put in countless hours doing whatever is needed. That is the environment in which Ginger was raised. And some farmers worked second jobs to stay afloat. Even that didn't always help.

They kept this all confidential. Ginger now knew the situation, in part. Fred didn't have a clue. Everything looked fine from his standpoint. But he was more involved in the plant and his bank project.

Fred was glad to see August 1st come around although things didn't look much better. He and Ginger talked about adopting and began to pursue this. There was an adoption agency in Alcoa, thirty miles away.

# Chapter 49

Bernie didn't grow up with a lot of money. Her dad received a good salary but there were two other children and money didn't go that far. When her father had a stroke, he needed to go to a care center, where he died shortly thereafter. The family wasn't prepared for any of this. Her brother was in college and her sister in high school at the time. Life had been a little rough for Bernie as she grew up and left home. But now things were much, much better. Except for what was happening in Emerald. This left a sour taste in her mouth.

She was hating Emerald as much as Fred loved it. She was excited about coming back to see Jeff, especially, but also some of her classmates. Unfortunately, the reunion wasn't what she thought it would be. Jeff and Anita were the perfect little couple, with the perfect little family and it nauseated her. She hated seeing them together. She also hated that Jeff wasn't giving in to her advances. But she wasn't giving up. *"Where was that old Jeff with whom she spent so much intimate time?"* She was very bitter. And seeing Fred and Ginger together, well, the four of them were just too much. They seemed to be having the time of their lives. Everything was going good for them, too good. Memories of her and Jeff haunted her, and she desperately wanted to relive them.

Gloria and Bernie continued the reignited relationship. They talked over the phone a lot. Gloria kept Bernie informed about all the trash going on in Emerald. Gossip was fast and furious. What Gloria didn't know for sure, she made up and she was pretty good. Besides the juicy stuff Gloria might bring up about the Emeralds, Bernie wanted to know what was going on with Scott McClary.

Gloria kept on top of everything. At one time Gloria had dreams of moving on but that changed after her college experiences left her sour. Gloria got married after her first year in college to a guy she met there. She was divorced by the end of her second year. The marriage lasted all of 9 months. He was a drinker. He was a violent drinker. He got mean and abusive when he drank. She was smart to get out of the marriage, but it tainted her terribly towards men in general. She never knew her dad. He walked out on her mom and Gloria barely knew her. Gloria lived with her grandma before getting her own place and worked as a bartender at *The Dock*.

The tree that killed her grandma totaled the house. Fortunately, insurance took care of replacing it. There was no mortgage. It was paid off years ago. Gloria was the only heir and planned to rebuild in the same location. It was like going home, only better. She had grown up in that house, but it was old, looked old and smelled old. Now she could live in something brand new. Olson Insurance had a lot of business to take care of, but they were very efficient. She could move out of the house she was renting. When Bernie came down from Minneapolis, there would be room for her. A new house would be built before the end of the year.

Bernie and Gloria did a lot of mean-mouth talking, but as far as Gloria was concerned, that is as far as it went. That wasn't the case with Bernie. Bernie was married to a man of influence. Now, he was a good man and honest man. He built his business from the ground up and was extremely fair. But he was married to a woman who was unscrupulous and could be very vengeful. And she demonstrated that. When she was able to see how the business was run, she saw the opportunity for growth and to accumulate power that could be used for any purpose she saw fit.

As she despised the two couples in Emerald who had what she wanted, she was going to make their lives as miserable as possible. Warped thinker that she was she even thought that when problems arose the marital bliss Jeff and Anita demonstrated might start to disintegrate. Bernie would be waiting in the wings once again for her former lover. She had the means to create havoc and was not above doing damage whenever the opportunity arose.

Carlson Industries was not only involved in land development but also diversified and involved with the production of machinery used in moving dirt around, big machines. This only made sense. They needed a lot of big, earth-moving equipment, it was a good investment. And who supplied the hydraulic cylinders to the company they invested in? Why, it just happened to be Fred's company or the one he co-owned. And whose contract got canceled after 8 years of faithful, excellent service? Once again, Fred and his employees got the raw end of the deal.

What had Fred ever done to Bernie? Nothing. But he was part of the two couples she despised. She would do whatever she could to make their lives miserable. Strike one! And that was just the beginning as far as Bernie was concerned. Just wait. There was more to come if necessary.

# Chapter 50

Fred and Ginger came back from the adoption agency with mixed feelings. They still wanted a child. But there weren't many babies coming up for adoption. At least that was the attitude they got from the agency. They were put on a list that seemed very long, but at least they had taken the first step.

It was a quiet drive back from Alcoa. Each had thoughts racing through their minds. Close to Emerald they decided to eat at *The Dock*. That would be a nice escape. It sounded good but didn't turn out that way. They missed being with friends. Their next stop would be a very familiar location in Emerald.

They went to see Jeff and Anita. Sitting in their backyard was where Fred and Ginger really *NEEDED* to be. A slight breeze kept the mosquitoes at a distance. The sun was getting close to the tree tops but hadn't met them yet. Some were taking their evening walk. Two dogs seemed to have new energy as they stood at the bottom of a tree wondering where that squirrel had gone. Anita was about to head the reluctant boys to bed. *"But we're not tired yet!"* Their droopy eyes told a different story.

*"How did things go in Alcoa?"*

*"Okay, I guess."* Ginger was frustrated. *"We filled out tons of forms and the people were nice."*

Jeff asked. *"Did they give you any kind of a time-table?"*

*"No."* Ginger answered all the questions. *"We are just on 'the list' now."*

For a moment they just sat there. Jeff got up. *"How about a beer?"* he asked heading for the house.

Fred was ready. *"Sure, sounds good!"*

Jeff returned with a couple bottles. No sooner had Jeff sat down than the phone rang. Anita had just put the boys to bed, was walking through the kitchen and turned back to answer it. *"Jeff ... John's on the phone."*

John was one of Jeff's older brothers who had dreams of playing pro-football. He was even picked up by the Green Bay Packers. His career never took off but as he was up in Wisconsin, he decided to stay there, make it his home. He was a coach at a high school near Green Bay. He loved it and the kids loved this big, bulky guy who used to be a pro. His nickname: *The Hulk.*

*"Hey, bro, what's up?"* The usual talk started.

*"Heard the plant was laying people off because business was down. Might be able to help. We got a company in town that makes firetrucks and they might be open to getting a new quote from somebody ... if I put in a good word, of course."*

*"Really, you have a good word to put in?"*

*"Smart aleck, tell Fred to give me a call."*

This was the first ray of sunshine for Fred in a long time. He jumped on the idea.

# Chapter 51

It was a barren lot. As Anita looked through the vast window in the front of their store she used to see five very prominent buildings that were part of the makeup of downtown Emerald for decades, but now she only saw backyards. To the south was a tavern, the post office and the bank. But there was nothing directly across the street from Emerald Grocery. No decisions had been made on what to do with this area. It was depressing. Life was depressing. Business had fallen off. With the layoffs at the plant, people weren't spending as much, they didn't have it! Some were going to Alcoa for groceries. She couldn't blame them, but that didn't help Emerald Grocery.

It was the 16th of October, 5:50 in the evening. They started the process of closing. They stayed open until 6:00 p.m. The last customer just headed out the door, so the store was empty except for Jeff and Anita. Anita would soon leave to get supper ready. Jeff would pick up the boys at Anita's parents.

The days were getting shorter and when the time changed from daylight savings time, it would really be noticeable. There were a few pickups on the street belonging to farmers who were *"getting the news"* in Ernie's before heading home. All the storefronts were getting dark. Anita was counting the day's total. A pickup screeched to a halt in front of the store. *"Who in the world...."* Anita thought. Then she recognizes Fred's vehicle.

*"Driving a little fast, aren't you Fred?"* Anita didn't even look up as Fred entered.

*"Who cares?! I got great news! We're back in business!"* Fred is in a better mood than he has been for some time. He's got a big smile and a precious document he can't wait to show Jeff.

*"What are you talking about?"* Hearing Fred's voice, Jeff came up from the back.

*"Just got back from Wisconsin. We sealed the deal with that firetruck company."*

*"You mean John's tip actually paid off?"*

*"Boy, did it. And, now get this, we have some leads to look at with a couple other companies."*

*"Sounds like you have some celebrating to do."*

*"Yeah, and I got some hiring to do that should make a lot of people happy."* Thanksgiving would be great this year. News traveled fast. It always did in the small town of Emerald. And this time it was great news. Rehiring took place the beginning of November.

The town was decorated, and the plant was doing well—people were cautiously shopping again. It was a good holiday season. Trees were selling very well and very quickly. Jeff wished he had ordered more. He had only six left.

Saturday, December 5$^{th}$, 1981 was a very cold day. The sky started with dark clouds that waited until noon to spit out flurries. The prediction was for single digits and heavy snow going into tomorrow. Snow puts everyone in the holiday spirit, especially the kids. Unfortunately, slipping and sliding on the ice can take it away almost as quick. No one likes dented fenders especially over Christmas vacation.

Through the afternoon the thick, wet snow invited kids to enjoy the winter wonderland. In the country it started to drift across the roads. Salt trucks kept roadways covered and snow plows were gassed up for their time of service later. When it started to really come down they wouldn't be able to keep up but that didn't ever stop them. Twelve inches of snow fell before the sun rose Sunday morning. That was too much for regular activities to take place. Tuning in the regional radio stations, most church services were canceled. No one could make it out and no place to park anyway.

# Chapter 52

Anita wasn't due till the end of December but felt ready to give birth already! Jeff was hoping it wasn't going to be today. It was doubtful he would be able to get out, the streets would be a challenge. If he got to the highway, it would probably be clear, but not the streets of Emerald. As it turned out, Anita was just uncomfortable. It wouldn't be today.

That Sunday saw neighbors digging out in boots and heavy parkas. Kids were loving the first blizzard of the season. Since it was a wet snow, an army of snowmen appeared as kids eagerly competed with their friends to see who would build the biggest and best.

Finally, the empty lot across from the grocery store wasn't so hideous. It was the perfect place to pile snow. Truckload after truckload deposited the white cargo creating the perfect spot for kids to gather. It looked like Mount Everest to the little climbers who couldn't resist the invitation to make it to the top and see the town from the new peak. There is nothing quite like climbing a mountain of snow, playing on a mountain of snow. It wouldn't completely melt until April.

Christmas activities filled the month of December. New Year's Day arrived and 1982 brought all the hope that 1981 brought a year earlier. Jeff left the house January 2nd to open the store and no sooner did he hang up his coat, but the phone rang. The baby was coming! Anita just called her mom to come over to watch the boys. Jeff's mom would take care of the store. It was a clear, bright day as they headed for the hospital. The highway was free of snow and especially ice. Traffic was light.

Well, it turned out to be a false alarm as can happen. Around noon the hospital sent the embarrassed couple home. Halfway home

Anita felt things were changing. *"Better turn around...NOW."* This time it was not a false alarm. At 12:14 the morning of January 3$^{rd}$, 1982, a little blonde to be named, Emily, opened her eyes to the world for the first time. The boys had a sister. Anita had the daughter she hoped for. For Jeff, life was perfect. Phone calls were made. Cigars handed out. What a great way to bring in the New Year!

Jeff wasn't even 30 and had a beautiful wife and family, two boys and a girl. He had his own business that was doing better and better. He was looking toward expanding. The future looked positive. God was smiling on him. But would it all continue? Why wouldn't it!

While most phone calls were of a good nature, one wasn't. Gloria shared the news with Bernie. Bernie hated to hear about the Emerald family's newest addition, but she would have been angrier if Gloria hadn't informed her.

She had already heard about the new contract for the plant. She tried to make sure it wouldn't go through but failed. She didn't have the connections. But she was always thinking and plotting. Life had made her hard and cruel and she wasn't even 30. It is amazing how two people can be so different.

It makes you wonder if Jeff had married Bernie would she have turned out different. Or was she destined to be this way from the start?

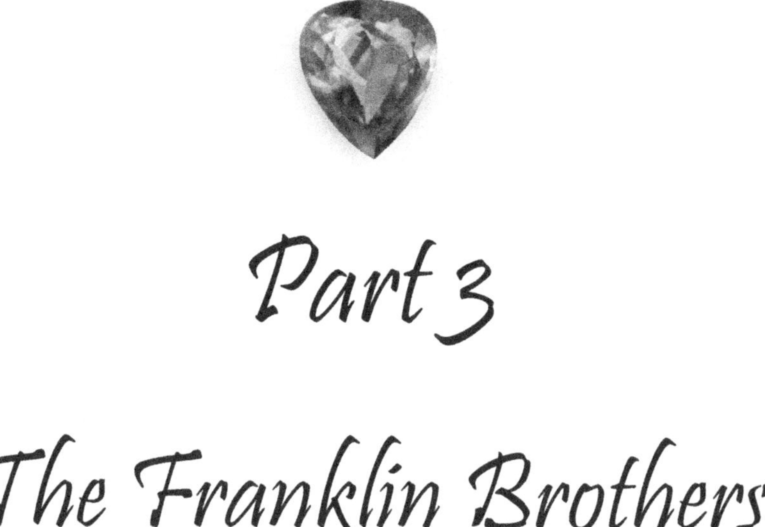

# Part 3

# The Franklin Brothers

# Chapter 53

Jewel Lake was a natural lake, three springs supplied it with fresh water. Kidney shaped and surrounded by trees at one time, it was a natural habitat for many of Iowa's water loving critters. Recognizing its beauty and tranquility, that changed over the years. A small island appeared a hundred feet off the north shore when the water level wasn't too high. It was a fishing lake—mostly carp and bullheads. It was a recreational lake, water-skiing in the summer and ice skating and snowmobiling in the winter, when cold enough. The church camp on the west side had a toboggan slide which was pretty much booked for winter nights by youth groups from the area, a very popular destination.

While Jewel Lake got its name from being only 5 miles outside of Emerald and closer to it than any other town, it was claimed by other towns in the county as well. At first, crude summer cabins popped up here and there. Eventually a state park was built complete with a shelter house, picnic tables, a dock, beach and changing booths for swimmers. It took years for it to happen, but homes were eventually built for year-round residence. The church camp expanded several times. A small grocery store tried to make a go of it but always had trouble.

A small restaurant also tried to survive, but never did until Fred intervened. Fred thought it had potential and bought the place, put money into it. He remodeled and gave it a new name. *The Dock* was paying off. It opened daily at 4:00 p.m. and stayed open until midnight,

2:00 a.m. on Friday and Saturday nights. It had a lounge and an elegant dining room. Pretty fancy according to Emerald standards.

Jewel Lake was experiencing kind of a boom. Some wealthier people from Alcoa, 25 miles east, purchased property and built small homes at first, but soon some pretty exclusive houses also appeared. You could tell money was being spent by the boats floating next to the docks. These people needed a place like *The Dock* in which to socialize. This was a dream come true for those wanting to get away for the weekend.

Gloria Pearson opened the lounge Tuesday through Saturday. She was hired as head bartender a month after the Grand Opening. Fred's brother, Paul, was to fill that position, but the fit wasn't good. Gloria already worked at a bar in Alcoa, and when there was an opening at *The Dock,* she applied and got the job. Living in Emerald, she was thrilled to work closer to home.

Gloria was 5'6" and a little on the heavy side. Her short red hair was easy to manage and suited her very well. She tried to wear makeup but never got the hang of it. She had a slight under bite, not real noticeable. She wasn't very attractive but knew her way around the bar. She talked with the regulars and knew more than she should as most bartenders do. She had a difficult time keeping secrets. She was quite the gossip. And she got away with it. Since she was good at managing the bar, Fred kept her on despite the loose lips. On the other hand, that is what brought some customers in.

When she took this position some of her old regulars followed her. That can be good at times, but in this case, she brought some not too reputable. Pete Franklin was among them. He was a drifter. Pete was a few years older than Gloria and had worked all over the county. He couldn't seem to hold down a job—had an attitude. He had gotten into a few fights. Some he started and some he didn't, just got beat-up. Pete got himself in trouble many times.

Pete got his curly brown hair from his mom and at one time he had a lot of it. Now it was shorter but still a little over his ears. He was all of 5' 10" and on the slender side. With a pug nose and a bottom lip that stuck out, he gave the impression he was pouting at times. He would stare a lot and you didn't know why he was doing it. He didn't either, it just happened. And sometimes the trouble he got himself into was a result of this mindless habit.

But Pete was nothing compared to his older brother, Darrell. Darrell was 6' 2" with greasy black hair that he liked to tie back into a ponytail. He had a big gut and most of the time walked around with his shirt unbuttoned displaying a t-shirt in need of washing. He always looked like he hadn't shaved in a week.

Darrell had a mean streak. He got kicked out of school more than once for cussing at a teacher. That seems unbelievable today, but it wasn't back then. He even spent some time in the county jail for pulling a knife on Stan Beckmann, town cop in Emerald. Darrell and Pete both rode Harley's appearing quite intimidating. Most people gave them a wide berth. But for some reason they were both close to Gloria. And Gloria didn't mind when one or both were around in case someone got a little out of hand ... whenever and wherever she was working. They were very protective of her, almost like big brothers.

# Chapter 54

Those dining out would often first go to the lounge for appetizers or just drinks, socialize a little and see who else was out for the evening. Tonight, was no exception. It was one of the first Friday night's people could get out free of a heavy coat. Spring appears as winter loses its punch, at least here. Flowers popping out of the ground emit their sweet fragrance hoping snow is gone for good. Trees are covered with little, green spots soon to be leaves providing shade. The air smelled fresh. It was time to open windows wide letting fresh air push out the stale winter odor.

Tonight, Fred and Ginger take Jeff and Anita out to dinner. It had been a long time since they were able to get together in such a way. They sat at the best table in the lounge, right next to the window, revealing a panoramic view of Jewel Lake. They enjoyed the sunset as the sun slid behind a variety of soft clouds on the horizon casting an array of pink, yellow and orange. Most of the ice had melted but a few patches were still floating. They would be gone within a few days. Lights were coming on around the lake.

Anita was especially glad to have an evening out. She had just gone back to work part-time but with their newborn, Emily, only a few months old, she was exhausted at the end of every day. Babies were more work and demanded more attention than she remembered. She wasn't complaining, just seeing the reality of it all. Anticipating this evening she took the whole day off. Jeff's mom, Bonnie, was able to handle what was needed at the store. Anita's parents were babysitting tonight.

*"Well, what are we going to have tonight?"* Fred lifted his eye brows asking this question as the group sat down in the lounge. He was

ready for a night of excitement. Enjoying some wine, cocktails or mixed drinks was pretty much the norm for this foursome. Fred rubbed his hands together when he didn't get an immediate response, *"Well?"* He kept looking at the others.

Jeff looked over at Anita and Ginger. *"Let's let the girls decide. What would you two like?"*

Anita knew exactly what she wanted but was hesitant to mention it. *"How about a pitcher of margaritas?"* She wasn't sure what Ginger might like.

*"Yeah, margaritas ... perfect!"* Ginger's eyes got wide and a big grin assured Anita she agreed. *"And a few chips and salsa, of course!"* It had been a long time since they enjoyed tequila.

Glasses are full, and everyone unwinds. *"Thanks for inviting us. It really feels good to be here and just relax,"* Jeff stretched out his legs putting his hands behind his head taking it all in.

*"It sure does,"* Anita rubbed her husband's back, *"and we don't need to be in any hurry tonight... at all!"*

*"No, we don't!"* Jeff sat up as the chips and salsa arrived. They all got close to the table and enjoyed the appetizer. It wouldn't ruin their meal. Nothing was going to ruin tonight's outing. At least that was the presumption.

The girls kept the conversation going and the guys sat and enjoyed their chatter and laughter. They were enjoying themselves and everyone in the lounge could tell. Checking out the rest of the activity, Jeff sat up, *"This place is really hopping, Fred. Is it this way all the time?"* Jeff was impressed. He hadn't been out here in some time. He dipped some chips in the salsa. There were only a couple of empty tables in the lounge at this point. All the booths were full.

*"Well, we do pretty good business,"* Fred was modest. *"It pays*

*the bills."* He looked over at Jeff. *"You know, Jeff, you should get in on what is happening out here."* Fred meant to approach Jeff with this idea but hadn't yet.

*"How so?"*

*"Have you thought about expanding, you know, maybe buying that old grocery store that closed ... again. You could really make it go with your business skills. I think there is a demand for something like that out here."*

Jeff hadn't heard about the store but wasn't surprised. Fred's suggestion was intriguing. *"Really?"*

*"Give it some thought."*

*"I will."*

*"Hey, our table is ready, let's go."*

# Chapter 55

The night started out slow with only a few customers and then it seemed someone opened the flood gate. Cars made their way around the lake and the parking lot filled up. Conversations made the noise level increase as the lounge filled. Gloria soon found herself wishing the crowd would thin out a little. She hardly noticed when the Kemps and Emeralds arrived. But then she heard Ginger with her unique laugh. And wherever Ginger was, Anita was probably close by. Fortunately, she wouldn't have to witness any more of their fun as they left for the dining room.

About 9:00 p.m. Pete Franklin drifts in. Gloria knows he wants a whiskey sour and prepares it without being asked. He's had a rough day but has cleaned up as much as he ever would to come see Gloria. He sits on a stool close to the end of the bar. The conversation went as usual. His paycheck for the week was too small for all his hard work. *(To be honest, it was generous for the actual work put forth.)* He was looking for another job that would pay more, where he could get the respect he deserved. Still, he was glad it was Friday. Gloria heard it all before and would hear it again. She talked when she could but was busy. Pete watched the crowd looking for any single women that might be present. None would want to be with him, but he could still look. He came up empty.

At 9:30 Gloria gets a surprise. Wiping off the counter she looks up and glances over towards the door that has seen a lot of action tonight. But the next person to enter would be the most interesting of them all. And the interaction she would produce would be memorable.

*"Well, my goodness, look who just arrived,"* Gloria smiled as Bernie's expensive perfume brought an appealing fragrance to the

lounge filled with less pleasing scents. She takes her time moving towards the bar, surveying the lounge, checking the crowd. She loved making an entrance.

Bernie replied, *"Thought I'd see how the other half lived,"* as she unbuttoned her coat and slid up on a seat at the bar directly in front of Gloria. Taking a deep breath, she began to relax and get settled.

*"What brings you down here?"* Gloria put a napkin on the counter and made Bernie her signature drink, a Manhattan. Gloria really didn't care why Bernie was down, she was just glad to see her. Outside of people she saw at work Gloria didn't have a lot of friends. *"Didn't think we would see you until the summer."*

*"Oh, I am sick and tired of winter in Minneapolis and it sounds like there is going to be one last blizzard. I had to get out of the cities."* She just drove down from Minnesota. Tired of winter, the Emerald area was her closest escape. And besides, she still had Jeff on her mind. Driving down the interstate, with every mile, another idea came to mind of how she might be able to make contact with him or better yet, really close contact. She would love to get him in a compromising situation and teach that *"sweet little Anita"* what was what. Any way she could make Anita's life a living hell, she would try.

Pete was taking it all in. He loved watching Bernie and Gloria gab away. As always Bernie was dressed quite well. You wondered if she ever dressed down. Bernie's *"casual dress"* looked better than most women when they get dolled up. Bernie was hoping to spend a few days in the area, maybe make contact with Scott McClary if something with Jeff didn't pan out. She preferred to stay in Alcoa, but as a last resort would stay with Gloria ... if Gloria didn't mind. Good time to catch up. Gloria was now in her new house and she had a guest room for Bernie. In fact, Gloria decorated it with Bernie in mind. Bernie hadn't seen it yet.

*"Okay, what do you have to eat? I'm starved. The trip was way*

*too long!"* Gloria handed her a bar menu featuring a wide variety of appetizers. Bernie started examining it to see what looked good. She wanted something spicy to go with her drink. Maybe just getting the sampler platter would do.

Pete decided he wanted in on this conversation. Bernie really intrigued him. She knew Gloria and that seemed strange to him. From the outset you might wonder what in the world Gloria and Bernie had in common. Regardless, Pete made the comment. He played with the plastic stirring stick from his drink. Taking it out of his mouth and pointing it toward Bernie he said, *"You don't look like a person who would eat in the bar. You look like more of a 'dining room' person."*

Bernie turned her head and gave him a weird look thinking, *"Who is this bozo?"* To her, Pete was the only drawback from sitting where she did. But when she came in, this was where Gloria was.

Before Bernie could answer Gloria quipped, *"Oh, she doesn't want to eat in the dining room. Some of her 'favorite' people are in there."* Pete had no idea what Gloria was talking about. He looked confused at the comment. It was normal for him. What Gloria said didn't make any sense whatsoever.

Bernie raised her eyebrows looking up. Her curiosity was getting the better of her. *"Oh, really? Who might those people be?"* Bernie was intrigued by the tease.

*"Oh, I don't know... maybe the Kemps ... and the Emeralds. Aren't they close friends of yours?"* Gloria smirked. That is all it took. The wheels started turning as Bernie took advantage of the opportunity. Her first encounter with Jeff in a long time was just in the next room. Things were looking up. Could it be this easy?

*"Yeah, right."* And with that Bernie stood up, took off her coat to reveal her curvaceous form. Displayed in a short, tight dress revealing an ample amount of cleavage, it would be just right to remind Jeff of what he was missing. She was slightly more *"bosomy"* than

Anita. The heels she wore made her legs look long and shapely. She enjoyed the guys checking her out as she sauntered toward the dining room. And Pete was among them although Bernie was way out of his league... and he knew it. But still, he could look, and he did.

# Chapter 56

Bernie looked around the dining room and saw her prey laughing and carrying on by the window. With her seductive walk she moved directly toward them. The couples were having a fabulous time and didn't have an inkling of the coming storm on the horizon. They just finished their entrees and were on their way to one of the fabulous desserts *The Dock* offered when Bernie struck. Standing behind Jeff she bent down close to his ear and asked, *"How is everything going?"* displaying a devilish smile. Her bosom was well displayed for Anita to notice—intentionally of course. And enough of her perfume was transferred to Jeff to be noticeable for the rest of the evening. She stood up and put her hand on Jeff's shoulder, standing between Jeff and Anita—slightly more toward Jeff.

*"Bernie,"* Ginger said, *"what a surprise! What are you doing here?"* Ginger was always doing that kind of thing. Innocently, she was nice to everyone, at least, at first. Bernie was no exception. And when Ginger gave the greeting it wasn't with the idea that Bernie was a welcome guest. It was more out of surprise. Ginger was a little too spontaneous at times which could cause problems. It did tonight.

*"Thought I'd spend some time in dear, ol' Emerald."* Bernie rested the side of her body on Jeff kind of rubbing her hip against his shoulder. Jeff was close to part of Bernie's anatomy he once knew ... exceptionally well. Her hip kept hugging his arm—his bottom lip came up over his top lip, eyebrows raised, not knowing what to do. He wouldn't admit it to anyone but Bernie's attention to him felt... he was flattered.

*"Would you like to join us?"* Ginger asked. And when she did, Anita wondered, *"What in the world are you thinking Ginger?!"* Anita

wanted to give Ginger a look indicating that but decided against it. That would be too obvious. Anita didn't want to give Bernie the satisfaction of knowing the feelings brought to the surface. If she were closer to Ginger, Anita would have kicked her but that may have been a little too obvious also.

Jeff just sat there smiling. He looked at Fred biting his bottom lip, trying not to notice what Bernie was doing, looking away. Ginger was talking more than anyone else. Anita, trying to keep her composure, thought, *"Ginger, just shut-up!"*

*"Oh, no,"* Bernie started to rub Jeff's back a little more, intentionally flirting, hoping to irritate Anita… it worked. She tried to arouse Jeff a little and put some slightly immoral ideas in his head—plant the seed. She didn't know it, but it worked. *"I don't want to disturb you. You all are having so much fun. Gloria said you were in here and it wouldn't be right if I didn't come in just to say, 'Hi.' I have to get back to the lounge."* She started to act like she was going to walk away but then hesitated a minute and looking at Jeff she said, *"Oh, by the way, congratulations on your little … girl, wasn't it? You have such a nice little family."* Then she looked at Anita with a belittling smirk as she squeezed Jeff's shoulder.

With her hand sliding across the back of Jeff's neck, slightly brushing his hair she left the foursome. Bernie took her sweet time walking back to the lounge, drawing attention from male diners. More than one wife noticed her husband taking advantage of the show provided by Bernie.

Later that night, the word *"hussy"* was used a lot. Anita was seething but didn't want Bernie to know at the time. She just kept smiling as Bernie interacted with Jeff. Anita was sitting there with her legs crossed and playing with her earring watching it all but then again, NOT watching it all. As she tried to inconspicuously watch Bernie walk back to the lounge, she was thinking a lot of things but the most respectable one we will say was, *"Oh, brother!"* The four would have stayed longer but the mood had changed. The thought of having dessert—completely gone. *"Check please!"*

Bernie could see from the mirror behind the bar when the couples left. The expression on Anita's face gave Bernie great joy. She knew she had succeeded in making her miserable. *"Who knows?"* she thought to herself, *"Maybe everything won't be so perfect between Mr. and Mrs. Emerald tonight. Maybe the seed took root and maybe Jeff might think about the old days."* She also noticed in the mirror that Jeff did look her way although they didn't make eye contact.

The two couples drove out in the same car and on the way home it wasn't quiet in the car. Bernie's perfume attached to Jeff's shirt would be one of the articles of clothing thrown in the hamper none too soon. Anita literally exploded she was so angry! This was a side of Anita most people never saw.

*"What is Bernie's problem?"* Anita sat with her arms crossed looking out the window paying no attention to the starry night. *"Why is she always like this?"*

*"Oh, don't let it bother you."* Jeff tried to calm her down.

*"And you, why didn't you do something?"* Her anger turned toward Jeff for a moment.

Jeff started to respond but didn't, knowing he might say the wrong thing.

Within the last year Bernie had just reappeared, but in those few months she had wreaked havoc. Part of the problem was that Anita wasn't feeling too attractive right now. She wasn't back to the way she wanted to be. Bernie looked too good.

# Chapter 57

Bernie was quite pleased with herself. Back in the lounge she sat on a stool next to Pete. Pete was surprised to say the least that he would be this close to such a *"looker."* She crossed her legs and Pete was more than surprised. He wondered why Gloria hadn't mentioned Bernie before. Gloria brought Bernie another Manhattan *(compliments of an admirer across the room)* and a sampler platter of appetizers. Pete, the big spender, was going to pay for it, but Gloria clarified where it came from. Pete looked around to see who it might be. He wasn't too happy with that gesture. The appetizers were on the house. *"By the way, what went on in the dining room?"* Gloria held her mouth indicating she knew exactly what happened.

*"Oh, nothing much, just said, 'Hello,' to some old friends."* She raised her eyebrows confirming Gloria's thoughts. Gloria worked basically for Fred but didn't like the company he kept.

Bernie's hate for Anita was growing. In her mind, Bernie was even more convinced Anita was the real root of her problems. Bernie never had any time for Ginger either. Ginger stole the crown from her. Bernie should have been Homecoming Queen in 1970. Bernie was more popular. Bernie was prettier. But she didn't even get elected to the Queen's Court! It was a total snub.

Sitting next to Pete wasn't very pleasant. He smelled of cheap cologne and sweat. But she felt he would follow her no matter where she went so she stayed put. When Gloria had to head to the other end of the bar, she asked Pete, who was continually ogling her trying not to look too obvious, *"So, what do you do for a living?"* She only half listened to his response.

*"She's paying attention to me!"* Pete thought. *"This was*

*great!"* Pete embellished his past and current abilities and skills. Bernie saw right through it. Pete didn't have a clue he was so transparent. Pete asked Bernie about herself and she informed him she was married to Robert Carlson of Carlson Industries which impressed Pete to no end. Everyone in the Midwest knew Carlson Industries. Pete thought this might be an open door to a better job. Later Bernie would have several jobs for Pete, but they wouldn't all be in construction. Pete would become invaluable to her.

Gloria finally made her way back, *"Hey, Bernie, guess who just walked in?"* Gloria nodded towards the door. Five burly guys made a noisy entrance. The third guy in Bernie knew very well and her eyes lit up.

*"My, my, the night is improving."* With a look of desire, Bernie watched Scott McClary strut in. *"I think I'll see what's going on."*

Scott felt hands squeezing his shoulders and the whiff of sweet perfume as Bernie bent down and kissed him on the cheek. *"How's it going, big guy?"* He was surprised, and his face got a little red while his heart started to beat faster.

The guys around the table were envious and would give him a hard time. "*Whoa, where did you come from?"* Scott couldn't believe his good fortune!

*"Came down to see you, of course. What did you think? Got time to get together later?"* Bernie poured on the charm. Their faces were inches apart as he turned to look at her.

Scott heard the invitation and immediately wanted to ditch his friends. *"Well, maybe,"* he teased.

*"Great."* And with that Bernie walked back towards the bar. She had made Scott's night. She hoped he would make hers... and he would. Scott excused himself from his friends and they found a table that had just opened and sat together leaving Pete at the bar with

Gloria. Pete's bottom lip stuck out even further.

Saturday morning Anita was still fuming. She didn't get much of a restful night's sleep. The evening she looked forward to and really needed was turned upside-down by a person who seemed to have no qualms about chasing her husband. It would take a while for her to get over it.

It would take a while for Jeff to get over it as well. He loved Anita, but the vibes Bernie was giving tormented him. He wouldn't ever intentionally cheat on Anita ... but things happen... don't they?

Trying to get his mind off Bernie, Jeff was also thinking about the lake store. Jeff had been considering expanding the business for a while but wasn't sure just how to go about it. There was a lot of competition from the big stores in Alcoa. Jeff needed to be competitive if he wanted to stay in business. The grocery store in the neighboring town had problems with declining sales and rising prices. It was about to close its doors. Jeff considered buying it. He could keep prices low buying in bulk the same way the chains did. Expanding seemed to be the only way of surviving.

He talked more to Fred about the possibility. Fred encouraged him to talk to T. J. McClary, bank president. He was always pretty good about giving out business loans. Jeff was a good business man. He had a good head on his shoulders. See what T. J. had to say. On Monday, usually one of the slow days at the store, Jeff walked down to the bank.

Emerald State Bank's new building ironically had the same floor plan as the old building. This really questioned the necessity of a new residence. But the ceiling wasn't as high, and it did feel a little more modern. They even had a drive-up window that the old bank couldn't have. Jeff went up to Vern Johnson, head teller, to find out if T. J. was available.

# Chapter 58

T. J. was out for the day, a little under the weather, but he could talk to Greg, T. J.'s oldest son, vice-president of the bank. T. J. would hopefully be back Tuesday. Jeff decided to come back some other time. He had nothing against Greg, he just wanted to talk to T. J. personally first. And he was trying to pull it all together in his own mind anyway.

Bernie was enjoying her time with Gloria and the feeling was mutual. After Friday night's little adventure at *The Dock,* Bernie pumped Gloria for more information about Pete. There was really a dark side to Bernie that intrigued Gloria, but, also, made her a little fearful. Bernie found out about the ex-con brother, Darrell, and this really got her thinking. She looked forward to meeting Darrell. But it was Wednesday and Bernie had to get back to Minneapolis. Business dealings were calling. She would keep in touch with Gloria... and Pete... and maybe Darrell.

Anita noticed Jeff was quiet in the evenings and seemed to be working on something. He was looking at prices and graphs and a variety of *"business"* related things. Trying to figure out if it would be profitable to expand, if he could do it, if it was a wise move for them. He went back and forth with it. One moment it was a good idea and the next it would bankrupt them. By Wednesday night he thought he had put a plan together. He wanted to bounce it off Fred first, but he wasn't available. Jeff decided he needed to take the idea to McClary.

Jeff finally met up with T. J. on Thursday afternoon and the meeting went well. T. J. invited Greg to sit in. He was grooming him for president someday. They thought Jeff's idea about expanding had possibilities. They would want to look at all the figures, of course, but they were receptive to the idea. T. J. especially liked the idea of buying the lake store because he had a weekend home on the lake and would like a grocery store closer on Saturday and Sunday. Jeff even had an idea who could run it. His younger sister, Beth, was getting out of the military and returning soon. She knew the grocery business. She could take it over.

Like her big brothers who were going to get out of Emerald and into pro football, Beth was also anxious to get out on her own. She was going to make a career in the military and see the world. But while home on leave a year earlier, cupid shot his arrow. David Clark, the youngest son of Harvey and Alma Clark, had a slight fender bender with her. This led to something more, romantically speaking. Letters flew back and forth over the next year and it looked serious. Neither knew for sure about the other, but both hoped it would lead somewhere and it did.

David was a carpenter, very handy with tools. He didn't work for anybody. He worked for everybody. He built houses. It might take a while, but if you bought one of his houses, you knew you had a good one. He was getting a reputation in Emerald and the county in general. He had helped in the construction of Fred and Ginger's house and then went on his own. Good decision.

The bank loaned Jeff the money and the store on Jewel Lake was his. The minute he got the funds he got nervous. He wondered if he had done the right thing. Anita assured him he did and that they were in this together. Remodeling was needed. He looked for someone who could handle it and David stood out as the best choice. But it had to be done now. He couldn't wait. Time was money. David could start in two weeks. Beth would be home in a month. The timing would be perfect.

Emerald Grocery expanded. If the lake store took off, Jeff would strongly consider the store in the neighboring town. But there was no guarantee he wouldn't be added to the list of others who tried to operate a store at the lake. He didn't want that to happen. There were a few anxious moments. But then he also thought how rewarding it would be to own a chain of stores. Was it possible?

The remodeling work moved along on schedule. David went the extra mile to make sure everything was done to perfection. He had high school shop students helping him and closely supervised everything they did. The store was looking better than ever. It used to look old and the kind of place you really didn't even want to enter. Not anymore! The smell of fresh paint and newly cut wood was enticing. People would slow down as they drove by to see what was happening with this old relic. There was a lot of excitement. The Grand Opening was scheduled for just two weeks. The Emeralds' were hitting a new milestone.

# Chapter 59

The blare of the siren woke the volunteer firefighters at 1:30 early Sunday morning. There was a fire out in the country somewhere, according to the siren, threatening to reduce someone's property to an ash heap. If it were during the day, smoke would be seen billowing into the sky like a thunderhead, but not at night. Stan Beckman got the call. The blaze was at the lake. It was the new store. It always takes a little longer with night fires to get people on the scene. Awakened out of deep slumber, sometimes you must reorient yourself a little as to where you are and what is happening. By the time the red trucks arrived, the store was totally engulfed, a complete loss. The building wasn't that big and went up fast.

How it started was a mystery. The electricity wasn't hooked up yet. It couldn't be an electrical fire. There was no gas hook-up. No greasy or oil-soaked rags left behind to provide the impetus for such destruction. David was sure everything was cleaned up before he left. It was part of his routine at every job site. An arson investigator from Alcoa was called in to do some snooping around, see what he could come up with. Emerald's new town cop was also asking questions. The only leads she got were from two neighbors who were night owls up watching *"The Man Who Shot Liberty Valance,"* an old John Wayne/Jimmy Stewart western. Both said they heard some obnoxiously loud motorcycles shortly before they smelled smoke.

John and Beulah Jackson's daughter, Liz, was Emerald's new *"police force."* She had just returned from Los Angeles. Her ambition was to be a part of *LA's finest*. That looked like meaningful and exciting work. It appeared to be the challenge she needed in her life. This was where all the action would be that she wanted to experience. But, after a while, she got tired of the gangs and high cost of living and missed the more subdued life of the Midwest. When Stan announced his retirement after 40 years of faithful service, her parents wrote her of the opening. They always worried about their daughter and her safety in dangerous and scandalous southern California. Liz jumped at the opportunity. She was a real catch and overqualified for the job as you might imagine. Stan agreed to stay on and work when needed. He was an old bachelor. What else did he have to occupy his time?

*"Well, well. What do we have here?"* Roger Poppe arrived Sunday afternoon to examine what was left of the newly remodeled structure now reduced to ashes. There wasn't much. And, that would help him as he started to sift through the material. The rubble had cooled off considerably. But there was still a hot spot here and there. Smoke lazily ascended indicating where raging flames had once been.

*"Don't know, can't figure out how it started. Any ideas?"* Liz was eager to get experience in the firefighting area, causes and such. She wasn't very familiar with things of that nature in this area of police work. That was handled by different people in her last position. But she was a quick learner and followed him around in his investigation.

*"Let's take a look and see what we can find."* Roger was an old hand at this and took his time strolling through the ashes looking at everything with a trained eye. His experience in such cases extended over the last 25 years. It didn't take long. It was obvious—arson. He pointed out to Liz why he was sure it was and even gave her the exact location it all started, in his humble opinion.

*"Who would do this, and why?"* Liz was going to solve this puzzle. Lots of questions—few answers. But it was her first big case and she was on it.

Jeff and Anita came out to look at what was left. This wasn't part of their plans and when they heard it was arson, well, that didn't make any sense at all! This kind of thing didn't happen around here.

These people were respectable people. They didn't go around setting someone else's place on fire. They both just looked around at what was left. Jeff walked around the perimeter. Anita stayed by the car. It reminded Anita of the mess across the street from the store when lightning hit the old bank building and fire reduced a quarter of the business district to nothing.

After the initial shock, Jeff started to look at the destruction as an opportunity to rebuild in a way that would truly make the store his own. He wasn't about to give up. The old store was just being remodeled, but now, Jeff could have David start from the ground up, build a store that would really fit his needs. It could be built a little further back on the lot, provide more room for parking, be more accessible in general. There were several new innovations he could introduce. It would really be a fresh start. This was a whole new way to look at things. *"Yeah, this could work out really well,"* Jeff thought, getting excited.

# Chapter 60

David got right on it and by the fall of 1982 the store had its official grand opening! Beth was back and enjoyed overseeing the newest facility owned by the Emerald family out on Jewel Lake. Her military experience helped her make everything run efficiently and look exceptional. David did a great job coming in under budget. And the store was a nice addition to the lake's general appeal. The first weekend the parking lot was always full, and people had to park along the road.

David's next project would be personal. There were still a few empty lots around the lake, not many but a few, and fortunately he found one a quarter mile directly north of the store just off a side road. He started to make blueprints a reality, building a house for him and Beth. He had proposed—she had accepted. A June wedding was planned. Even though he was the youngest of the three brothers he would be the first to marry.

David's older brothers, Dwight and Dwayne, were men of sizable stature, both bachelors. They drove cattle trucks. They were big, but they were also teddy bears. They wouldn't hurt anyone. But to look at them you wouldn't know that. Quite often they were hired as bouncers for teen dances. They would walk around in bib overalls, huge biceps. They were in school the same time as Jeff's brothers. They all played football together. The Emerald Eagles were unbeatable for several years in a row in those days. Everyone talked about those memorable years.

Back in Emerald, Liz wondered if she brought something back with her from California. She has gotten calls about break-ins and thefts. Emerald wasn't known for such activity. People here left their doors unlocked at night and weren't concerned if windows were left down on their cars sitting outside overnight. The crime rate in Emerald was almost nil. But recently there had been trouble. One farmer had the hose on his gas barrel cut and all the gas stolen. No one had any idea who was responsible. It was making residents a little bit jumpy.

In response, Liz started to do a lot of cruising in the wee hours of the morning, keeping an eye on what was happening, looking for anything unusual. Stan agreed to keep an eye on things during the day when he was on duty, occasionally, and on the weekends. He was also doing some patrolling. He was just as puzzled by what was taking place. In all his years as town cop there had been no problems to speak of, at least, nothing like this.

There were only two taverns left in town, the pool hall and Ernie's. Liz talked to Ernie and Rusty, the owner of the pool hall, asking each to let her know if they saw or heard anything. Quite often the tavern might be the place where gossip would generate, and some leads might come. Emerald was their town, too, and they would let her know.

Rusty always had a baseball bat behind the counter and everyone knew that. No one fooled around with Rusty. He listened a lot to conversations although he appeared not to. He had strict rules that needed to be followed when in his establishment. But he hadn't heard anything out of the ordinary. By the way, no one ever actually saw Rusty ever *use* the bat.

It was 3:00 in the morning. It had been a quiet night. In fact, it had been a boring night, the kind Liz enjoyed. She had enough excitement in her life. Stan was sleeping at the station and got the call: a fire out at the lake. The siren went off and Emerald's volunteers responded quickly. Liz put the lights and siren on and headed out. It was supposed to be the store again. But nothing was amiss. False alarm.

Driving back into Emerald she drove through the business district. That is when she saw the broken glass. Emerald Grocery had been vandalized.

# Chapter 61

Every so often you hear it. A couple tries to have a baby. They have difficulties, go through all kinds of procedures and tests. Nothing seems to work. They feel miserable and look for other options. Adoption seems the only hope they have of ever having a family. They start the lengthy and expensive process. Anxiety mounts.

Then it happens. The wife gets pregnant and the couple is ecstatic. That is what happened with Fred and Ginger. She had been pregnant twice before, each time miscarried. Now she was pregnant again and had reached her sixth month. She had never reached this point before. The two were cautiously making plans.

Anita didn't want to be cautious at all. *"Well, we have to get a shower planned."* It wasn't the first time the suggestion was made.

*"Not just yet, Anita."* Ginger kept putting her off.

Anita was getting frustrated. *"Why not?"*

*"We don't want to jinx it."*

*"Nonsense! ... Really? Well, I guess I don't blame you. But let me know WHEN we can."*

Business at the plant was better than expected. Those laid off were called back and two full shifts were in operation with overtime activities most weeks as well. Word spread, *"If you wanted a job, Emerald is the place to go. And more specifically, Emerald Hydraulics."* Fred even hired his brother, Paul. Paul was good in sales. He really knew how to schmooze. He seemed to have the gift. And he brought in the business. He traveled a lot and it was paying off.

This also helped when it came to housing. New houses were built, and old ones were selling at a premium. There was even talk of building a tract of homes south of town, between Emerald and Jewel Lake. It was good farm land, but the town was bursting at the seams. Houses were needed! When Emerald Hydraulics was successful, others also benefited.

Emerald was a bedroom community for Alcoa. Harvey Clark, mayor, had a lot to do with reducing property taxes to the bare minimum, making Emerald look more attractive, inducing people to relocate to this pleasant little borough. The news went out and it worked. The town population increased. Businesses were profiting and expanding.

Fred had a lot on his mind with a new family starting. But he still thought about his lost bank project. *"Doesn't that look pathetic?"* Fred was standing with Jeff in the grocery store looking across the street.

*"Well, it isn't pretty, that's for sure."* Jeff didn't like the sight either and was hoping someone would do something to give an inviting appearance to the downtown area. The debris had long been removed, of course, but it still looked bleak and barren. They both stood with legs slightly apart and arms crossed, rubbing their chins.

Anita walked up the aisle and saw the two in a serious stance. Seeing them standing the exact same way doing the same thing, she couldn't help herself. *"What are you two knuckleheads up to now?"*

# Chapter 62

Fred didn't mind the comment. *"Oh, hi, Anita. I just don't like that empty lot over there. Something needs to be done. We've got to get downtown looking better ... better."*

*"Well, talk with Harvey."* Jeff suggested, remembering Fred's suggestion to him about the lake store. *"Maybe you can get something going with the town council."*

Fred didn't respond immediately. He acted like he hadn't even heard Jeff. *"Good idea, maybe I will."* And Fred was off. He always had a million ideas going around in his head.

Three fillings, two wisdom teeth extractions and six general cleanings filled his day. Harvey Clark was glad to see the day end. He hadn't been feeling well but, trooper that he was, he tried to never cancel an appointment. He was locking up and heading home. But before he made it to his castle Fred made his appearance. *"Hey, Harv, got a minute."* Fred put his hand on Harvey's shoulder as they walked together to the post office.

Harvey wondered what was next and tried to act glad to see him. *"Sure, what's up?"*

*"How you doin' Harv?"* Without waiting for a response Fred continued, *"Say, Jeff and I were talking about getting something done with that terrible eyesore on West Main. We have some ideas we'd like to fly by you and the council. Any chance of that happening?"* It was all Fred's idea, but he thought attaching Jeff's name might carry a little more weight.

Harvey wanted more details but really didn't want to prolong this conversation. *"What you got in mind?"* He knew how Fred could be. What he really wanted was something down in writing to evaluate before moving to the next step.

*"Oh, just a proposition ... I'll write it up and bring it to you. What do you say?"* Fred was on the agenda for the next meeting.

If it wasn't Ginger's baby shower it was Beth's wedding shower. Anita was involved in both. Beth and David reserved a Saturday in June for their wedding. Anita and Jeff's 8-year-old son, Jake, would make his debut as ring-bearer, dressed in a little tux with tails and everything. Anita seemed to take it all in stride while still very involved at the store and now in school, both Jake and Jared were getting older.

Both showers were held in St. Paul's basement. Ginger had given the *"okay."*

Ginger's baby shower was scheduled for 2:00, Sunday afternoon. Sunday afternoons were the best time for ladies to attend. Ginger and Fred were well-known and well-loved in the community. Guests started arriving at 1:45, people always came early. They wanted to get a good vantage point to see who else came and be the first to talk about them... and others. The church door banged to let you know someone had arrived and you waited to see who came down the steps. That was possible for the first few arrivals, but it wasn't long before conversations took over and few paid attention anymore.

The program began at 2:30 p.m. The ladies quieted down each finding a place to sit. Fifty females of various ages filled the chairs. The sweet smells of various perfumes mixed with the general smell that goes along with church basements were predominant. Anita got everyone's attention, gave the proper welcome, instructing the participants on the first game, when two additional ladies started down the steps. There were always late arrivals. Everyone waited.

# Chapter 63

Keeping secrets in Emerald isn't easy. The rumor mills get going and anything you would want to keep quiet gets spread and embellished. Ginger's baby shower was no secret. The whole town knew about it. But it was one of those events where invitations were sent to ladies close to Ginger. Proper etiquette dictated an RSVP. Anita needed to know how many to expect.

Gloria Pearson didn't get an invitation. Imagine that! Neither did Bernie Carlson. They weren't offended, but it wasn't going to stop their attending. Planning and conniving was in full swing and the results were about to be seen.

Bernie and Gloria made their grand entrance. Being the host, she was, Anita let them crash the party. What was she going to do?! Most of the ladies didn't know the history here. Had they known, all eyes would have been on them to witness what kind of interaction might take place. Jeff's mom, Bonnie, knew as did Clara, Anita's mom. They could see the fire in Anita's eyes and her general body language tightened up at the appearance of the late arrivals. They were proud of how she handled herself. Ginger was also happy that her good friend remained gracious. The whole afternoon could have been a disaster. But that would have been a different Anita. The party continued, no one being the wiser to the brewing tempest.

Opening her gifts, Ginger opened Bernie's card with five, crisp \$50 bills inside. A generous gift, but at the same time, impersonal. While Fred and Ginger were well off, the cash would come in handy. They would have to buy three of everything. The doctor informed them they were having triplets, very apparent from Ginger's appearance!

As the ladies enjoyed the refreshments of punch, cookies and little sandwiches with the crust cut off, Bernie worked the room. She went from one lady to the next being as sweet as she could be, not missing anyone. She put on the charm matched by her big smile. Many knew her mom, so she was repeatedly asked, *"How's your mother doing, dear?"* Bernie hadn't seen her mother in years, more Bernie's choice than her mother's, but she made up something anyway. She was very good at that and seldom got caught.

Those who didn't have the inside scoop commented, *"Isn't it nice for her to come all the way from Minneapolis just for the shower? She's such a nice young lady."* Even in Emerald some secrets can be kept, people deceived. Bernie was good at pulling the wool over the eyes of many, but four people present wondered what she was up to.

Gloria followed Bernie like a little puppy. She didn't have a lot to say but enjoyed being close to Bernie. It made her feel special. All the guests received their special *"Bernie"* greeting and the two sat down to enjoy the gathering. They drank a little punch and chewed on a cookie before deciding it was time to leave. Eye contact between Bernie and Anita was very subtle, but it was there. Bernie made her next move.

*"Look out, here they come."* Anita groaned. *"Get the 'smiles' ready."*

Bernie discarded her plastic cup, smoothed her skirt and headed toward the stairs with Gloria close behind. The two walk toward Anita and Ginger to say their *"Good-byes."*

*"Well, Bernie, how nice of you to come all this way."* Anita is polite and cordial but also a little sarcastic. She felt the undercurrent present. No hurtful words were spoken but neither were fooled by the pleasantries expressed by the other. At least by this time Anita wasn't feeling the previous jealousies. Anita had her exquisite figure back, looking more attractive than Bernie. Bernie noticed but tried to feign she didn't.

*"Nonsense. Friends do this kind of thing for friends all the time,"* Bernie replied. *"How much longer do you have?"* She looked at Ginger not caring in the least for her answer. It was all meaningless small talk for those watching.

Ginger was deceived by Bernie's demeanor thinking Bernie was really interested in her condition. *"A few weeks yet but I am hoping it will be sooner."* She went on further explaining her condition not realizing Bernie wasn't listening anymore.

Anita was hoping these would be the last words she would hear from Bernie and would just take the opportunity to pass Anita by on her way out. Not gonna happen!

*"And what about you, Anita? When are you going to have another baby? After all, you and your hubby haven't wasted any time having your first and then your second and then your third. You just seem to be having fun making babies."* Bernie was as nasty as she could be... smiling the whole time.

*"Why don't you just shut-up,"* Anita thought. But Anita wasn't going to let this opportunity get by without making a cutting remark on her own. *"Well, Jeff and I are very happy with our life together for right now. Why, just the other night before we went to sleep we were lying in bed, talking about our life together and Jeff asked if I thought we should have any more children. Well, we talked about it for a while and then... uh... we went to sleep."* Anita pretended she was embarrassed by how far she went telling something so intimate.

Ginger was shocked by what she heard. She couldn't believe what Anita was saying. She was stunned. Finally, Anita said, *"We love the family we have. But should we decide it is time to add another one, we'll let you know."* Oh, yes, Anita had other thoughts as well.

# Chapter 64

Bernie was caught by surprise. Her mouth was hanging open as Anita started to reveal a little of their private life. She didn't know what to make of Anita's response. Her sarcastic smile dimmed but then returned as not to be out-witted. *"I see... well we better be going. Maybe we will see you around."* The two headed for the steps, quietly whispering.

*"Not if I see you first,"* Anita thought, *"good riddance!"*

Bernie was also down for another reason. A business proposal is being presented to Ginger's parents. Carlson Industries is interested in developing land around Emerald. The rumor is out: if any farmer around Emerald is willing to sell land, they will get *"top dollar."* Bernie knew Ginger's parents were in financial trouble and would jump at the chance to sell. The next day, as a representative of Carlson Industries, Bernie made an appointment with Louis Price to talk about a proposal. Monday afternoon they sit around the kitchen table discussing the future.

The offer is not for *"top dollar."* It is the most Carlson Industries will pay. Bernie talked her husband into this project but hadn't been completely truthful. She wanted to be involved in what took place around Emerald and do it as cheaply as possible. This was her *"baby."*

Business man that he was, Robert Carlson realized what was happening. Even so it looked like a good investment. He let Bernie take on the project and was glad to get her out of his hair. Through it all Bernie was getting great experience enjoying it. Her personality impacted the way she would work the deals. It wasn't the way Robert would do things.

Well, the offer was made and was a joke. Louis and Clara were embarrassed to let anyone know how little their property went for. They never told anyone the exact amount. Ultimately, Louis and Clara were relieved it was all over.

They had a huge sale selling tractors, wagons, and all the farm machinery. The two found a house in Emerald that met their needs. Louis worked at the plant in a job Fred provided. Bernie, meanwhile, was going to make a fortune.

The city council meeting is always the second Monday of the month. Harvey called the meeting to order precisely at 7:00 p.m. The agenda items were discussed in the proper order. Harvey had his own copy of *Robert's Rules of Order* to insure proper procedure.

Most items take care of themselves. Still, some things must be discussed. Members let their feelings be known. *"We need a new lawn mower to mow the cemetery."* Should they buy it locally or not? Hard to see this as being important but to some it was. Things get a little out of hand. When that happens, Harvey suggests something go to committee or be tabled.

Finally, time for new business. Fred has been waiting for his opportunity. Listening to the council, Fred didn't know if this group could handle his ideas or not. But he was going to put it before them to see the outcome.

Fred handed out papers and started talking. The evening was getting late. *"Thanks for giving me time on the agenda. I appreciate it and I think you will also appreciate what I have to share. It could help bring new life to downtown Emerald once again. I will try to be concise."* Fred presented his proposal. A mini-mall would replace the vacant lot attracting new businesses. Emerald needed this facelift.

His delivery was professional. Any PR person would have been proud. But the council just sat there. Some eyes were heavy as the hour was late. A couple were invigorated by it but were also bean counters with challenging questions. This wasn't the response Fred hoped for. Fred came to the conclusion they weren't ready for this proposal. It was too radical for this council.

*"Looks good, Fred. I have one question though, where would the money come from?"* And then other questions and soon they were off topic. The gavel came down and everyone is quiet.

Then came the death blow. *"I think it needs more thought. Good idea, but let's think on it. I move that we table Fred's idea."* The council did what they almost always did with something new—tabled the idea. To Fred it meant his idea had been shelved... for good. Might as well get a shovel and bury it.

Fred felt bad about this, just like when the bank went up in flames. But he took it. The council members could not be pushed to do something they didn't want to do. There might come a time when they would be ready for such a change, but it wasn't now. It took more than this to deflate Fred and all his ideas. He sulked for a while but got over it and learned from the experience.

# Part 4

# Tornado

# Chapter 65

Beth Emerald and David Clark are married and live at Jewel Lake. They have a beautiful home and expecting their first child. Beth is doing a fantastic job managing the lake's grocery store. It is just right for her and working with her brother, Jeff, is a dream come true. David is continually on call. He never looks for work. It looks for him. His reputation puts him in demand. He is booked 6 months in advance.

Fred and Ginger are busy with their three little jewels. They have passed the terrible-twos and in their third year. It turned out to be a good thing for Ginger's parents to sell the farm. Their three grandchildren demand a lot of attention which they are willing to give.

The year is 1986. Jeff and Anita have done so well with the store at the lake, they purchased the grocery store in the neighboring town. Now they have a chain! They have three children, all they will have and are happy—quite the family.

You wouldn't know the Emerald area from the way it was 5 years ago. Jewel Lake has become a recreational spot; new homes have been built around the lake. Some are right on the water and some on the other side of the road circling the lake. And Carlson Industries is busy with their new development south of town. Big, earthmoving machinery has come in to change a huge farmstead into substantially smaller plots—houses being sold at premium prices. Bernie has taken special pride in this project. She is quite the business woman. Little does she know, but those big machines are using hydraulic cylinders made at Emerald Hydraulics.

Fred's business is doing very well. Hiring Paul was a good move and Fred took the opportunity to buy his partner out. He was now sole owner of Emerald Hydraulics.

Bernie was spending way too much time in Emerald as far as Anita was concerned. And she was becoming more blatant in her pursuit of Jeff. Rumors were started about affairs that either of them might be having or had in the past. Things like, *"Jeff sure spends a lot of time away from home. Is it really all business?"* and *"Anita sure is friendly with some of the customers more than others."* Some even questioned who Emily's father really was. *"Did Emily really look like an Emerald?"* How ridiculous! That one really made Anita angry. When confronted, Bernie denied any involvement in such ... talk. It all came from gossip at *The Dock.*

Bernie's marriage was hurting. It never was a good marriage. Robert got married too soon after his first wife died. He was still on the rebound. Ultimately, Robert felt he deserved what he got. But it was wearing him down. He was getting old before his time. They had no kids. He had no kids. Since no prenup was signed, Bernie would get everything when he died. There were times when he saw how much she was spending, he wanted to die. She wasn't what he expected. He wasn't what she expected either. Bernie had Scott McClary, down in Emerald, making her happy. It was mutual.

And then there were the Franklin brothers. They were always around. They both had jobs in Bernie's project, but didn't work all that hard. And ever since they spent time in Emerald, it wasn't the nice community it had been. Hearing the loud roar of their Harley's ruined the small-town ambiance. There was a price to be paid for growth in the community.

The Olson Insurance Building on the corner of West Main and Diamond, right next to Emerald Grocery, was built years ago and had been a bank to begin with. It mirrored the old bank building which used to be right across the street. At one-time Emerald had two banks but few remembered those times. Harold Olson bought the building back in the 60s after renting space for several years.

Harold got in the habit of dropping in to see his daughter, Anita, around 10:00 every morning, have a cup of coffee with the retirees and shoot the breeze. It was good public relations and handy as Emerald Grocery was right next door.

Summer began with kids taking advantage of their new freedom. Any number of bikes went through town during the day. Ad hoc baseball games were organized either at the city park or the diamond behind the school. Most summer days looked the same. This day in early June was no exception.

# Chapter 66

It was a beautiful day and business for Harold was good. He was the only insurance agent in town, had been for years. Everyone came to Harold. Everyone knew Harold. Everyone trusted Harold. And he could be trusted. He took a personal interest in all his clients. He made sure they were paid for any claim ... yesterday. Most people he knew by their first name—along with their family history.

Harold loves his daughter. He never expected that she would marry Jeff but was happy she had. He knew she was a beauty from the day she was born. She was not only physically attractive, she had a marvelous personality. And he knew many young men pursued her throughout high school. Every week a new prospect came. Some would make fine son-in-law material, but Anita never was interested. He thought she would go away to college, find a guy, get married and never return to Emerald. He even thought, after he retired, he and Clara would have to go wherever Anita was to be around grandchildren. When Anita and Jeff married, that was the best day of his life. Well, third best. The first, when he married Clara Jessup and the second, when Anita was born.

And he was ever so proud of his grandchildren. Jake, Jared and Emily were the best. Jeff and Anita were doing a great job raising them. Eleven, eight and four. Jake was already helping around the store. And little Emily, pictures of Anita at her age were almost identical.

Anita could set her watch by when dad came in. The mornings weren't usually that busy and sometimes she would be able to sit and have coffee with him. Before he left, she always gave him a hug and a peck on the cheek. She just turned 33 but if she tried to purchase liquor, out of town, she would get carded. The years, few as they were, had been very kind. Her figure was better than it was in high school. She still wore her hair long. Sometimes she had bangs, sometimes not. Still gorgeous.

Harold went back to his office and would head home for lunch in a couple hours. Today was like the hundreds of other days he had lived. He shuffled papers around, filled out necessary forms, spent time looking out the window, talked with his secretary, met with some old clients and answered a few phone calls. That was his morning. When lunch time came he walked home.

It was all of five blocks from home to office. He almost always walked now, except in the winter. He walked by the bank and greeted T. J. as he was leaving for some business lunch. Harvey was filling a tooth or pulling one, couldn't tell which strolling by the dentist office. Harold wondered what Clara was preparing for lunch. He would be happy with leftovers but thought everything was gone from last night's supper. Oh, well. It was the perfect day for a walk. The sky was beautiful. There were some clouds bunching up in the west that might produce something later, but also a lot of blue sky. As he gets a block from home he hears the noon siren and most work in the community stops for the next hour.

By 1:00 p.m. Harold is back in his office. Sitting in his leather chair, he glances at the pictures on his desk. Pictures decorate his walls but the ones around the perimeter of this old piece of furniture he treasures the most including one of his bride, his daughter's graduation, and a picture of Anita and her family.

Dark clouds have moved in and the wind has picked up. *"Olson Insurance, Harold speaking."* Harold answers to hear the familiar voice of his wife of 35 years.

Clara calls a couple times a day and whenever she needs to report something special or serious. *"Hi honey, just heard there is a severe thunderstorm warning out. Thought you'd like to know. Could you tell Anita?"* The message comes at 2:30 p.m. when his secretary was away from her desk. It was obvious that something was building up and making its way toward Emerald. It is good to know if the forecasters are thinking it might turn into something.

*"Thanks, will do. Let me know if you hear anything more. You keep safe at home."* Nothing to worry about—happens all the time. You get lulled into a sense of security you shouldn't always assume.

Harold left his office to convey the message in person. It had gotten windier! He is surprised how fierce the wind is as he makes his way those few feet to the grocery store.

*"Wow was that loud!"* A crack of thunder broke the silence. *"Look at that lightening. I hope it doesn't get too bad."* Anita didn't like lightning. When lightning hit the old bank, the flash was a little much and ever since that time she was more cautious, gave it more respect.

*"It probably won't but keep an eye out anyway."* That was the typical response to any storm coming through. Harold had seen a lot of storms in the past. No big deal.

# Chapter 67

Harold has a hard time concentrating. Wind gusts come and go. One minute you think you are going to blow away and the next… nothing. But those moments when it is nothing start to be fewer. *"Boy, it's really getting windy out now!"*

*"Yeah,"* Anita responds, *"I think we're in for a good one."* They are on the phone with this conversation.

*"You doing okay?"* Harold always looks out for his daughter's safety. It hasn't been this windy for a long time. The clouds race east but then slow down. They are various shades of gray, displaying an attitude.

*"We'll be okay over here, dad, if it gets too bad we'll head for the basement."* She said, *"We,"* meaning her and any customers. Jeff was at the lake store.

*"If you want, come over to our basement. It is probably stronger."* Harold offered. His building was brick and mortar, and he was sure it would be standing long after every other building in town was gone.

The storefront awnings are relentlessly whipped back and forth. Trees are swaying. The huge elevator garage doors are lowered as a precaution. Gene Porth went out to pull the doors down when a sudden gust took his cap off before he could pull it tight on his head. He watched it bounce down the alley and disappear. The streets are devoid of traffic with small pieces of trash flying around. And then … then the wind stops. Gene realizes what might be happening.

When the wind suddenly stops, everyone gets nervous, not a

good sign. There is a good chance all the wind is being sucked up in the vortex of a tornado. Unfortunately, that is exactly what is happening this time. It is quiet, perfectly still for a few seconds, extremely eerie! Then there is the sound, the frightening sound of a freight train rolling through. In an instant, everyone loses power—no electricity! Everyone feels helpless and defenseless.

The violent twister comes down directly onto the Meyer farm two miles outside of town hitting the barn that has been a fixture for 50 years. In seconds it is gone. Hay stacked in the mow flies everywhere. The wind lifts the huge barn door ripping it off the building and sets it to the side intact. The remainder of the building is reduced to toothpicks. Fortunately, no livestock were inside the structure. Quonsets are next. Tractors and trailers are thrown like discarded toys from a child's sandbox. Finally, the call comes in about the funnel cloud from Clyde Lenz just coming in from the field. One long siren blast tells people to take cover. Many will wait until they personally see the twister coming. Emerald is next. It won't be pretty.

The city park has a new shelter house a year old. A few months later it will have another new one—this one will be history. The wind blows through it, picks it up forty feet and releases it. The foundation now holds twisted pieces of lumber. St. Paul's will lose its bell tower and half of the roof. The huge bell, rung for the past 82 years, falls into Jewel Lake like a meteorite, scaring some fishermen not knowing what fell. It will be a story told and retold. The bell will stay in the lake and be viewed by future divers. The two houses across the street from the church are demolished. No one is home in either place. On to the business district. It seems this is what the tornado was created for and is now aimed at. It moves on. It lifts for a block and hovers giving some hope of deliverance but then it slams down.

It stops in midair deciding upon its next target. The new bank is destroyed. T. J. McClary is on the phone with Fred when the building explodes. It is T.J.'s last day on earth. His body is never recovered. His son, Greg, was playing golf at the lake and was on the 12th hole. It was his day off. He could see it all from a distance but has no idea how bad it is. The rest of the bank employees were in the basement.

The tornado jumps over the post office next to the bank, sparing it, but Ernie's tavern has the south wall ripped away leaving one farmer sitting at the bar, not knowing what has happened. Ernie was standing behind the bar and is lifted and transported to the post office roof.

With no buildings to the north, the tornado crosses the street to Emerald Grocery. The front window is hit by flying debris. It takes Anita by surprise and she moves quickly before the window is shattered. She wastes no time heading for the basement.

But the tornado has a real interest in the structure next to Emerald Grocery. The Olson Insurance Building gets the brunt of the tornado's force. This strong building appears to be a challenge. Stones in the building have seen many windstorms and countless blizzards. It has withstood the force of Mother Nature for decades. Today it would not. It is a total loss.

# Chapter 68

The tornado isn't through with its destructive rampage; it has just started! It gains strength and determination to do more damage. Moving on, 75% of the business district is wiped out, completely gone. Grace Methodist is gone. The funeral home is gone. The new gym is gone. And then it heads toward Emerald Hydraulics. And here... here there is no basement. There is no storm cellar. There is no protection, nowhere for employees to flee. Fred watches with horror as he sees the twister traveling toward him, he can't do a thing about it. He can just imagine the carnage. Machines can be replaced. Lives are something else. Where could his employees go?!!

Debris is flying everywhere. Tree branches, bicycles, cars, furniture—the tornado has a mean streak. While this is the most perfectly shaped tornado he has ever seen, the perfect funnel, Fred is scared to death. It is about to cross the highway to go that extra quarter mile to devour his plant. At first, there is no hesitation in fulfilling its desire.

But then, and this is odd, it stops for a moment at the highway as if to make sure there is no traffic. Right between a gas station and an implement dealer the twister pauses. It is a brief pause before it gears up and proceeds. And then ... then it gives the hint it might lift back into the sky from whence it came. It had jumped over the post office to get the rest of the town. Was it playing a trick on Fred? Was it doing some teasing, cruel as that might be? Did Emerald Hydraulics have a bulls-eye on it? Was the tornado preparing to come down like it did on the barn, sending pipes, machines and most importantly, people in all directions? The tornado looked like it was bouncing along as it traveled.

The tornado descends as it comes to the plant's entrance. But giving it a second thought, it ascends. The destructive journey is over, its task complete. The wind dies down.

Fred breathes a sigh of relief. So does Ginger, watching it all from her front porch. Her home, south of town, has been spared. Bernie viewed the destructive path from her house in Carlson Estates. Her development is intact—no damage whatsoever, not even roof damage. Jeff watches from the lake. The terrain is flat, and he witnessed all the terrible, frightening activity. He has no idea of the damage done. He wastes no time getting back to Emerald. Is his wife okay? Are his kids safe, his mom?

The highway is clear, but the streets of Emerald are not. Debris everywhere, Jeff can't get very close to the business district in his car. He parks and walks. People have emerged from their caverns of safety and are stunned viewing the damage. Jeff gets his first glimpse walking through the once well-groomed neighborhoods. Still he has no idea how hard downtown has been hit or if it was hit at all. Walking up West Main he notes the bank is nowhere to be seen. Some cash is strewn around the area. Little is left on the foundation. Ernie's looks very strange with the south wall gone. Otherwise the place seems intact. But when he sees his store, his heart sinks. The roof has partially collapsed as the south wall was blown away. Most of the shelves are still standing with all their products arranged like nothing happened. Only a few have been blown over. The coffee pot has coffee in it and hasn't been disturbed. But he cares only about one thing right now—Anita.

*"Anita?" "Anita?"* Silence. He assumed she took cover in the basement and by now would be back upstairs. Surely, she is around somewhere. Maybe she is with her dad, surveying the destruction. Maybe she is somewhere else around town. Maybe she is with her mom and their kids or his mom. With most of the buildings downtown gone you would think she would be easily visible... somewhere. But she wasn't.

Jeff makes his way to the back of the store to the basement door. It is blocked. Now he reasons to himself why she isn't out yet. *"She probably tried to get out but couldn't."* He can't get the door open but finds a pry bar to help. He yells to let her know he is there to get her out. It will just be a few minutes. She shouldn't worry. But he hears no response. With the door open, he looks down the stairs.

*"Anita?" "Anita?"* More silence. *"Why isn't she answering?"*

The power is off, all is dark. He runs back for a flashlight. It is dead. He rips open a pack of batteries and voila, it works. He points his flashlight down the steps to find her. He shines it around. The basement is empty. No one is there.

# Chapter 69

Liz Jackson was in Los Angeles long enough to see the damage an earthquake could do. She experienced a small one and it was scary. To her, it was unnerving. She grew up in the Midwest. Tornadoes didn't bother her as much. At least you knew when they were coming and could seek shelter or get out of their way. *Usually,* you knew when they were coming. The weather would feel funny and the siren would go off. Maybe you might even witness one being formed in the distance. When it appeared, you took cover, headed for the basement or cellar or drove in a different direction.

And everyone would generally be safe if they followed those rules. That is the way it was supposed to happen. But this time it didn't. There was little warning and much, much destruction, more than this little town had ever seen. Liz was at the police station when it hit. It was one of the few buildings still standing downtown. She took cover but now it was time to see how everyone else was and to offer the much-needed assistance as people tried to put their lives back together. Did everyone survive? Who needed help?

Viewing the destruction took her breath away. Coming up from the basement, nothing was amiss inside. Everything looked like it did when she headed downstairs. Looking out the front window, nothing looked the same. She started to walk up East Main. *"Wow, I had forgotten how bad storms can be."*

*"Pretty bad, isn't it?"* Her deputy, Stan, joined her, looking over the town. The cleanup would take a while. He lived a couple of blocks east of the station. His house had escaped with only a few shingles ripped off as far as he could tell. His front yard was full of branches.

*"Yeah ... yeah it is. Let's look around."* They start to walk north,

taking their time. It was still very quiet. So much to see—so much destruction! They kept their ears open. You could hear voices from blocks away. Strange!

They step over some rubble and almost trip on boards sticking up. The two chairs from the barber shop found a new home in the middle of the street. No damage although they were very much out of place. A real mess! You never knew what you might find... anywhere.

*"Help! Anybody out there? Can someone help? Anybody out there?"* A familiar voice beckons and they wonder whose it is. It demands attention. It stops and then starts again.

Liz looked at Stan, *"Did you hear that? Where is it coming from?"* They listened as the plea continues.

*"I think that's George Plummer's voice."* A printing press had been shoved here and there until it found a resting place trapping George in his own basement. This heavy machine kept George trapped. Liz and Stan pry it enough so the door will open giving George a way of escape. As he looks at what used to be his place of business, he can't believe what he sees. His means of trade has been tossed to the wind. The newspaper side of him looks for his camera. This all needs to be recorded for historical purposes. But more important, he wants to get home to see about his family, everyone's top priority.

Before they move on they make sure George is okay. *"I think I'm fine. Just a little shook up. Wow! What a mess!"* He makes sure his camera works as he snaps a few pictures before heading home.

*"One down...how many to go?"* They continue walking down the street. They can hardly take it all in. Then they see a bizarre sight.

*"Would you look at that?!"* The pool hall is gone, walls, bar, everything. Everything except for the 8-ball table. The balls are racked waiting for the next players. Two pool cues are there with a little cube of chalk. Nothing about the table looks disturbed.

*"I just can't believe it, Stan."* Liz looked over what used to be a very vibrant town... albeit years ago. Still, only hours ago, actually *MINUTES,* these places were inhabited by customers going about their daily routines. People were moving around town doing this and that. Now there basically wasn't a town at all to do anything in. You just saw the remains of what once had been.

*"Neither can I! You can't even tell where the drug store was. Nothing is left!"*

Then they make their way towards Emerald Grocery. They see a lone figure looking through it all.

*"Anita?" "Anita?"* Jeff is yelling for his wife. He continues to get no response but is unwavering in his determination to find her.

*"Anita missing?"* Liz asks. She knows them both very well.

*"Yeah. I thought she'd be in the basement, but it is empty."*

*"Anywhere else she might have gone?"* Liz starts to ask *"professional"* questions hoping to help Jeff look at the situation in a logical more than emotional way.

*"I'm hoping so. She might have gone next door to be with her dad."* And in making that comment he turns to face the mess where Olson Insurance had been. This was where he was now going to expend his energy and efforts.

*"That's a mess over there. But it was a strong building."*

# Chapter 70

Volunteers made their way downtown looking for the injured or … the trapped. The farmer in the bar was still sitting there, stunned. He looked at the post office roof and saw Ernie. He didn't know if Ernie was dead or alive. He was just … there. Soon he saw Ernie's arm move as Ernie's hand went up to his head.

Ernie opened his eyes to see the sky before he pushed himself up. Looking around he looked straight over at the farmer who was only 6 feet away when the tornado hit. They looked at each other and the farmer got his answer. This was one of the good stories.

Ambulances from neighboring towns arrived. A film crew from the television station in Alcoa showed up. This would be the lead story tonight—The Emerald Tornado. The injured were taken to hospitals in Alcoa. Dr. Floyd was on the scene directing most of what was going on, medically speaking. A few in town were injured and he went to wherever called. Ginger got downtown as soon as her parents could watch the girls.

Thankful that Emerald Hydraulics had not been hit, Fred knew a lot of damage had taken place in the town itself. The tornado cast all kinds of debris inflicting a lot of damage as he watched it approach. His home wasn't in the tornado's path, so he went to where his help might be needed most. He joined other pilgrims walking randomly through town offering assistance.

*"Good, God!"* Fred said as he looked at the business district. His walk from the plant hadn't prepared him for what he saw. He wondered where everything was. So much had been picked up and moved to some new location, in some cases miles away!

He surveys the area. *"What a mess. How's it going? Anybody hurt?"* Fred finds his wife who has been busy working side by side with Dr. Floyd. Some of the injured are waiting for the next ambulance. Most don't need medical attention to that degree. There are a few broken bones but mostly rattled nerves.

Ginger could handle a lot of the scrapes and scratches. What she couldn't handle was the absence of her friend. She looks at her husband who sees she is worried, *"We haven't found Anita yet."* Her eyes indicated her deep concern. But she also knew her close friend would have taken the proper precautions. Still, where was she?

*"What do you mean? Wasn't she in the basement?"*

*"No. And that is where she should have been. And she is not at her parents or Jeff's mom's either."*

Fred starts to search the crowd for his friend. *"Where is Jeff?"*

*"He was working to get through the debris at Olson insurance, trying to get to the basement. Anita might be there... there he is."* Ginger pointed him out. There were maybe... 15 guys helping, actively working and an even larger number standing around watching as only so many could get in to help at one time.

Fred makes his way over to the group clearing the bricks and other building materials. Rubble is everywhere. Jeff doesn't even notice Fred at first. *"Need some help?"* Fred pitches in next to Jeff, moving one of the workers over.

You could see in Jeff's face he was optimistic Anita was in the basement. They just needed to get the bricks and plaster out of the way to get her out. Hope springs eternal. Jeff wasn't about to think the worst. That just could not be possible. He wouldn't accept anything other than that Anita was alive somewhere just waiting to be rescued. He keeps thinking she is alive in the basement, safe with her dad. This was a strong building. This is where she just HAD to be! She was waiting for him. And he was going to rescue her.

It was starting to get warm. The clouds that offered protection from the sun as well as the destruction that descended on the town were long gone. The sky was clear, and humidity returned. The workers are sweating up a storm.

After a half hour it doesn't look much different. *"How many bricks were in this building anyway?"* Jeff had been bent over for a long time. He stands up straight and stretches a little. This clean-up is taking longer than anyone expected. There were still a lot of bricks to clear. That was okay, just as long as Anita was safe. It wouldn't be a problem. No matter how long it takes, as long as she is safe, they will get her out.

*"Take a break, Jeff,"* Harvey Clark encourages, *"they are bringing a bobcat over from the elevator to help clear a lot of this. It'll go faster."* The elevator experienced a little damage but nothing crucial or life threatening. When Gene Porth heard about the search effort at Olson Insurance he got on *"Gertrude"* one of the three bobcats they had and headed in that direction.

Some debris is too heavy to be moved manually. Won't be a problem for *"Gertrude."* Jeff steps back. He and Fred see someone has sent water. They each get a bottle and down half the refreshing liquid and pour the rest over their heads.

# Chapter 71

*"Get out of the way, guys."* Harvey yells as Gene moves *"Gertrude"* in to help. It is a welcome sight!

Gene found another hat to wear and it sits sideways on his head. He is very serious offering aid in this rescue attempt. He brought several straps and maneuvers in as close as he can. He takes over the mission as he gets off the bobcat to insure straps are where they should be and won't slip.

*"This will make things go a lot faster."* Volunteers step back to let this little machine do the heavy lifting. It starts to scoop up bricks and move them to the side. Some pieces of the building stayed together when the building fell. They were much too heavy to be moved by hand. No problem now.

Gene carefully removes debris not wanting to do any more damage and risk hurting survivors. As the third load of bricks is brought out it became apparent.

*"Oh, no."* The sight takes on a whole new perspective.

*"What?"* Not everyone realizes what has happened.

Harvey sees that the first floor collapsed and the whole building has fallen into the basement. *"This isn't good."*

*"I hate to say it but I'm afraid if anyone was down in the basement ... they probably didn't make it."*

*"Then don't say it!"* That is the feeling by everyone.

It was time once again for bricks to be removed one at a time.

The loader on the bobcat is filled with whatever needs to be removed. Only a few guys can get in at a time to help. Volunteers take turns and are reluctant to be relieved. Then there was another big section of bricks still together, once a corner section of the building. The bobcat empties its load and comes back to lift this huge, heavy section. A strap is put around this bulky mass. It is extremely heavy, and *"Gertrude"* is doing a lot of grunting and groaning attempting to elevate it. The back wheels go up until volunteers climb on to bring the back down. Finally, there is extra strength and the huge load ascends. As it was lifted a gruesome sight is revealed.

*"Look. Is that what I think it is?"* An arm is uncovered. All you could see was someone's left forearm. The hand had been crushed and mangled. The wristwatch wasn't damaged and still working. The protection the basement gave to Harold Olson in the past was not provided on this occasion. The collapse of the floor killed him instantly. That was the only blessing anyone could see. A new respect for this terrible site was felt. This was where a person lost his life.

Now the question was, *"Is anyone else under the rubble, specifically... Anita?"* And for the first-time people were hoping Anita *WASN'T* in the basement! Could she have met the same fate as her dad? Everyone was praying she hadn't!

Power still wasn't restored so a generator was brought in and lights were set up to illuminate the area. Removal of debris continues at a slower and extremely painful pace. With every brick removed, workers hold their breath, hoping no one else is in that death trap. Because they fear the worst, they encourage Jeff to stay at a distance as the search and clean-up continues.

This is hard for Jeff. For a while he nervously stands by the coffee wagon supplied by ... someone. Then he gets close to the site pacing back and forth trying to look in. Finally, he lets the workers do what they need to do. Fred tries to encourage him while himself fearing the worst. Ginger tries to keep his spirits up talking about all the places Anita might be. But you could see it in her eyes that she fears she has seen her best friend alive for the last time.

Then once again, all work stops. The hunched over workers slowly straighten up. The bucket on the bobcat is only half full so onlookers know something else has been discovered. Something else or someone else captures their attention.

*"Doc, you better get over here."* Why that was said, no one knew. Dr. Floyd couldn't help anymore if someone, anyone was crushed under the weight of the once majestic building.

*"Uh…we've uncovered a hand."* Hearing those words, Jeff runs over. Actually, it is before those words are said. When everyone got quiet Jeff knew something was up. No one tries to stop him from seeing what is going on. They can only imagine what is going through his mind. They think about what it would be like to dig through the rubble searching for their own loved ones. It gets very quiet. Jeff peers into the hole.

The hand is pinned down by another large section of the building. It is somewhat in a shadow and not very easy to see. It is a bloody hand indicating that whosever lifeless hand it is; they didn't die right away. Their heart kept pumping out the fluid of life.

# Chapter 72

Jeff climbs down to examine the hand. The bobcat will have to be brought in to uncover the rest of the body. He is fearful. The blood on the hand has dried. He touches the cold extremity but almost immediately is relieved to see it is not Anita's hand. This isn't the delicate hand of a 33-year-old. This is the hand of an older lady. Jeff has mixed feelings. He also knew Mrs. White, Harold's secretary for many years, and is saddened by her death but relieved it is not Anita's hand. Another life was claimed. But the big question still looms, *"Where is Anita? Where could she be?"*

Darkness comes, and the light is needed even more. Power has been partially restored. Some lines are still down. The sky is clear, and the moon is half-full. Stars look down on the rescue efforts but offer no encouragement.

At 3:00 in the morning the basement of Olson Insurance has not produced anyone else. No one else was in the basement, thank God, when the building fell. The last bricks are removed and Gene and *"Gertrude"* head back to the elevator. It has been quite a night.

Jeff was relieved Anita wasn't there but beginning to really wonder. *"Where could Anita be? Had the tornado whisked her away and landed her safely in some field? Where was she?"*

Tornadoes can do funny things. In some cases, debris could be picked up and thrown great distances, landing miles away, not to be found for years. A farmer might find books or a chair or some such material while looking for livestock in a pasture. Hunters might find bones from an animal or human long after the storm had occurred. Jeff was hoping he hadn't lost his wife to such a cruel fate. Not knowing would be the worst.

Volunteers didn't know what to do. They didn't know where to search. The obvious place for Anita was in one of the two basements but she was in neither. No one felt comfortable going home. Most just stood around talking, speculating. Then some did begin to leave. The television crew decided their story was complete and packed up. One ambulance was still around but no one needed transportation. The paramedics were questioning what to do.

Jeff knelt, exhausted, looking into the empty basement. Then he got up and went over to Fred and Ginger. They were watching him, wondering what his next move would be ... should be. He looked drained. They all felt that way. Sitting down he put his head in his hands and rubbed his face. *"Where is she? Where is she?!"* He didn't expect an answer. It was the same question everyone else was silently asking.

Fred pats his buddy on the back. *"We'll find her. She has got to be somewhere. We'll find her!"*

Jeff opens a bottle of water and is refreshed as he sits there for a few minutes, now not looking at the empty basement any longer but looking at his store. Taking a deep breath, he gets up and starts walking in that direction. He didn't know why he went there, but this was a place of comfort for him. He had grown up in this building, what was left of it, and he and Anita had built up the store over the years.

Kind of in a daze after all the fruitless searching for Anita, he picks up items to put back on the shelves. Jeff went over to the cash register and there under the counter, undisturbed, was Anita's purse where she placed it that morning, undisturbed. Seeing the purse, he picked it up and that was it. That was all it took for him to break down. He couldn't hold back any more. With shortness of breath he started crying uncontrollably. He was exhausted physically and mentally. It had been too much! Fred and Ginger saw what was happening and went to comfort and support him.

Then, miraculously, as if God were sending a signal, the street lights came on. The REC *(Rural Electric Cooperative)* had been hard at work reconnecting lines so the streets of Emerald were lit once again. The power was restored to many homes as well. Seconds later the lights in the grocery store returned to reveal that most items were still on their shelves. Only in one area, where the cereal boxes are, was anything majorly disturbed.

With the lights on, Jeff was joined by others as he started to do some cleaning up in a vain attempt to get things back in order, a simply ridiculous gesture, but something to do to relieve the tension. One volunteer started to move a shelf that had tipped over and as he did he got a surprise. He yelled, and everybody came over. Cereal boxes were on top of ... someone, there was someone's foot.

# Chapter 73

The *Dock* opened earlier than usual because of the storm. A lot had happened in the community. A tornado had ripped through Emerald. Frank Anderson, manager, knew there would be people needing a place to go so he opened shop, so to speak. Later, when he heard about all the destruction and the search efforts in downtown Emerald, he sent the coffee wagon over along with some things to eat and bottles of water. He knew it would be welcomed relief.

He called the lake grocery store to see if Beth and David had heard anything. No answer. He assumed they went to check on their families. There was power at the lake but none in Emerald. The sun was shining as if everything was fine. But it was a day of great destruction, sadness and confusion.

*"Wow, what a day! Glad you're open."* Bernie was Gloria's first customer. It was just the two of them for a while. With no power at home Bernie decided to take off for a while and since getting into Emerald was almost impossible she went to a place where she felt very comfortable. Everything in Carlson Estates looked fine from what she could see, no collateral damage whatsoever but also no power.

*"Yeah, Frank called to see if I could come in a little early. Think he thought we might get a crowd in here and we might as the day goes on. Not a problem. Didn't have any 'juice' at home anyway. Actually, I was surprised the phone lines were working."* Gloria almost felt more at home in the lounge.

*"I wonder how bad it was in town."* Bernie was curious. *"I tried to get in but it looked like it was quite a mess, some streets were blocked*

*off, so I came out here."* She had no idea what the storm had done.

*"Well, my street had a lot of branches down. I had to drive around a couple of big ones, didn't know if I would get out or not, but I made it. I didn't see any damage otherwise."* Gloria lived south of the business district and was completely unaware of the destruction.

*"I wonder if it will be on the news tonight."*

*"Probably. I saw a news van on the way into town on my way out here."*

*"What do you have to eat? Anything good?"* This was typical Bernie, more concerned about herself than anyone else.

Later business did pick up. Many Emerald residents were looking for a place to get a hot meal and relax a little after all the excitement. Without power televisions wouldn't be working and they also wanted to see if there were any reports of the storm on the news. Everyone was shaken by what they witnessed. Emerald had never experienced a tornado before. And the destruction had a tremendous impact.

Bernie was extremely happy none of her homes in Carlson Estates were hit. If anything, she might profit from the whole situation. She had homes already built to sell to those who might find themselves, homeless. She didn't feel the least bit bad about having such thoughts. She was a businesswoman.

*"Let's see if there is anything on the news."* Gloria turned the set on and went to the station out of Alcoa.

> The 6:00 p.m. news was just coming on. *"My goodness, there is nothing left!"*

*"It's all gone!"* The camera panned the downtown area. *"Where's the drug store? Where's the pool hall? I can't believe it is all gone."*

# Chapter 74

"W*hat's Ernie doing on the roof of the post office?"* It was a while before someone got a ladder to get Ernie down. *"Isn't that Delbert Kraft sitting in the bar?"*

*"Well, that is his usual spot."*

Then they talked about the corner of Diamond Street and West Main. Bernie knew that address. She had walked by Olson Insurance hundreds of times and knew Emerald Grocery was right next door. She saw the destruction. She saw Jeff's store in pretty bad shape.

*"Look, Olson Insurance looks like it collapsed."* They listened closely to what had happened. No bodies had yet been uncovered and so no one had any idea about Harold, Mrs. White or where Anita might be.

*"Is that Jeff in the background?"* Bernie thought out loud. She was leaning forward concentrating on the screen with great interest in what was being shown.

Gloria was searching the screen. *"Where?"*

*"Right there. See. And there are Fred and Ginger."* She wondered why she didn't see Anita. Oh, that is right. The ever-sweet Anita is probably making sandwiches for all the volunteers. *PLEASE!* She was so sickened by *"sweet"* Anita. Sweet Anita was the perfect little wife and baby-maker for ***her*** beau, Jeff. She hated her. She wished she was gone. Dare she say it, *"She wished she was dead"?* She didn't say it, but she was always thinking it. She had no idea that the tornado may have fulfilled that wish!

It is interesting, at the same time, Jeff was asking where Anita was, so was Bernie. Both had an interest, but for different reasons.

As the day came to an end, Bernie made her way home and drifted off to sleep in her comfortable bed. She had no idea of the excavation continuing in downtown Emerald. She assumed the four people she despised were okay and their lives were going on as normal albeit, the little disturbance of the day. They would all survive and move on. If anything, they would all be applauded as heroes or *"Citizens of the Month"* for all the work they had done. Bernie didn't have a clue. And Bernie didn't care.

# Chapter 75

Dr. Floyd was there in an instant. Everyone's mood changed from utter despair to optimistic joy. Jeff never thought to dig through the area where the shelves had toppled. He never gave it a thought. The cereal boxes were moved away and there was Anita. The striking blonde was on the floor looking as if she was resting after a long day at work or in a pose for some commercial. Jeff cried out, *"Anita!"* He almost caused another shelf to topple in getting to her.

Dr. Floyd checked her vitals. *"Was she alive or dead?"* Everyone collectively held their breath. Some were certain she was gone. Another casualty for this horrific day! Just looking at her you couldn't tell. She looked at peace.

*"I have a pulse!"* With those words paramedics moved into action, getting her on a gurney. They rolled her into the ambulance and were off to Trinity Hospital in Alcoa. This was the first bright spot of the day! The sun wouldn't be seen for a couple hours yet but just finding Anita changed everyone's outlook. They hoped and prayed she would be okay.

Jeff rode with his bride in the ambulance. He wasn't going to leave her. He had her again, but he wasn't sure for how long. He held her hand and told her, *"Everything is going to be alright."* He cried tears of joy looking at her beautiful, unmarred face. He kissed her cheek, smelling the perfume he saw her spray on 24 hours earlier.

The thirty-mile ride through the dark countryside took 15 excruciating minutes. Liz Jackson made sure there was no traffic in the way to keep Anita from getting the needed medical attention. Sirens were blaring. They took Anita to emergency where she was examined. One by one, causes for her condition were checked off the list. No internal bleeding. No concussion. No bones broken. She didn't have a scratch on her. Miraculous! They did everything they could to find anything wrong. They found nothing. But she still hadn't awakened. Her heart was beating strong. Her breathing seemed okay. It appeared she was in a coma.

They took Anita to intensive care for continued observation. For six days Jeff stayed by her side. All he could think about was his beloved. When he had those moments he slept, he dreamt of her. When he was awake he replayed different times of their life together. He was totally consumed thinking about Anita. He could not envision his life without her.

He thought back to the night they first kissed and the days following. At that time, he was distraught at what Bernie had done. He was more than distraught. He felt he had no future. He didn't care about anyone or anything, but Bernie. Bernie knocked the wind out of his sails with her rejection.

And then Anita entered his life although it seemed to be kind of through the back door. He wasn't expecting it. It came completely by surprise. He remembered seeing her sitting in the café as he came back from the restroom. Sitting in the booth wearing a miniskirt revealing those long, shapely legs, *"Wow!"* He never saw her the same way after that. He felt like a teenager in love for the first time.

But he also remembered the night they drove back to town at the end of their first date, her head on his shoulder. That was indeed the turning point. The days after that in the store were days he would have worked for free. He couldn't wait to see Anita's smile. He made sure he was always there when she arrived, eager to get the door. She liked the attention. She liked Jeff. And that kind of surprised her.

Those early days didn't go as smoothly as Jeff or Anita would have liked. They both had feelings of doubt as to where this relationship might lead. Anita never had a steady boyfriend. It wasn't that she didn't want one. It was just that none of the guys she dated *"fit the bill."* They all lacked something. Whether she had changed or had just never seen Jeff in this light was anyone's guess. But Jeff was her first. And she wasn't at all sure about where this was going either, although it started out pretty good. It was all because of Bernie.

Jeff and Bernie had been together for a long time and Anita felt that Bernie could *"re-enter"* the picture at any time and then, where would she be? Would that relationship be rekindled? Would Anita suddenly be ... dumped? She never dated anyone on a steady basis. Jeff had no idea she had those thoughts until she opened to him later. To Jeff, everything was very plain and obvious, after he got over the jitters and finally asked Anita out.

Jeff had no qualms about the relationship. At least he didn't the day he walked into Olson Insurance. He was confident of what he wanted to do, of what he was going to do. Mrs. White was out for a moment and Harold just got off the phone. Jeff could see him sitting at his desk. Just a little nervous, he knocked on the doorframe. *"Mr. Olson, may I talk with you."*

*"Sure, son, come on in."* Harold almost always had a smile on his face. *"What's on your mind?"*

Jeff came into the office. He had never been in it before. It looked very impressive and intimidating. Harold had all kinds of papers scattered which looked like forms of some kind or another. Jeff took a moment to gain a little more confidence when the phone rang.

*"Excuse me for a moment."* Harold apologized for having to take the call.

# Chapter 76

In a way, Jeff was glad the call came when it did. As he looked around he saw Anita's graduation picture on the desk. It was the *"sign"* he needed to do what he came to do. He looked on the walls and noticed other pictures of the family as if they were saying, *"Go ahead, ask already!"*

Finally, Harold got off the phone. He apologized again for the interruption. *"Now, what's on your mind?"*

The call was a serious one though and Harold didn't have the previous smile. It made Jeff nervous. *"Uh ... I want to do this right ... um ... Mr. Olson, I'd like to ask Anita to marry me and ... uh ... is that okay with you?"* Jeff looked nervous as he spoke. He didn't look up until he finished the question. He was even shaking a little.

Harold raised his eyebrows, he hadn't anticipated the request. But now the smile returned. *"You're asking for her hand?"* Harold enjoyed this act of chivalry. He tried to look serious as Jeff sat there but his heart wouldn't allow it.

Jeff thought it was obvious but with respect clarified what he said, *"Yes, sir."*

Harold's cheeks looked like they were filled with marshmallows as he smiled in appreciation of Jeff's gesture. *"You bet! And thanks for asking. I never expected that. When are you going to ask her?"*

*"I'm thinking ... maybe this Friday night."* Jeff said with relief that this was over. He revealed a generous smile. Harold got up and shook Jeff's hand.

*"Do you think she will say yes?"* Harold asked. Jeff was pretty

sure she would but now that Harold asked, he wondered and began to have doubts. Did Harold know something he didn't know? How embarrassing it would be if after going to all this trouble talking to her dad and asking permission if she said, *"No!"*

To Anita it was just another Friday night. It was no different from other Friday nights she and Jeff went out. It was somewhat understood they would go out on Friday nights, but Jeff still made a point of asking every week. She thought it was silly, but gave that adorable smile and always said, *"Yes."* Deep down, she appreciated not being taken for granted. No one likes that. They had been dating for six months.

Jeff made reservations at *Lee's* in Alcoa. This was *THE* place to go in Alcoa. But it wasn't cheap. In fact, it was very expensive. Jeff got a loan from his dad for this night. Jeff told his parents that tonight he was proposing. He thought if he told them it would boost his confidence. It didn't. But since Harold knew and no doubt his wife, it was only right to inform his parents of the plan. After he picked up Anita, they were on their way. Later, Jeff's parents called Anita's house to talk with her parents. They tried to find out what Anita's response would be. Her parents couldn't say for sure, but everyone assumed she would say, *"Yes."* Everyone was *HOPING* she would say, *"Yes."*

This restaurant was very classy and very dark. Each table had the glow of a candle centerpiece. Reading the menu was a challenge, the light was so dim. Jeff was nervous and started to feel very warm and uncomfortable. He wished he was old enough to legally have a drink but that was still a few months away. Anita was calm projecting the appearance of being self-confidant yet not arrogant. She was beautiful as ever too. Jeff told her this would be a *"dress up"* date. He was going to wear a coat and tie. They did this every so often. It was kind of fun.

Anita wore a blue dress with short sleeves and a matching jacket. The dress was down to right above her knees and not exceedingly tight but very eye-catching. Her delicate neck was adorned with a gold necklace carrying a gold cross. Dangling pierced-earrings, very appropriate. Her hair was a little longer than shoulder length and her bangs, perfect. Wearing heals made her appear a little taller. Jeff and Anita made a great looking couple. Anita was noticed as they walked in. When she sat down and crossed her legs she appeared to be a real beauty. Guys were envious of Jeff, as well they should be.

*"This is really nice,"* Anita smiled as she looked at Jeff and took his hand.

*"I was hoping you'd like it."* Jeff smiled as he looked into her sparkling, squinting eyes trying to see what was going on in that beautiful head. He confessed to himself that he had no idea!

# Chapter 77

Jeff looked at her. Her blue dress made her blue eyes sparkle in the candle light—especially in the candle light! It also made him very nervous. *"What in the world made him think this beautiful, young woman would want to spend the rest of her life with him? Look at all the guys she dated and none of them were worth a second date... most of the time. Was this just a pipe dream? Was he crazy? What if she said, 'No'? She WILL probably say, 'NO'!"* He was having second thoughts. *"Should he ask her or not? If she said, 'No,' everything would be awkward in the store from then on. This is a terrible idea, just terrible! She will quit, and I will be the fool and I won't ever see her again."*

*"Would you like something to drink?"* The waitress came to get their orders. Both got water and a soda. Jeff wasn't very hungry, was rapidly losing his appetite and had no idea what to order. He had everything planned, but now his mind was blank. He thought of all the scenarios of how this evening could end. He thought they were thinking along the same lines, but now he wasn't sure. This whole idea could be a terrible mistake.

*"Have you decided what you would like?"* That pesky waitress was back again. Anita looked over at Jeff to make sure he was ready to order. Getting the signal, he was ready she proceeded. Anita had been studying the menu and decided on the Fettuccini Alfredo.

Jeff thought to himself, *"Whatever Anita orders, I'll have the same."*

Most of the conversation was initiated by Anita. Distracted, Jeff couldn't remember much of what was said. She laughed at him and wondered if something was wrong. Something was up but she wasn't sure what it was. She had no idea what was coming, *NONE!*

The meal over, now is the time Jeff was going to *"pop the question"* right there in *Lees*. The ring was in his pocket. He wanted to create a memory they would have forever. But he didn't. For some reason it didn't seem right. The atmosphere was all wrong; too many people around. If he was going to be rejected, he didn't need to be humiliated in front of a lot of strangers.

Instead, he helped her with her coat and then went to get the car. Anita waited at the door. He drove up, got out and opened her door. She got in and slid to the middle, right next to him. It was a quiet drive back to Emerald. Anita rested her head on Jeff's shoulder, putting her hand on his thigh. They listened to the radio. No words were needed. He pulled her close. Entering Emerald, they pulled up to her house.

Their custom was to spend a little time in an intimate embrace and maybe talk about the evening. His arm still around her, she turned more towards him as he put the car in park. But tonight, was different, Jeff started to talk. He looked at Anita at first but then looked away. Looking into her eyes was too much for him. Looking straight ahead, he spoke as if he were reciting something memorized, which is exactly what he was doing. He knew precisely what he wanted to say. And then he turned and looked at Anita, *"Uh, Anita ... would you marry me?"* His eyes indicated sincerity but also fear. *"It was now or never,"* he thought. Then there was silence.

Now it was her turn to act nervous. She did a good job. Looking at him, Anita put her hands over her nose and mouth. That scared him to death. Then he saw a tear forming. *"Oh boy! That could mean anything. It could mean she was sorry for leading him on. It could mean she was going to break his heart. It could mean that maybe they needed to take a break. It could mean she liked him but liked him as a 'friend.' No guy wants to hear those words after he has proposed. It could mean the worst."*

*"You want to marry me? That is why you were acting so strange tonight."* Anita could barely get the words out. She began to sniffle a little as a tear fell.

Still Jeff couldn't tell what her response would be. His anxiety level sky-rocketed. *"Yes, Anita, I want you to be my wife. Will you marry me?"* Jeff was getting scared! But he was also determined and focused. He thought maybe he needed to say more, possibly explain how he came to this conclusion. But doing, it would be like explaining a joke—what's the point?!

The tears started to flow. *"Yes. YES!"* No more words needed. Lips were used for something else! Jeff had his answer. Anxiety was replaced with ecstasy and dreams of the future.

About to get out of the car, Jeff remembered the ring still in his pocket.

*"What's the matter?"* Anita wondered as Jeff hesitated.

Jeff reached in his pocket. *"Have to make it official."* Anita watched as he pulled out the symbol of his love and gently holding Anita's hand, placed it on her finger. More tears. Holding her hand out, she couldn't believe it was real. She was engaged!

The cork was popped, and champagne was poured. Harold and Clara knew tonight was the night. They didn't know if they should wait up to find out if he would go through with proposing or not. They decided to wait and when Jeff walked Anita to the door, they could tell they would soon have a son-in-law. When Jeff opened the door for Anita, her parents were there with huge smiles. Looking at dad, Anita started to cry. She went to her dad first, giving him a great big hug and then to her mom. She was a *"daddy's"* girl.

# Chapter 78

*"Let's see the ring. Wow! That is pretty."* Harold smiled ear to ear. Anita held her hand out to display her new piece of jewelry.

*"Thanks, daddy."*

*"I'm so happy for you sweetheart. So, have you set a date?"*

*"Mom, we just got engaged!"*

*"Oh, I know, but we ... you need to make plans!"*

Harold suggested before it got too late, Jeff and Anita should go to Jeff's parents. They would like to hear the good news first hand.

Jeff got Anita back around 1:30 a.m. Her parents had already turned in, but this was a night this couple didn't want to come to an end. Anita said, *"I can hardly wait to be Mrs. Jeff Emerald."*

*"That sounds pretty good to me, too."* He kissed her holding her like he never wanted to let her go.

*"Would you like some coffee?"* Jeff awoke at the nurse's question.

Anita was resting in intensive care, looking so beautiful and at peace. *"Please wake up. Please."*

Bonnie brought the children to see mom. They were told she was just sleeping and someday, someday very soon she would wake up and come home. Jake, the oldest, was not so sure about the explanation given. His siblings accepted it without a second thought. Looking at her it appeared like she was just taking a nap. Before they left, each kissed her on the cheek.

It was that same warm, soft cheek they kissed so many times before. Emily got close to Anita's ear and whispered, *"Goodnight mommy."* Jeff watched and turned his head, starting to cry. *"How could God do this to him? Why? Why?"*

Every day was pretty much the same with nothing new to report. The doctors were hopeful but also concerned. She wasn't on life support but wasn't responding to anything either. They were about to move her to a regular room, considering their next steps. How long could she go on like this? Jeff wasn't about to leave her side.

Once again, Jeff had too many cups of coffee. He needed to use the restroom. He knew where it was. He knew where everything was in the hospital. When he came out, the nurse's station was deserted. Where was everyone? Looking around, his heart almost stopped. Everyone was in Anita's room. He ran to find out what was going on.

# Chapter 79

Those six days Anita was in a coma were excruciating for ... Bernie. Once she found out about Anita's condition, she kept on top of everything. She watched the news footage of the basement exploration at The Olson Insurance Building. When she found out Anita wasn't making sandwiches, but they were still looking for her she was surprised and intrigued by the possibilities. And before she heard the news they had found Anita in the store, Bernie had thoughts, *"Please, please let Anita be down there."* She was disappointed Anita wasn't at the bottom of the building with *"dear, old daddy."* Bernie wanted to see Anita's crushed and mutilated body underneath all the bricks.

Getting the news Anita was found, but in a coma, her prayers counteracted Jeff's every step of the way. She wanted Jeff back in a terrible way and thought it was now possible. The tornado might have taken care of all her problems! Spending time with Scott was supposed to have an impact on Jeff, make him jealous, but it hadn't. She enjoyed being with Scott even though that wasn't her original intent. She reflected on the past with Jeff and it was eating her up!

You wonder what goes through the mind of someone like Bernie. Did she really think she could do something, anything to win Jeff back? Even if Anita died, would Bernie be in his future? Obsessed with him, she thought she just might.

Gloria had a contact in the hospital where Anita was, giving her daily updates on Anita's condition. She knew on a regular basis if any changes were taking place. She reported everything to Bernie. With every passing day, Bernie's hopes grew. *"Another day closer to death."*

Bernie even had a plan. She always had a plan. She thought to herself, *"One day she would go visit Jeff sitting at Anita's side. She would console him, tell him what a good wife he had. But, if he needed someone to talk to, well, Bernie, would always be there. Remember how close they had been in the past. It could be that way again, well, in a platonic sort of way (for right now)."*

RIGHT! Even Bernie didn't believe Jeff would accept that line. So ... she didn't go.

# Chapter 80

Opening her eyes, she saw an unfamiliar ceiling. An antiseptic smell was prominent. An IV taped to her arm irritated her. A group of smiling strangers were staring at her. *"What is going on?"* Then Jeff broke through and she felt relieved. Finally, someone she knew. She still didn't know where she was or why she was there? Anita didn't remember much of anything.

She remembered going to work that beautiful June morning, but after that, nothing. No recollection of talking to her dad or the storm warning. She didn't remember the front window breaking or being knocked down. Six days of her life were gone, never to return.

She also didn't know about her dad and Jeff wasn't in a rush to tell her. All he can do now is look at her and hold her. With tears of joy he held his wife tighter than ever. To him, she had been resurrected from the dead. She appreciated the affection, with no idea of what everyone had gone through. As far as she was concerned, she was asleep and had just awakened... period.

He started to tell her about that fateful day. She couldn't believe the destruction and damage that took place. But before the explanation got too involved, he thought, *"We need to call the kids and let them know 'mommy' is okay!"*

Hearing Jeff's voice, Bonnie asked, *"Is everything okay?"* expecting the worst.

*"I'll let you decide."* Jeff handed the phone to Anita. Hearing Anita's voice, Bonnie started to cry. She talked with Anita a little and then, one by one, Jake, Jared and Emily all got to talk with *"mommy"* – who decided it was time to wake up. They were all anxious as they

awaited their turn. They knew it was good news as Grandma Emerald had a huge smile.

Emily asked, *"When are you coming home, mommy?"* They were more excited than she was. She hadn't realized the time she had been away and the worry it caused.

Hanging up the phone her eyes got big as another thought came to Anita. *"Let's call daddy next."* Those were chilling words. Jeff had to explain what happened. As he looked at her, he started to look down and Anita knew something was wrong. Avoiding all the gruesome details, he told Anita her dad didn't make it through the storm. She didn't need to hear anything more than that right now, possibly ever.

The news crushed her. She loved her dad. Her dad meant everything to her. And now he was gone. She didn't get to go to the funeral or see him one last time. Now she was holding on to her husband... now the only man in her life. As close as Anita and Jeff were, as strong as their love for one another already was, it got stronger that day.

For some, hearing this news would have dropped them into deep depression. There are times when that just can't be helped. It didn't happen with Anita. She was sad and would be for some time. Memories haunted her. There would be times she would look for her dad and wonder where he was and then remember. But she had friends to help her and a husband who would do anything for her. Two days later she was home. On the way they went through downtown. Jeff wasn't sure that was a good idea, but Anita insisted. Seeing her dad's office building completely gone was the worst part. She started to cry. She knew she would.

But then, in typical Anita fashion, she said, *"We have to go see mom."* She knew her mom needed even more comfort. She must just be devastated. Anita and her mom became very close after that. Anita would call her every morning. She found out what a wonderful mother she had. And Clara would appreciate her daughter's affection.

The kids were playing in the backyard when Jeff and Anita arrived. They had been waiting for mom and dad to get home but got interested in other things. Hearing the car doors slam they looked at each other with expressions of surprise, dropped everything and took off running to give *"mom"* the proper welcome. Anita wrapped her arms around all of them as they just couldn't get enough of one another. Life was back to normal in the Emerald household, at least the new normal.

*"Who could that be?"* Jeff was just getting supper ready for their first night back home. Anita was sitting on the couch with the kids, resting. She still felt a little weak and would get back into things when she regained her strength.

# Chapter 81

Jeff walked through the dining room to open the front door. *"Surprise!"* Fred and Ginger brought over a casserole for Anita's first night home. They were all smiles and a little tearful. This had been a tough time for everyone.

*"Well, come in."* Anita joins them in the entryway, *"You're just in time for supper"* not realizing they had brought supper with them. Ginger gave Anita a big hug holding back tears. Fred did the same.

*"No, we don't want to intrude. We just wanted to drop this off and leave. Let you two be together with your family."*

*"Forget it. Get in here."* Such arguments happened all the time. These two families spent a lot of time together. In fact, when Emily saw it was the Kemps, she was out the door in a flash to talk to the triplets.

Halfway through the casserole, they realized this wasn't going to be near enough. They called *The Dock* to have a couple pizzas delivered. What Jeff was preparing was put on hold. This was no time to be in the kitchen. They were all enjoying being together again.

Later, sitting in the back yard, they talked about the whole experience of the last couple weeks.

*"I can't believe you are sitting here with us. You don't know what you put us through."* Ginger pretended to scold Anita for the scare they experienced. At the same time, they appreciated the fact they hadn't lost her.

*"Well, thanks a lot Ginger."* Anita fired back. *"I didn't plan it, you know."*

*"Don't do it again."*

A cool breeze in the back yard felt good. The sun was heading downward. The relationship these four people had grew deeper that night. None of them would ever take one another for granted again.

As the night progressed the girls talked on their own. Fred looked over at Jeff. *"Jeff, what do you think is going to happen downtown? I mean, you got any plans?"*

*"Haven't thought about it a lot. Had other things on my mind lately,"* looking at Anita. *"Why? You got something planned?"*

Fred had ideas he wanted to share. *"Let's go for a ride."*

*"Now?"* Jeff had no desire to leave his reunited family.

*"Yeah, now."* Fred looks at the girls, *"Okay if we take a spin around town, girls?"*

*"Get out of here. I want to talk with Anita alone anyhow."* Ginger had no idea of what they were talking about. Right now, the guys were more of a distraction as far as she was concerned. Anita looked at Jeff and gave him the *"go ahead"* look. She knew they would have time to be together alone later. She was enjoying just being home for right now.

And they were off to hear of Fred's vision for the *"new and improved"* Emerald. Jeff went along for the ride, but his mind wasn't on Emerald or Fred's plans. What was up front in his mind was Anita.

And right now, he was just enduring Fred and all his talk. Jeff was waiting for them to get done with their ride around town. Jeff was waiting for them to go home. Jeff was waiting for the kids to go to bed. Jeff was waiting to truly be alone with Anita, the resurrected Anita. It had been a long time... and Jeff was waiting.

# Chapter 82

Bernie got a phone call from Gloria with the news that Anita regained consciousness and was expected to be released in a couple days. Bernie had almost talked herself into going ahead with the plans she had of going to talk to Jeff at the hospital. Now that was out the window. *"Anita dying was too much to hope for,"* she thought.

But she also had other things on her mind. The rebuilding of Emerald was one of those things. Prestige and power took hold of her. She invested in building 50 luxurious homes and they needed a town to go with them. Jewel Lake was a nice attraction, but the town of Emerald was needed to complete this picturesque community. She wasn't sure the direction this would take. She had a lot of weight to throw around and hoped her influence might have an impact of profound proportions.

Fred, on the other hand, knew exactly the direction it needed to go. And he put his money where his mouth was. He personally had plans drawn for the *New Emerald*. It would be the *"Jewel"* of the area, new and better than before. Businesses and people would flock to Emerald if his plans were followed. Maybe now the city council would be more receptive to his plans.

If anything was going to be done, it had to be soon. Businesses needed to be up and running, not just sitting and nursing their wounds. The people of Emerald needed a working town. This couldn't take years or even months. Some kind of plan needed to be presented to give hope for the future. Fred asked Mayor Harvey Clark to call a special meeting of the city council as soon as possible.

*"Gentlemen, I have a proposal that is genius, if I do say so*

*myself. It will make Emerald the real 'Jewel' of the area, pardon the pun, if, and I say, 'If' we are bold enough to take it. I think we are!"* Fred was excited at this opportunity. He learned from his last bout with the town council and was prepared for this second endeavor. What could he lose? He had a lot to gain and so did everyone else in the room.

The council really did need direction now. Some had thoughts about what could be done to rebuild the town, but no real organization was involved. Everyone was doing their own thing. Taking personal responsibility is a good virtue but Fred wanted to join everyone together to move forward. Problem was, most people, most businesses didn't know how to go about getting that done. Fred did.

*"Okay, Fred, what do you have?"* Harvey moved it along. He had no idea what Fred would suggest and thought the members might get a little bored. That wouldn't be the case. And Fred didn't need much encouragement. He got right into it.

# Chapter 83

*"Picture this: We start from scratch, make this a real 'planned' business district?"* Fred had rehearsed his proposal to get it just right. He wanted to get it down and be able to answer any and every question or concern that might come up. There would be no *"tabling"* action this time.

The most negative members of the council challenged Fred with their standard question. *"What do you mean?"*

It didn't faze Fred. *"I mean we wipe out anything that is still left and start all over!"* Some were really taken back by this. Fred rolled out his plans.

*"Whoa! That is a little radical, isn't it?"* One member commented. Looking around the room for support, he didn't get it like he thought he would. Other council members were intrigued by what Fred put together and were willing to give this some serious thought.

Fred got a big smile, took a drink of water, looked around the room, and continued. *"Maybe, but I think the results will pay off."* Fred laid it out. Members of the council stood, looking at Fred's plans. Fred saw in their eyes they were surprised and a little skeptical. He was ready for that this time.

Blueprints have a way of exciting people. Even those skeptical started thinking. You could tell members were excited studying Fred's plans. They pointed out how maybe some area might be improved. Parliamentary procedure was not the focus anymore. Excitement was picking up steam!

West Main would have businesses on the west side of the street only. East Main, the same on the east side. In the middle, would be a park—*Emerald Memorial Park*. Here is the center of the business district, and what a *"center"* it would be with a swimming pool, playground and a beautiful fountain right in the middle. Fred was getting more and more animated describing every detail.

But then the usual questions came up. *"How in the world would it get paid for? Would they have a bond proposal? Could they get a loan from the bank? T. J. had disappeared, thanks to the tornado. He was pretty supportive of council ideas, of Fred's ideas. T. J. was a hometown boy. But who knew how the next president would feel?"* They thought his son, Greg, would be appointed but nothing had yet been done. Money was the big question. It always came down to financing.

All in all, it was approved, and Fred would go out and promote it with the council's blessings. A new Emerald was about to come into existence.

How long do you think it took before Bernie found out about the plans? They looked good. What looked even better was having her finger in the works. She could control a lot of things and make life easier or harder for people, as the case might be. She liked the plans. Maybe Carlson Industries could be involved here. She would have to talk to Robert.

# Part 5

# The Killer

# Chapter 84

You wouldn't know the town of Emerald in 1991. Those coming back for their 20th year class reunion would be very surprised and, in some cases, a little disappointed. Some of their old, familiar haunts were gone. It happened in a lot of small towns. People would leave, and businesses couldn't be sustained. In some cases, buildings just fell on their own, not getting proper attention. But that was not the case with Emerald. Emerald was doing very well. It was all new and expanding. Over 2,000 people now called Emerald, *"home."* It was the largest the town had gotten to date, bursting at the seams.

The '86 Tornado wiped out most of the business district, rebuilding took place and was nearly complete. Fred's plan was followed ... with just a little tweaking. It was financed through insurance claims, bank loans and grants from the state. Carlson Industries also did some financing and building. It was all very impressive and quite inviting!

For the first time in a long time, Emerald once again has a movie theater. Carlson Industries built it and it is called *"The Carlson."* Unique name, right? There are three screens. It was built facing south looking at Memorial Park. The outer façade looks very elegant. In the lobby one complete wall is a waterfall—classy.

On West Main, going from north to south, we have the new bank. Ironically, it is built in the same location as the old one destroyed in the fire. The post office is next. And built pretty much directly across the street from where it once stood is Emerald Grocery and adjoining Café. Next is Hakeman's Cards & Things and Ernie's Pool Hall. At the end of West Main, you find Cooper's Barber Shop and Hair Styling.

On East Main at the corner of Diamond, the new combination of City Hall/Police Station/Fire Station is located. Next door is *The Emerald Examiner* with state-of-the-art printing capability—courtesy of Carlson Industries. On down the line is the town library, Douglas Hardware, Richard's Clothing, Odiot's Appliances, and Emerald Cleaners.

The Olson Insurance Building is on Pearl at the south end of West Main. Next to it is *The Clinic* and then the new Drug Store. Even though Harold Olson died in the tornado, the name was kept in honor of his many years of service. Dr. Floyd is now the full-time physician at *The Clinic* since the population has increased. Ginger is the full-time administrative assistant/nurse now that the triplets are in school. And they also have a receptionist and part-time nurse on staff.

The outer façade of all the buildings gives an old, small, town appearance. There was a lot of discussion here and there but for the most part, very few hang-ups as the town was rebuilt. Big posters publicized the way Emerald would one day look when completed. It was very exciting and got people involved in their town like never before. People were proud to say they were from Emerald. The city attracted a lot of attention from other towns, especially Alcoa.

The business district all centered on Memorial Park. All the businesses faced it. The park is a little different from what Fred envisioned. The north end has flag poles and a plaque honoring those who died in the tornado. There were fourteen in total. The flag poles form a semicircle around the fountain which has a green glow to it in the evening. At the south end is the swimming pool and playground.

The swimming pool is a *"first"* for Emerald. The town never had one before. This, also, was supplied by Carlson Industries. In the middle stands a shelter house, used more than you would think. A new shelter house was built out at the city park and it was also used but the one in Memorial Park was larger and more of a casual meeting place. In addition, it had an enclosed kitchen where food could be prepared and served. This was the center of activity during Emerald Days. The downtown park was used more than the city park. It had more attractions and was more convenient at times. Kids would play here when parents were shopping. Teenagers used it as a place to hang out.

# Chapter 85

Insurance was the greatest help to Jeff and Anita. They survived off the other two stores during reconstruction, but also needed some financing from Emerald State Bank. They incorporated a café into the new building adjacent to the post office. *"Bonnies Café"* as it would be known would have hours from 6:00 a.m. to 6:00 p.m. initially. Jeff's mom, Bonnie, managed it hiring a short-order cook who did a superb job. She enjoyed coming in early to talk with the breakfast crowd and usually stayed until after lunch.

Jeff and Anita's children have grown. Jake is 16, Jared—13 and little Emily is 9 ... going on *16*. Emily looks like Anita did at her age. Neither Jake nor Jared are athletic but are somewhat involved in other school activities. Like Jeff, at their age, they are learning the grocery business, the family business. Jeff has a slight touch of gray around his temples. His hairline has receded a little, hardly noticeable. Anita is still Anita. She has the *"mom"* look about her but is still very attractive. She continues to work the cash register and wherever else needed. She enjoys working with her husband of 17 years.

The guy not keeping much of his hair is trying to expand Emerald Hydraulics, yet again—and is succeeding. Fred is balding. Ginger finds hair on his pillow and in the shower on a regular basis. He has tried to do the *"comb-over"* but it is a losing battle. Fred is adored by his girls: Michelle, Miriam, Millie and of course, Ginger. Fred's investments are paying off and the family is not hurting. They give back to the community as they always have.

Bernie hasn't changed much. But there is something of interest here. She now has controlling interest in Carlson Industries. Her husband, Robert, is completely out of the picture. He died, actually was murdered, under very suspicious circumstances. It appeared to be a botched burglary attempt. Nothing of any real value was taken though. He was shot with a small hand gun he bought at Bernie's request. She said she didn't feel safe when he was out of town. She insisted he get her one just for protection purposes. The gun was kept in the bedside table on her side of the bed.

The only finger prints on the gun were Bernie's which would be logical even though she never fired it. But the prints weren't found where you would find the finger prints of the killer. And Bernie had an iron-clad alibi. At the time of the murder she was hosting a small dinner party in a private room at *The Dock* on Jewel Lake. The murder went unsolved and went into the cold case files.

# Chapter 86

Bernie now divided her time between living in Carlson Estates and Minneapolis where her position as head of Carlson Industries dictated she spend more time than she desired. She liked having power and control along with people at her beckon call but didn't like being away from Emerald and especially Jeff. He was still on her mind. He was someone out there she couldn't have. It frustrated her!

Down in Emerald, she had the best of all the houses. Many influential people from Alcoa purchased houses in Carlson Estates. It became a status symbol. Her relationship with Gloria is still intact. Scott McClary has moved in with Bernie. He takes care of her house when she is not around and is generally in charge of the development. He is living the good life off Bernie's wealth the same way Bernie lived off Robert's wealth.

But before we enter 1991 we spend a little time in the late fall of 1990.

*"All right! That fire looks great!"* Jeff loves the atmosphere a fireplace gives. His home doesn't have one, but Fred's does.

*"Come on in where it is warm."* Fred welcomes Jeff and Anita. It is a nippy November afternoon, just the kind that makes you feel good to be indoors. The weather outside is typical with light gray clouds protecting the barren landscape.

*"Gotten chilly, hasn't it?"* Ginger comments from the kitchen hearing her dear friends enter. The triplets were helping her and hearing it was the Emeralds they got excited thinking Emily had arrived. But not this time.

Fred explains, *"Thought the fire would inspire us."*

*"Make us think of warmer days, you mean?"*

Jeff sniffs the air a little and asks, *"Hmm.... What do I smell?"*

*"Just another of Ginger's great appetizers."* Fred smiles, *"She's trying something new on you."*

*"I love being a guinea pig!"* Jeff heads toward the kitchen. He picks up something freshly baked and burns his fingers in the process. *"Ouch!"* He drops it immediately and shakes his hand trying to cool the burning sensation before he puts his hand in his mouth and then under the faucet for cooling relief.

Planning for the 20th year reunion of the class of '71 is underway. It is basically the Kemps and the Emeralds, but anyone who wants to join is welcome. Another couple does come that recently got married and wanted to get more involved. Most classmates are willing to just let *"others"* do it all, typical.

So, the six of them sit in the living room, talking about what to do to make this reunion better than the last. This all happens after they talked about old times and memories for the first half hour or so.

Getting the list of addresses out, the girls talk about invitations. The guys talk about what activities might be fun. Basically, they just talked. You could tell it was going to be the females that did most of the planning. What else is new? The girls head towards the dining room table where they can get more organized and write things down while the guys stay in the living room. Who knows, maybe the television will get turned on. Is there a game on this afternoon?

As everyone gets up to take their new positions, the doorbell rings. No one pays much attention that someone else has arrived. *"The more the merrier!"* Ginger answers the door to welcome two more classmates. They thought they would like to be part of the committee and help. They had never done that before but ... well, why not see if they could help. They were willing to give it a try.

Ginger is very gracious, *"Hey! Great that you could make it. Get in where it is warm!"*

*"Sorry, we're a little late."* The voice is familiar but not welcome. Anita knows who it is and looks in that direction with a little fire in her eyes.

Ginger is friendly as always. That is her nature. *"We just got started. Let me take your coats."*

*"Hello, everybody,"* Bernie said sashaying in Jeff's direction. Neither she nor Gloria really wanted to help with the reunion. Bernie didn't even know about the planning until Gloria mentioned it earlier in the afternoon. Then the wheels started turning. Bernie couldn't pass up the opportunity. Bernie never gave up. Whenever she could cause trouble, she did. Whenever she could be close to Jeff she took it. She planned on being close to him today.

# Chapter 87

Bernie hadn't slowed down a bit. She was still considered very attractive. Her wardrobe was never wanting, she spent a lot on clothes. She had gained a little weight, not much, just a little. Most guys wouldn't see it as they drooled over her. They were too impressed with the tight, low cut sweaters she had a habit of wearing. But when Anita looked at her, all she thought was, *"What a big butt Bernie has."* Anita had her moments. And now it wasn't because of any jealousy. If anything, Bernie was a little jealous of Anita's figure. Anita's taste in clothing was superb and she looked good in anything.

The new members were told the plans thus far. There were two groups working on two different things and basically just getting started. The girls were working on invitations and food around the dining room table. The guys were working on … other activities. Anita wasn't too happy to have Bernie sitting at the table with her, but she would at least not be flirting with Jeff.

*"I think this group needs a little female input,"* Bernie said as she placed her hand on Jeff's back and sat on the arm of the couch right next to Jeff. *"What do you think, Jeff?"* He didn't answer—pretended he didn't hear. Bernie and Gloria stayed with the guys.

The other girls move to the dining room. Bernie sat where Anita could see her, and both knew it. The vibes were what you would expect. The other couple had no idea what was going on. They were just enjoying being there. Bernie managed to sit next to Jeff, a little closer than Anita liked. In fact, Bernie could feel Jeff's presence right next to her and she kind of got excited. That *"big butt"* Anita noticed was sidled right next to Jeff. Bernie hoped Jeff felt a little excited as well. She scooted close to annoy Anita but was enjoying the fringe benefits nonetheless.

To be honest, feeling Bernie so close did send him back to those nights out on a country road. And it did excite him more than he wanted to admit to himself. He kept thinking, *"That was a life-time ago. Now it was time to get down to business."* Jeff's feeling for Bernie would plague his mind. He loved his wife and couldn't imagine not being with her, but still, there were times when Bernie's pursuit was hard to ignore.

Everyone stayed longer than expected. Jeff and Anita were waiting for people to leave so they could visit with Fred and Ginger allowing Anita to do a little *"venting."* But Bernie and Gloria just stayed and stayed and stayed. Finally, it got so late, Jeff and Anita had to get home to make supper and get Emily to bed. It was a school night. As soon as they left it wasn't long before Bernie and Gloria also left. They went back to Gloria's and spent time talking about the afternoon before Bernie returned home to enjoy Scott's company. Her thoughts continued to be centered on Jeff. Scott was merely there for her pleasure … until she could have Jeff again.

Anita held her tongue all the way home. Jeff could tell she was irritated. She held her tongue as she prepared the evening meal. She held her tongue until she and Jeff were alone in the bedroom. And then, she continued to hold her tongue. She wasn't saying anything. She got into bed and rolled over with her back towards Jeff and said, *"Goodnight."*

Jeff leaned over and kissed his babe on her neck. *"I love you,"* Jeff whispered. Jeff knew she wasn't mad at him. At least he didn't think she was. She was just mad. There were times when Bernie got to her and when Jeff didn't react more negatively to Bernie's advances, that did irritate her. Still, she was just mad. She rolled over and looked at him with her beautiful squinting eyes, smiled and kissed him as well.

Anita and Ginger were on the phone the next morning talking up a storm. Ginger was at *The Clinic,* Anita at the store. Both were unusually busy for Monday morning and decided to have lunch together at the cafe to talk further. They could have gone on for hours but didn't have the time right now!

Well, lunch never happened. An emergency right before noon brought in two students from school with nasty scrapes from falling on the frozen playground. Anita and Ginger didn't get the opportunity to talk again until both cooled off a little. Probably a good thing.

# Chapter 88

*"Done any ice-fishing yet?"*

*"Tried. That damn ice was really thick. Took me forever to get through."*

*"Catch anything?"*

*"Nah. But had a little whiskey and it was fun being out there."*

*"Didn't really care if you caught any, did you?"*

*"Whatever makes you think that?"*

It was time for winter fun. St. Paul's youth group was having their turn at the toboggan slide at the church camp on Jewel Lake. Twenty-three youth enjoyed this Friday night event. Parkas and boots were a must even though the female attire was more colorful than their male counterparts. You still had to look attractive, maybe a little like a snow bunny?

It was clear with a full moon, stars were abundant, giving permission for a possible romance somewhere. And it was cold, really cold! The temperature on the digital thermometer at *The Dock* read 17 degrees as it intermittently allowed the time to be revealed. A heated clubhouse provided a place to congregate for those who had enough of the cold. Cookies and hot chocolate were in abundant supply. But outside, couples enjoyed standing next to the fire barrel, looking at the flames, holding on to one another. It was a great place to snuggle and wrap your arms around the one you were with.

Three long sleds were available. Each held up to six people. Jeff and Anita were chaperones and went down the slide a couple times.

Anita enjoyed Jeff's arms around her squeezing her tight. She remembered the invitations she got when in high school. Plenty of boys had the opportunity to get their arms around her and longed for more opportunities. But seldom did that happen.

Their son, Jake, was more like Anita in high school than Jeff. He was handsome, but like Anita, shy. He tried to get over that, but it was taking time. He wasn't interested in any *one* girl. He was interested in all the girls but hadn't found any interested in him. He had heard the story how his parents got together—hundreds of times. He thought, *"Maybe someday."*

Not far from this fun venture a lady nursed a Manhattan in the corner booth of the lounge with her favorite male companion as of late. Bernie and Scott were regulars at *The Dock*. Bernie wasn't much for eating at home. Scott didn't mind. He enjoyed his free ride. Bernie watched the fun the youth were having.

It was a distant memory for her. She and Jeff spent many winter evenings involved in all the activities others were now enjoying. Actually, they did much more. But now things were different. She couldn't see Jeff and Anita but knew they were there. She kept on top of things, most of the time. She knew they were there and hoped something bad would happen to Anita. Maybe she would fall through a thin spot in the ice and drown or catch pneumonia and die.

The Franklin brothers, Pete and Darrell, enter the lounge and seeing Bernie sitting alone head directly to talk with her when they almost run into Scott coming out of the restroom. They stopped cold in their tracks and turn in another direction. Scott didn't know anything about the relationship Bernie had with these two and Bernie didn't want him to know anything. She told them to stay clear of her whenever Scott was around.

The brothers head for the bar acting like that was where they planned to be all the time. They looked over to see if Bernie noticed they were there and might give them some kind of signal. They tried to glance that way and make it look like a casual glance, but it never did. Neither were too swift in this area of subtlety.

# Chapter 89

Bernie knew they were there, but never let on. Later, Bernie and Scott went to the dining room. The brothers stayed in the bar. They wanted to talk to Bernie, but she left before they could. This was the only place they were to be seen together. She made that very plain. And if they ever wanted to talk to her, contact would be made through Gloria first. They knew the rules but didn't always follow them. Before they left, they told Gloria they needed to talk to Bernie and it needed to be sooner than later.

*"We need to ask her."* Pete was insistent and nervous. His bottom lip extended even further when he got this way.

*"I know we do but we got to do it right."* Darrell stated.

*"You should have just given him it all, the way Bernie said."* Pete lays the blame on Darrell for why they need to talk to Bernie.

*"You idiot, that's not the way it works."*

*"Well, then you shouldn't have...."*

*"Shut-up."* Darrell gets fed up with Pete's inability to understand how life works. Darrell isn't far behind.

Ultimately, through Gloria, they did get $500 from Bernie which they called, *"spending money."* They needed it for a specific purpose. Bernie simply saw it as being a retainer for their services. They came in handy at times. It was a small price to pay. And if they couldn't do the work for her, they knew who could.

That was how it worked getting rid of her husband. Bernie got tired of Robert but not of his money. Robert was not the person she thought. Or, maybe her expectations had changed. Hard to tell what Bernie thought but she didn't want to be married anymore... at least to Robert. He was older but wasn't getting older fast enough. He could live on for years. Now, he was getting in the way of her plans.

And besides that, he started to clamp down on her spending. She was getting out of control. He put her on an allowance for a while and she stayed within the limits. Then he relented and let her spend as much as she wanted. She went out of control again. Finally, he told her he had had enough and wanted a divorce. It was just a threat. He wasn't going to act on it, but Bernie didn't know that.

Bernie got very concerned. The marriage had its good points but as of lately the relationship had become a little rocky. Bernie didn't like the thought of being out on the street. Then again, she wouldn't be poor. She would make sure to get a good cut of Robert's wealth. But that didn't satisfy her. No matter what she might get, she would want more... need more.

But Bernie didn't have all the facts about Robert. He didn't always tell her everything. She wished him dead. That wish would come about by natural causes as time went by and not very much time. If she would have just been patient, Robert would have died within a year. Cancer was eating away at him. He knew it. She didn't.

# Chapter 90

*"Had either of the Franklin brothers ever killed someone?"* Bernie amazed herself in even wondering that. But now she thought about her future. She was careful approaching them. They weren't the most upright guys, but she never talked to them about anything like this. She tried to feel them out. When that took too long she just came out and asked, *"Just curious, have either of you ever ... killed anyone?"*

Darrell said, *"Well I thought about it once. I could probably do it, if I had to."* He was smug in his response. It made him feel tough making this brave admission. He tried looking cool and confident in this declaration.

Pete looked at him with a mean, yet inquisitive expression, *"Really?!!!!"*

*"Well, the guy would have to be a bad ass as well."* Darrell justified his comments. Pete agreed with the added explanation, shaking his head.

But Darrell hadn't ever done it and, deep down, he couldn't do something like that. He talked big but that was it.

*"I think I know someone who might do it ... for a price."* Darrell added scratching his two-day growth of whiskers. He gave his version of the *"stink-eye"* wondering if Bernie was serious.

Bernie decided. *"Get in touch with him. But don't let him know who wants it done. Tell him he'll get $10,000 if he does the job."* She started to leave the lounge.

*"$10,000! Maybe I could do it."* Darrell had second thoughts.

*"Find the guy, Darrell."* Bernie wanted someone she could count on. She headed out the door and Darrell and Pete stood there looking at one another and then left themselves.

Emerald Days took place the second weekend in June. Along with it, the Class of 1971 had their 20th year reunion. Most classmates had seen the changes in Emerald, but some had not and found it hard to believe this was the same town. *"Is this the same place?"* Most liked it, but some wanted it like it was growing up. You don't want to mess with *"home."*

Registration at the shelter house in Memorial Park saw 90 people, including spouses from the class that numbered 58. Fred and Ginger greeted everyone. They plan to ride together in the Emerald Days Parade on a float supporting the sign, *"Class of '71."*

Friday night most classmates hang around the shelter house talking. Some hit Ernie's. No meal is planned until Sunday at noon. A tour of the school will take place, but beyond that, everyone is pretty much on their own. So much for all the *"activities"* the guys thought up! Nobody minded there weren't formal activities. You didn't really need something planned to mingle.

Saturday morning George Plummer gets a picture of the class for *The Emerald Examiner*. Bernie is in the picture but won't be riding on the float/hayrack. She wasn't a farm girl then and she isn't one now. The short parade started at noon. The Homecoming Queen for 1971 was to be featured. This was something new. While Ginger was kind of embarrassed by it, she wore her crown and gave the wave.

*"Looks like there won't be room for everyone on the float."* Fred makes the observation as he and Ginger are pretty much in charge of what is happening.

*"More people came than we thought."*

*"Oh, well, the parade isn't that long. Some can walk."*

Sunday morning the sky is not as clear as it was Saturday. Thin clouds provide shade that seems to fit the mood of most people as they need some relaxing moments after all the excitement of the past two days. Sunday noon the streets appear quite different. The carnival is gone having packed up during the night to head to their next venue. The streets are no longer blocked. Trash is all over. The cleaning crew will have a job. In some areas they have started, but Sunday morning is Sunday morning, and they are either slow at getting to it, in church yet...or bed.

Potato salad, Maid-Rites and baked beans are on the menu for this last hurrah. Great meal! Enough beer has been consumed for a while and enough of the sweets, cotton candy included. The class probably won't get together again for another ten years. The group is kind of subdued today. Some already headed home depending on scheduled flights, etc.

Everyone is getting older which is evident by the conversation centering on what is important in their lives. Careers were a topic at one time, then children, houses and the list goes on changing with every reunion. Nothing is going to change much for most of them but before the next Emerald Days celebration, at least one will die, and another will be accused of murder.

# *Chapter 91*

Jewel Lake sees a lot of action on the Fourth of July. The state park is crowded. Forget about getting on the golf course without reservations. Fishing is out of the question with all the boats and water-skiers. When the sun sets, and stars make their appearance, a barge in the middle of the lake provides a spectacular fireworks display. People park on country roads to catch the colorful spectacle. Sometimes it is hard to find a place to park. The show goes on for a half hour.

*"The weather is sure cooperating."* Fred is loading up the pontoon with all the necessary refreshments. They plan to be on the lake most of the day. As the lake will be crowded they will meet other boaters, a very sociable crowd.

Jeff looks up as he carries snacks on board. *"Yeah, hardly a cloud in the sky."* The Emeralds and the Kemps enjoy the 4th on the lake together.

*"That is what we like, right Ginger?"* Anita started to take off her cover, pulling it over her head to expose a revealing swimsuit. It was brand new and a little daring. Anita wanted to surprise Jeff. Uh, Fred also noticed, by the way.

*"Whoa, Mrs. Emerald, you didn't get much material with that bikini."* Jeff was captivated by what he saw. Anita had nothing to be ashamed of! She gave that swimsuit the perfect form.

*"You like?"* Anita raises her eyebrows putting one hand on her hip posing like a model. She gives an inviting look while Jeff gives a smile indicating his thoughts.

*"I like!"* Jeff had no qualms about letting anyone know he loved his wife. He realized the treasure he had.

*The Dock* opens early on the Fourth selling hamburgers and hot dogs outside at a rapid pace. Smelling onions frying, you are instantly hungry. They do a bang-up job this Fourth. Not many were in Emerald this day. The part-time cop, Stan, keeps an eye on things, though. Liz Jackson is visible at the lake in full uniform. That was part of her jurisdiction via special agreement. Rarely was there any trouble, but when alcohol is involved you never know. Police presence makes you feel safe and secure.

It always takes longer for the sun to disappear on the Fourth. Days are still long. The darkness must be intense before the fireworks begin. The Kemp pontoon was full. It was a tradition for the Kemps and the Emeralds to watch the fireworks together. Jake and Jared didn't mind although, getting older, there were times they wished they could be with their friends. That time would come soon enough. Meanwhile they all enjoyed being out on the lake.

Beginning with the first *"pop,"* the typical responses are made to the fabulous colors competing with the stars. Seeing the mirrored image in the water doubles the beauty. One bang after another. One pop after the other. It goes on and on. Towards the end you wonder if this is the last one or not. Then another goes off and still another. Finally, the last one soars into the sky, and you see the humongous, bright, red finale followed by applause as another beautiful Fourth concludes.

But another pop is heard, and another bright, red finale takes place, but it is not in the skies over Jewel Lake. This finale has nothing to do with what is in the sky and there is no applause. It all takes place in the lounge at *The Dock*. It signals the conclusion of a life.

# Chapter 92

Outside, Frank Anderson is enthralled by the fireworks when he hears a *"pop"* that doesn't come from the heavens. Not knowing what he heard exactly, he decides to go inside to make sure everything is okay. Heading towards the door he is brushed by someone leaving, searching for the darkness. Frank enters to see everyone staring at the bar.

Behind the bar, Gloria Pearson is shot and hemorrhaging. She gasps for breath. The Franklin brothers try to help her but are at a loss as what to do. Frank yells for someone to call 9-1-1. Liz Jackson is there with paramedics in less than two minutes. Liz gives the order, *"No one leaves the lounge."* Gloria is taken to Mercy Hospital in Alcoa, arriving in critical condition, goes right to the operating room.

This is where Liz takes her experience from being part of the LAPD analyzing what happened and investigating. The Highway Patrol assists but Liz is in charge. This is a first at Jewel Lake.

Twenty people are in the lounge enjoying the comfort of air conditioning and relief from mosquitoes, watching the fireworks. Gazing at the display in the sky they weren't focused on the bar. No one was an eyewitness to what happened. The story was the same: While watching the fireworks, they heard a *"pop"* behind them. Turning around someone ran out the door. No one could identify who it was.

Everyone was questioned. Liz was convinced most patrons were telling the truth—except for two of them. The Franklin brothers were in the lounge and everyone in local law enforcement gave them a second look whenever anything suspicious took place. They took them outside and questioned them separately. Pete was questioned by Liz and Officer Michaels took Darrell.

Independently, they both said they didn't know anything. Gloria was their friend and they were *"real sorry"* about what happened. But they didn't know anything. They didn't fool anybody. They knew more than they were telling. But for now, they had to let them go. Meanwhile there was a murderer out there ... somewhere.

As people left Jewel Lake, they saw police cars with lights flashing, but didn't think much of it. Someone is always getting picked up for drunk driving, underage possession of alcohol, illegal fireworks or ...something and, it was the Fourth. It wasn't until the next day that word got out: Gloria Pearson had been shot. She was still in critical condition. The bullet had been removed but she hadn't regained consciousness. The police were hoping she would identify her shooter.

Before that could happen, she died. She was in intensive care for two days. Bernie was out of town on other business but when she heard what happened she was there within hours. Gloria didn't have a lot of friends. Bernie was her best friend, her only close friend. Bernie took care of the funeral arrangements—paid for it all. But that wasn't going to be the end of it. Gloria was Bernie's go-between and Bernie felt she might, indirectly, be responsible for Gloria's death and wanted to get to the bottom of it. She also felt a little concerned about her own wellbeing. She just had a funny feeling about it all because the Franklin brothers were present when it all happened.

The Franklin brothers came together to Carlson Estates. It wasn't a social call. Bernie told them when to come, ordered them to come. She wanted to know what happened—who shot Gloria, and why? She was pissed. They rode up on their Harleys. She was waiting on the porch. They went inside to get a tongue lashing.

Pete looked down the whole time, his bottom lip protruding. Darrell clinched his mouth. Both were silent for the longest time. Pete was first to speak. *"It was an accident, pure and simple, nothing else."*

Darrell said, *"Shut-up,"* but he wouldn't. Pete had to get it off his chest. He kept it secret long enough and felt guilty.

*"Gloria should not have been shot. No one saw that coming."*

# Chapter 93

Bernie crossed her arms and wore an angry expression. They saw this before and didn't like seeing it now. She was pissed, and she showed it. *"Okay, so what happened?"* Still they were quiet.

Pete took a chance looking up and said it was all Darrell's fault pointing at his brother before looking down again. When Bernie gave Pete and Darrell the money to have her husband killed she gave them the whole $10,000 to give to ... whoever it was that was going to make the hit.

From Darrell's vast knowledge of the underworld, basically via television, he knew that was not the way it should be done. *"Half should be given up-front and the other half when the job was done."* That is the way it works. *"Dumb broad!"* He didn't say that to her face though. But when he contacted Bud Cross from Chaska, Minnesota, those were the terms. Bud agreed without a second thought.

Darrell met Bud in Alcoa a few years back. They were in adjoining cells. Both were booked on being drunk and disorderly. They weren't together to begin with but ended up there regardless. Ironically, Bud was in a bar where Gloria was working for several years. Bud and Darrell didn't become friends, really, but got to know each other. Bud hinted he had killed in the past and that got Darrell to thinking he might do this job as well.

Bud did the job, but Darrell was slow in getting him the other half of the money. Darrell bet some of it on a *"sure thing"* that didn't turn out to be so sure. He bet only a thousand but lost. He gave Bud $4000, but Bud wanted what was promised and now ... with interest. Darrell was trying to get it for him. That is why they asked for some *"spending money"* from Bernie earlier. The $500 they got just took care of the interest as far as Bud was concerned. On the Fourth he came to collect the rest. He had waited long enough.

The fireworks were lighting up the sky when Bud entered the lounge. He knew the Franklin brothers would be there seeing their cycles outside. They were talking with Gloria at the end of the bar, closest to the door. Bud came over and was in no mood for chit-chat. Gloria had no idea who he was, didn't remember him at all, and didn't want to know. He looked intimidating. She was glad the Franklin brothers were around. Their mere presence often discouraged anything inappropriate from happening. Believe it or not she felt safer when they were around.

*"Hey, Bud, what you doin' here?"* Pete asked.

*"You know what I'm doing here. You got my money?"*

Darrell sat up on his stool looking a little concerned. He knew what was on Bud's mind. *"Yeah, we got it. I mean, we are going to get it. We just haven't picked it up yet."* The conversation continued and became heated. Bud pulled out his gun keeping it somewhat hidden as not to arouse any unnecessary attention. No one else noticed him, they were enthralled by what they saw in the sky. Eyes were focused in the opposite direction.

Gloria saw the gun, got a little nervous, *"I think maybe you need to leave,"* she said, looking at Bud and nodding toward the door. Her intimidating comment didn't even begin to work with Bud.

*"I need my money... NOW!"* Bud looked pretty mean in Pete's eyes.

*"Bud?"* Pete was surprised with the gun and looked at his brother.

Gloria spoke a little louder, *"Mister, I think you need to leave."*

At the same time Bud thought she was reaching under the bar for ... maybe a gun?

*"Keep your hands where I can see them."* Then he turned toward Darrell, *"Am I going to get my money or is someone gonna get hurt?"* He leaned on one foot posing the threat.

Then Gloria moved in a way Bud thought she was going for a gun and nervous as he was, he shot her in the abdomen. He surprised even himself by his action. Realizing what he did and that the crowd was starting to look his way, he ran out the door almost knocking down Frank Anderson.

That was the story.

# Chapter 94

All was quiet. Bernie's arms are still crossed. *"You pair of knuckleheads. You idiots. That is what you are. You two are dumb as dirt!"* Bernie fumed! She thought for a moment, *"Where is Bud now?"*

*"Don't know."* They shrugged their shoulders looking down.

*"You don't know? How did I ever get mixed up with you two?"* Bernie was disgusted. The brothers kept from making eye contact. Bernie paced the floor contemplating her next move.

She would get them the extra thousand to take to him. Then she thought she better get two thousand, just in case. That was a mistake. Now Bud got the idea he could do some blackmailing, get more money. And Bernie found herself in an even deeper mess.

Gloria's murder upset the whole town of Emerald. No one in Emerald had ever been murdered. No one from Emerald had even been shot. Liz didn't take this lying down. She was sure the Franklin brothers knew more than they were letting on.

This also led to the hiring of two new deputies to assist Liz. The town council had been debating over the need for more police. Emerald had grown, and it wasn't the quiet little town it used to be. This shooting at Jewel Lake was the turning point.

Meanwhile, Frank Anderson decided extra security was needed at *The Dock*. Never needed it before but no one had ever been murdered there before. There was the occasional rumble when guys had a little too much to drink, but never anything like this. Frank thought maybe it was a botched robbery attempt and installed security cameras in various areas including the parking lot. It was an overreaction, but that is what happens when you are scared and uncertain about your safety and the safety of others.

Gloria was a good employee and replacing her wouldn't be easy. She was dependable. She was honest. And she was good to the customers. At her funeral there was a big bouquet of flowers from *The Dock*. Fred, who owned the place, was saddened by what happened. You don't want your establishment to get the reputation for being dangerous. That was the business side of his brain. The compassionate side felt bad for Gloria. She wasn't his favorite person, in part, because of her relationship with Bernie, but murder… no one would wish that on anyone.

The clues Liz collected led nowhere. After a month, Gloria's murder was still a mystery, but Liz did not stop her investigation. She was watching anyone that looked the least bit suspicious when they came into Emerald. And she kept her eyes on the Franklin brothers. The Highway Patrol kept an eye open for their vehicles also. The brothers knew they were under surveillance and kept their noses clean. Bernie gave them money to pay off Bud and then told them to stay away from her unless she contacted them. She didn't want anyone thinking she had anything to do with Gloria's death. They stayed away.

# Chapter 95

The community-wide Labor Day picnic in Memorial Park brought out the whole town. It was also a kick-off for the new school year. The pool wasn't open, but the playground was available, and the kids took full advantage of it. An estimated 300 people showed up. The park looked full and every parking space was taken. Those who lived close enjoyed the walk up town.

Even though it had been two months since Gloria's murder, it is still a hot topic. *The Emerald Examiner* kept the community apprised of what was happening with quotes from the police and possible leads. People living at a distance kept their subscription up to date appreciating *The Examiner* now, more than ever. This was quite the news and a mystery for their hometown.

The following Wednesday night, the Franklin brothers were at Ernie's. On Wednesday's, Ernie had a pizza buffet at a very low price. He never appreciated the Franklin brothers showing up. His profits, slim as they were, would not be as good. But they were there drinking beer and eating pizza, having a good time. The crowd wasn't too bad either tonight. In fact, it was pretty good. There were people Ernie didn't recognize and he liked that. New customers—always welcome. When a booth opened, Pete and Darrell claimed it. Walking to the booth they looked like they owned the place, giving their tough and cocky stroll. Sitting down with their backs to the wall, their feet rested on the seat, they watched the crowd. They would have looked intimidating except for a *"dumb"* look about them. Those getting close could tell it had been a while since wash day.

Pete happened to be looking at the door when Bud Cross entered. Pete motioned to Darrell, pointing towards the door. Darrell lost a little color in his face. Bud stood there for a moment looking over the crowd when he found the brothers. They were stuck and had that *"deer in the headlights"* look about them. They couldn't go anywhere even if they wanted to. Bud pushed Darrell's feet off the bench and sat down resting his elbows on the table. He took a drink of Darrell's beer, a bite of his pizza, *"How are things going?"* Bud gave a smile with his head bent downward. He enjoyed intimidating them.

*"How do you think things are going?"* Pete tried to whisper. *"What are you doing here?"*

*"I heard about Emerald. Thought I would come to see what it was like."* Bud justified his presence smiling and giving a sneer at the same time. He looked around and didn't think too much of what he saw.

*"You better not stay."* Pete spoke without thinking.

Bud gave a defiant, angry look Pete's way. *"I'll stay as long as I want!"*

Then Liz Jackson opened the door, walking in, taking her time. She would do that on busy nights, just to make sure everyone was behaving. Bud had never seen Emerald's top town cop. He was impressed. In her police uniform she looked very official and every bit a woman. She kept herself in shape. Her long hair was pinned up to be out of the way if she encountered trouble.

Some high school boys saw her as being one of *Charlie's Angels*, a show seen in reruns. When she was off duty out at the lake you could see their reasoning. Liz was Homecoming Queen in year's past and hadn't lost her looks. She was known for being very athletic and intimidating when it came to obeying the law. You didn't want to have a stare down contest with her.

Nevertheless, high school guys joked about *"being picked up"* by her. Bud was thinking the same thing. He was thinking he wouldn't mind if this cute little cop picked him up… for … anything. He might even enjoy it. *"And she might enjoy it as well"* … he thought.

# Chapter 96

Bud was an idiot, a total idiot and a narcissistic fool. You didn't want to mess with Liz. She finished first in her class in L.A. in martial arts. She was 5'7" of trouble for anyone messing with her. Her colleagues knew that along with some perps she had taken down.

She looked around and was on her way out when she glanced over at the three stooges in the booth. None had too smart of an expression on their bearded faces and none looked her way. She strolled over, *"How's it going boys. Who is your friend?"*

Pete looked up, *"He's just from out of town."*

*"What's your name?"* Bud thought she was asking too many questions and kept his mouth shut but Pete supplied an answer to every inquiry Liz made. Pete didn't want to look suspicious. But in what he did they looked even more suspicious. She left Ernie's but kept an eye on the door for when this trio left.

Not long after Bud got up. *"I'm getting out of here."*

*"Good idea."* Pete said.

*"Shut-up! I'll be in touch."* It is a quiet, humid evening as Bud heads for his pickup. He doesn't notice Liz across the street. She is in the shadows. She lets Bud leave before getting into her patrol car.

While Liz was following Bud out of town, Pete and Darrell left Ernie's and made a beeline to *The Dock*. They knew Bernie would be there. They told her about Bud and she wanted to know what he wanted. They didn't know. They told her about Liz coming in and that upset her even more. They felt kind of important relaying this news bulletin.

Bernie was not in control and she liked being in control. Now this *"Bud"* person was giving her problems. Bud was the one she used to get rid of one problem in her life, and now she needed to find someone to get rid of Bud. She would give this some thought. Once again, she wondered why she ever got involved with these bumbling idiots. She asked them to leave and ordered another Manhattan. She would be in touch.

# Chapter 97

As the calendar turned to November, Emerald was still concerned about July. A murder was yet to be solved. This was still on the minds of many. But it was not on anyone's mind more than Liz Jackson's. Using all her training to figure out who did it, and why, she came up with nothing, hitting a dead end.

Quite often, if a person commits only one murder they can get away with it. The same is true with robbing a bank. Rob one and you are okay. Don't make a pattern of it. Liz didn't want another murder, but she wanted to catch whoever killed Gloria. And she wasn't making any headway.

It was the first Monday after the first of the year. Pete Franklin came into *The Clinic* with what he called *"an infection."* Dr. Floyd looked at it and could tell his wound was infected, but before it became *"an infection"* it was a gunshot wound. When a doctor suspects a gunshot wound, he must inform the authorities. Pete thought he told a pretty good story but when he saw Liz walk in, he knew he hadn't. She questioned him. He was very evasive in his answers. He couldn't wait to get out of there.

Working in *The Clinic*, Ginger sees everything and while she is not a gossip, she does share quite a bit with Anita and then Jeff finds out. Jeff isn't real familiar with the Franklin brothers since they originally lived in Alcoa but is very supportive of local law enforcement. As a new member of the town council, he will make sure they are paid well and have all the support they need. He remembered the help given when the tornado went through Emerald.

Bud had come down and gotten in an argument with Pete and Darrell when things got out of hand. They had been drinking and one thing led to another. He wanted to know who was paying him because he needed more money. It was just as Bernie feared. She was being blackmailed. The brothers weren't going to give up Bernie's name. Bud threatened them, but they didn't back down.

Bud looked at the brothers sitting in their kitchen, *"You think I'm kidding?"* He put down his beer and whipped out his pistol, waving it around. Of course, this got their attention and they got nervous. *"Do you think I'm just fooling around? Well, do you?"*

Neither answered. They didn't think Bud really wanted an answer. They sat up, very conscious of where that gun was pointed.

*"You two are nothing more than a couple of morons!"* He got angry at their silence and shot Pete in the side. It was not a serious wound or life threatening by any means, it did need attention. They hadn't taken proper care of it; hence the reason Pete was at *The Clinic.*

But now things were getting serious. Bud wanted to know about the person who hired him. The brothers were scared to tell Bernie, but they had to. They had to reveal their loyalty. Bernie heard the news and took it in stride. She had been giving this all a lot of thought and concluded she would take care of this herself. Hiring someone to kill someone else was getting too involved, too complicated. If she wanted something done right, she had to do it herself.

She surprised the brothers telling them, *"I'll take care of it all. You don't need to worry. Tell Bud the next time you see him the person that hired him wants to meet him... but don't use my name."*

They think Bernie is biting off more than she can chew but are glad they have something to tell Bud. They hope he won't be waving his pistol around.

Bernie puts her plan together. Where and when will be very important. It must be done in just the right way, so her involvement will not be detected. She must get rid of Bud and make it look like he mysteriously disappeared. Well, maybe a little too dramatic. This is something that needed to be carefully planned.

# Chapter 98

"*How do you plan the perfect murder?*" Bernie is thinking about that along with getting rid of at least one other person. She isn't the first to contemplate something like this. But this is *HER* first time and she wants to plan it perfectly. How does a person get to this point in their life? In her mind she thinks her hands will be clean and she might even look like the hero if everything goes according to plan.

Pete and Darrell tell Bud, the person who hired him is ready to talk. They set up a meeting. Bud likes the sound of this, telling the brothers the person should bring money. The message is conveyed.

Bernie thinks this through taking yet another step towards the dark side. She plans to do something most people would never think of doing. Has she lost her conscience completely? It would seem so. You might hate someone, but you don't think about taking their life. She has never taken a life. She doesn't know if she could ... personally. She had her husband killed, but she wasn't involved in the messy aspect of it. She had someone else do it. Someone else pulled the trigger. Someone else saw the blood. Someone else dealt with the lifeless body. Someone else cleaned it up afterwards. Could she be that *"someone else"*? She wasn't sure. Having her husband killed didn't bother her. She wondered if it would. And even when she saw him in the coffin, nothing, absolutely no feeling came forth. What was she made of?

The brothers gave Bernie a picture of Bud, so she would know the person to look for. When she saw the picture, Bud looked like the kind of guy she thought he was. He looked like he wasn't too smart. He was smarter than Bernie gave him credit for, but that was the way Bernie looked at everyone. She didn't have a high opinion of anyone other than herself. She decided her story to Bud was that she was just another go-between. The real person with the money still didn't want to be identified. She figured he would buy that, if enough cash was on the table. He was only interested in the money anyway.

The meeting was to take place on the seedier side of Alcoa in a tavern that had seen better days. Then again, maybe it hadn't! Bernie dressed for the meeting in clothes that would not be noticed or remembered. She didn't want anyone remembering her visit. She wasn't looking for lustful looks on this occasion. The people in this place were not ones she wanted to impress.

Pete gave her a description of Bud's vehicle. She didn't want to enter until she was sure Bud was present. And she didn't want to be in there any longer than necessary. The meeting was to take place at 10:30 p.m. She arrived at 10:20 and spotted Bud's pickup. She parked her BMW 50 feet away and sat there for a while. Her car looked out of place sitting next to rusted out pickups. Ten minutes passed, she went in.

# Chapter 99

Opening the door, she got a strong whiff of cigarette smoke. No one looked up as she entered. The bartender hardly noticed. There were only 6 people in the bar counting the bartender. It smelled of stale beer and had a dirty, uneven, wooden floor. The pub was small: four booths, two tables with a total of six chairs and an *"L"* shaped bar with nine stools. The bartender wore a long sleeve white shirt with the sleeves rolled above his elbows. Wiping off the bar, his tongue played with a toothpick hanging from his mouth. The television had a game on that a couple of people were watching. It was the only sound in the whole place. Bud sat in the last booth, somewhat interested in the game, nursing his third bottle of beer. The place wasn't well lit suiting Bernie just fine. She approached the booth, *"Mr. Cross."*

Bud looked up responding, *"Maybe. Who wants to know?"* He thought he was being cleverly evasive. He was really acting like a jerk. He heard this line in a movie and thought it was a good one, so he used it as often as he had the opportunity.

*"I believe we have some mutual, shall we say, acquaintances... the Franklin brothers?"*

*"Yeah, okay, I'm Bud Cross. And you are...."* He gave her the *"once-over"* which she didn't really appreciate but that was all part of the game.

Bernie sat down, *"I am the person with the money."* She didn't want to be this close to him, but she slid into the small booth nevertheless. The place was dirty. She had to do what she had to do. Tonight, she was going to get *"dirty"* in a variety of ways.

*"Okay."* He went on to say, *"I thought I was going to meet the person who paid to have her husband knocked off."* Bud didn't like it when details changed, made him nervous. He gave her a squinted eye look.

*"I'm not that person,"* she lied, *"does that make a difference?"* She just looked at him. For a moment they had a *stare-down* contest. Bernie was good at this. Bud was the first to look away.

He looked a little confused. *"Where's the money?"* Bernie pulled out an envelope with ten one-hundred-dollar bills inside, briefly looked around to see if anyone was watching and slid it to him. He looked around as well and then lifted the flap to checked it out. It was all there.

*"The person I'm representing has another job for you. Interested?"* She didn't wait for a response. *"It would be for more money. It would mean killing another person."* Bernie didn't waste any time. She was very straight forward. This wasn't a social visit and she didn't want to spend any more time in this place or with Bud than she had to.

Bud was taken back a little by this. Bernie's husband was the second life he had taken. It was the first where he used a gun. He beat the first victim to death in a fist fight. It was almost an accident. He shot Robert in their bedroom after he had knocked him out.

He had to make it look like it was a burglary gone wrong. But he didn't care much about moving the body around. His rearranging the scene didn't fool anybody, but the Minneapolis P.D. didn't let on they knew what might have really happened or what they really knew.

## Chapter 100

Bud was told Robert was a vicious, mean man who threatened his wife on numerous occasions. He was supposed to have been *"sleeping around,"* even bringing other women home. It was an *"in your face"* situation. He was portrayed as a lady's man. On top of that, he was violent and beat his wife. The wife left as often as she could, she was scared. If she ever mentioned divorce, he said he would kill her. None of that was true, but that is what Bud was told. It made him feel like he was a *"knight in shining armor,"* coming to the rescue of a damsel in distress. Bud needed to hear this to do what he did. He liked to justify his actions, in his own mind.

He had it all planned how he would kill Robert. Bud was given a key to the house, so a quiet entry was not a problem. A floorplan was provided. Bud was careful not to do anything that might awaken Robert. His mission was to make it look like a burglary gone wrong. Robert was asleep and snoring when he received a blow from Bud knocking him unconscious. Bud then pulled the frail body out of bed and laid him on the floor close to a bureau where Bernie's jewelry was kept. He shot Robert in cold blood with one shot in the heart.

As he looked at the corpse he wondered about the guy. He didn't look like the person he thought he would be. He certainly didn't look like a lady's man! Robert wasn't a big guy. He looked kind of thin and a little frail for someone who beat his wife. He didn't look mean. But then, what did he know? He had simply helped a woman in need. He might mete out justice at the right price, for the right reason and for the right person.

Bernie tells Bud that the person she is representing has someone else that needs to be taken out. And here, Bernie's story-telling ability flourishes. *"This person is pure evil. You wouldn't be able to tell from appearances, but you can't depend on how a person looks to get the full picture. Don't be fooled. This person has hurt a lot of people. This person can't be trusted. The world would be a better place if this person never lived."*

She went on and on and it would really have been a good description of herself, but she didn't realize it. *"Are you willing to take another life?"* She looks at Bud and for a moment, Bud just looks back at her. He has gotten caught up in her diatribe. He doesn't know what to say. He is trying to take it all in before he answers.

Then the door to the bar opens. In walk two patrolmen standing in a very official pose, hands on their utility belts, they look around the dimly lit establishment. The quiet atmosphere is disturbed by a neon light starting to buzz. Bud faces the door and is the first to realize they have lawmen in the room. Recognizing one of them, he puts his head down and raises his hand as if scratching his forehead to hide his face. Bernie notices Bud's actions and turns to see what is making him nervous. Seeing the lawmen, she also turns slightly and tries to look inconspicuous. She puts her head down and wipes her nose. The conversation between the two comes to a halt. The bar isn't crowded. The patrolmen just stand there for a moment appearing very intimidating. Bud doesn't think they are there for him, but he doesn't know for sure and isn't taking any chances.

The patrolmen make their way across the floor. As they approach him he appears nervous. One is standing on either side. He is sitting on the third bar stool from the end where he has been since 9:00 p.m. He has had more than enough to drink. Ivan Trek had beaten his wife and 4-year-old son for the last time and now he is headed for jail. He isn't interested in going anywhere and the alcohol dictates his actions. Any logic in what he does is missed on everyone else. He finds out these cops are ready for him. He isn't much of a match as he swings widely and then falls to the floor. They cuff him and lead him to the patrol car.

Bernie is shaken up by the scuffle and decides to finish the conversation later. The patrolmen haven't even noticed these two in a back booth. They were interested in only Ivan. Feeling guilty and suspicious she wants to leave.

*"When?"* Bud asks.

*"We'll keep in touch."*

This has been quite a night for Bernie. She thinks she has covered her tracks but wonders if she has made any mistakes. She has never done this before! She makes her way home but doesn't go through Alcoa. Instead she goes around it, leaving the same way she came. There aren't that many BMWs around and, like we said before, she didn't want to be noticed.

Getting back, she drove past Carlson Estates and on into Emerald itself. It was getting close to midnight, she decided to drive around for a while. She wasn't tired and needed to calm her nerves. Her mind was racing 90-miles-an-hour. She slowly drove around Memorial Park in downtown Emerald, not really looking at it. She was just there.

But when she saw Emerald Grocery she cursed it as she unhurriedly passed. Its very presence mocked her, and she despised it. There were six vehicles parked in front of Ernie's. Liz Jackson was making her rounds in the patrol car. She was cruising through the streets observing what little was going on. Bernie hoped Liz was focused on something other than her and wouldn't give her a second look. Then Bernie drove down to the south end of town. She drove by Jeff and Anita's. She loathed this couple. She detested their kids. She despised their place in the community. Bernie had become very bitter. She hated them but at the same time wanted to know anything and everything going on in their lives.

As she got close to their house, there was activity in their front yard. Pretty late for company. Their guests were just leaving the house.

Who else would it be other than Fred and Ginger? That was another couple she didn't have time for, but they were not despised quite as much. Actually, believe it or not, Bernie still had a thing for Jeff, but it was starting to wane. But Anita, Anita she hated as she always had. Many times, she had wished her dead. Maybe it would happen soon.

# Chapter 101

As children get older there is a point where you wonder when or if you will ever have time for yourself again. They demand so much time and energy. Most of the time, you just want to make sure they get their homework done or make it to practice on time, memorize lines for a performance or any of a vast number of other activities in which they are involved. You put your life on hold, doing what you can for them. Then again, in some ways you might find yourself reliving your early years through them.

Jeff and Anita were doing that somewhat through Jake. Jake was finally interested in a girl. He had always been interested in her but was too shy and felt awkward around her as can be the case with so many his age. She would come in on Saturdays with her mom to do the weekly shopping. Of course, Jake would be working at that time, and was very busy and very important, too important to really notice any customers.

Her name was Arlene, Arlene Plummer, one of George and Vera Plummer's children. George was the editor of *The Emerald Examiner*. Arlene was a cute, little brunette, also shy. The possibility of these two ever getting together would seem remote. Someone would be needed behind each of them, pushing them together, or it would never happen. Anita watched it all. She saw how her first-born acted when Arlene came in. She felt for Jake seeing how nervous he was. And she also noticed Arlene look his way several times. Arlene was 14 and Jake, 16, a freshman and a junior, who knows what might develop?

The fathers didn't know each other real well. Jeff always placed ads in *The Examiner*. George appreciated his business and gave him a good deal and the ideal place for ads on the back page. There wasn't a

Chamber of Commerce in Emerald yet. If there was, they might get together for that. Anita and Vera didn't have a relationship other than she was a faithful patron and had been for years. The Plummers also lived in town but not in the same area. They lived in the north part—the Emeralds in the south. Even though Emerald wasn't that big geographically, it still made a difference. While everyone knew each other to a certain degree, Emerald was also growing and not quite as intimate as it used to be.

When Anita saw the attraction, her motherly instinct kicked in and she wanted to encourage it. Maybe she would invite the Plummer family over for a meal, something like that. She tried to be subtle but wasn't subtle enough. Jake hated the idea. He didn't want anything like that to happen. *"Stay out of this mom!"* He was angry at the mere suggestion!

Anita understood. But she planned a get-together of sorts anyway that wouldn't put Jake on the spot. They had a gathering at their place including six families, all with children around the same age, and the Plummer family just happened to get invited. It would all be very casual, something outside for the most part, maybe throw some hot dogs on the grill, nothing fancy. Jake eventually warmed up to the idea and it turned out very well.

Of course, Fred and Ginger and their girls attended and were the last ones to leave that night. Bernie saw them coming out of the house that late hour. They didn't notice her drive by. They weren't looking, and they didn't care. They were all tired. It was late enough, and they usually didn't stay out so late, but they hadn't had so much fun in a long time, they were going to make an exception. The three little ones had to be carried out as they were close to being in dreamland.

It was hard getting out of bed the next morning for most everybody in the Emerald household. But Jake was the exception, he had no problem. Actually, he didn't get much sleep. He was thinking of Arlene. He would be thinking of her a lot. The previous night had been a huge success as far as he was concerned. When could they do that again? That is what he wanted to know. He was wondering how Arlene felt. She seemed very nice. And she was so easy to talk to. Jake was starting to feel different about himself, a little bolder, a little more courageous. Amazing what one night can do!

Jeff, on the other hand, dragged himself out of bed swearing that he would never stay up so late again. He always did that even though he would do it all again without a thought. Anita made it to the store by 9:00 a.m. It was just another day for the rest of the family.

The spring of the year makes you feel alive. At least it does when you have been cooped up all winter with snow days and blizzards. The clean, fresh air makes you want to get out and enjoy the warm weather even when the temperature is barely 40 degrees. Grass is starting to green-up. Some flowers are popping out and the trees are starting to bud. The meadowlarks decide to serenade anyone listening. Spring is wonderful and is often a time to fall in love. Jake was filled with that feeling.

# Chapter 102

Jake was about to do something he had never done before. *"Mom, can I talk with you ... about something?"* He takes a bold step. Mom is the best one to talk to about this. Still, it is not easy. It would be awkward talking to dad. Mom would understand.

Anita has no idea what he wants but gives the *"mom"* response. *"Of course, what's on your mind?"* She doesn't even look up. If she had she would have noticed, he was getting red in the face.

Jake was nervous. *"Uh... I've been thinking about ... uh ... asking someone to the prom."* He looks at his mom wondering what kind of response this comment might bring. He had been looking at the floor before that.

Anita was glad to hear he was going to the prom! *"Really? Anyone I know?"* She tried not to act too excited. Inside she was about to burst. She couldn't wait to tell Ginger! She didn't look at him or smile or anything, she didn't want to embarrass him. She thought she might.

*"Yeah...uh... maybe ... Arlene Plummer. But I don't know. She's just a freshman and ... I don't know if she could go or not or even if she would want to go. What do you think?"* This was a very important question and Jake was looking for a definitive answer. He needed encouragement.

It was the first time he ever talked about *"girls"* with his mom. Anita was thrilled but, once again, tried to control her feelings. She was going to be very careful in how she handled this. *"Well, you won't know until you ask her."* After replying she gave a side glance to Jake. He was thinking. It was weighing on his mind. This was really going to be a huge step for him. Not only would it be the first time he ever asked a girl out, it would be to an event that was pretty much *THE* event as far as high school was concerned. Before he left his mom, she gave him a hug and a little more encouragement. She thought about bringing up a little of her history with Jeff but decided against it. He had heard that story enough.

It was a couple weeks before it happened, but Jake finally got up the nerve. It was very awkward for both. He got the words out. Arlene didn't know this request was coming. She was caught off guard and it was very apparent in the stunned look she gave. That scared Jake at the time, but he let it pass. They had been talking during school and spending a little time together, but she didn't think he was that serious about her. She was just a freshman! She would have to ask her parents. She talked to her mom first. The answer, of course, would be, *"Yes."*

Both sets of parents would be there but for different reasons. George would be taking pictures for *The Examiner*. The Prom would be pictorially documented in the weekly edition to come out the following Thursday. Jeff and Anita would serve as chaperones for the dance along with three other couples. It gave Anita the opportunity to wear a formal once again.

When the big day arrived, Anita helped in the kitchen preparing the meal with the other mothers but left around 3:00 to go home and change. Her job in the kitchen was done. The doors would be open at 6:00 and the meal would be served a half-hour later. The dance would start at 9:00 and the whole affair would end at midnight. The big event was about to begin.

# Chapter 103

This was Arlene's first official date. Her parents didn't want her dating until she was 16. That seemed to be a rule in Emerald for most families. But because of the circumstances, an exception was made. Arlene was 5'5". She could easily wear heals and not even come close to Jake's height, but she wasn't that comfortable in them yet.

Her formal was very simple yet nice. Jake found out what color it would be and, with mom's advice and suggestions, bought a corsage that complimented it. To Jake she was the most beautiful thing he had ever seen. He was swept away!

Jeff drove Jake over to Arlene's to pick her up. That was part of the deal. This was not going to be a *"car date"* for the two of them even though Jake had his license. One dad would take them, the other would bring them home. Everyone was okay with this. The two on their first date were nervous about everything the way it was. They didn't need anything else to think about, although they were both wondering about any possibility of a kiss before the night was over.

They sat in the back seat but not real close. The conversation was rather stilted. It would get better as the evening progressed and no parents were around, close by, at least. Both had butterflies that would be calmed down once they got inside among their friends. Jeff tried not to ask any embarrassing questions or start any boring conversations. He was just the chauffeur, right now, not dad.

Pulling up next to the school, Jake immediately got out to open Arlene's door. He was the perfect gentleman. Other couples were arriving at the same time. Some were on their own and some had their parents dropping them off. Jake took Arlene's hand and they walked into the school, heading for the gym. They met some of Jeff's classmates as they entered. Arlene was the only freshman at this event. Jeff watched it all and smiled. Then he headed home to pick up his own date for the evening. She wouldn't disappoint him.

Shortly after the talk Jake had with his mom, the Kemps and the Emeralds were together in the lounge out at *The Dock*. They started reminiscing about the past. Fred couldn't help but ask Anita, *"Do you remember when I asked you out?"* She was the only person he ever asked out in high school.

She was the very first person he asked out. One day they met on the sidewalk and walked the rest of the way to school together. It all happened by accident, but later Fred planned it, so it would happen a couple more times. After Anita gave him a smile that seemed to say to him, *"I'm really kind of interested in you,"* he decided to take the plunge. Of course, all his friends encouraged him. It took quite a bit for him to take such a bold step.

Anita gave that look. You could tell she remembered it very well. *"Yes, I remember."* She didn't sound real excited. Fred was surprised in her response, just the fact she *DID* remember. He never forgot it.

*"You know, you broke my heart when you turned me down,"* Fred explained, *"but I was also relieved!"*

*"Really?"* Anita was surprised.

*"Yeah,"* Fred continued, *"I had no idea what we would do or how I should act. I was a real mess until you turned me down."*

She said she really had no interest in going out with him but was flattered he asked. She didn't say it in a cruel way. She didn't have a huge interest in any *"one"* guy in high school. Didn't bother Fred. He was madly in love with Ginger... and his three princesses. Anita was surprised that she was the first person Fred had ever, *EVER* asked out.

Jeff pulls in the driveway still thinking about the couple he delivered to their first night of memories. Jeff goes up the back stairs into the kitchen. He is looking at his watch and hopes Anita is on schedule. Sometimes she is a little late but not often.

*"You ready?"* He yells. *"We're cutting it kind of close."* He comes into the living room adjusting his coat a little. It feels tighter than it used to. He gets to the stairway, looks up the steps and there she is, standing at the top of the stairway. He is wearing a black tuxedo, but no one will notice anything about him or what he is wearing. What he sees takes his breath away.

Anita has her hair pinned up and is wearing a strapless light blue formal. Tight around the bodice, it flows with very sheer material downward. A matching shawl is worn just below her shoulders. She walks down the steps with all the grace and charm of a beauty queen. The formal is not that much different from the one she wore to the prom her senior year. Jeff wouldn't have known that. He was so focused on Bernie at that time. Tonight, Anita would be noticed by the other *"older"* people there but to the younger crowd, not so much.

*"This is the way the mother of one of the juniors is supposed to look? You bet it is!"* as far as Jeff is concerned! *"Wow! I don't know if I want to share this vision with anyone else tonight!"* Jeff says as he starts to get some serious ideas of how the rest of the night will go *AFTER* the prom! Anita feels very good in the fact Jeff likes what he sees. She gives a smile of satisfaction, raises her eyebrows and the two are off.

# Chapter 104

Jeff attended both proms with Bernie during their junior and senior years. He couldn't remember if Anita attended either. She attended every prom since she was a freshman—different guys every year. But Jeff had eyes only for Bernie in those days. Now he saw Anita for the first time in a formal. Sometimes he wonders how he could have missed her all those years. She wonders the same when it comes to Jeff.

Anita takes Jeff's hand going down the steps, out the back door. He opens the car door and she slides in. The school is only a few blocks away, taking seconds to get there. Jeff lets Anita off at the door, parks, and then escorts her in.

Dropping her off, he walks about a block. On his way, Bernie drives by. She eyes Jeff in his tux and almost stops to talk but decides against it. He has filled out as a man does, looks very masculine and very desirable. As she drove on, she saw Anita standing in her formal, waiting for Jeff. Bernie had no idea they were chaperones. She didn't even know it was prom weekend.

Bernie didn't have any kids and didn't keep up with school activities. She had other things on her mind. But seeing Jeff in his tux brought back memories. When they were in school none of the guys wore a tux as a rule. All the girls had formals, but guys wore suits and sometimes, just sport coats. The prom hadn't changed much over the years. The same format was used without much deviation.

Back in 1971, however, after the dance, kids drove to Alcoa or around the lake. Sometimes they would go to a drive-in. Some couples would double up, but Jeff and Bernie never did. They were into each other. How could things have changed so much?

She remembered how involved they got after the last prom. Being together in the front, or back, seat of a car, in the middle of the night, with no one else around, was too tempting for some couples. They were no exception. It was rumored, by those who think they are *"in the know,"* that Bernie and Jeff had gone all the way... on a regular basis. After all, they were going to get married sometime in the future, why not take advantage of the opportunity to be alone and...? Only Jeff and Bernie knew how far they went.

Bernie drove around the block in time to see Anita take Jeff's arm and disappear into the darkness. Bernie cursed them both and continued to scheme.

# Chapter 105

Emerald Days was expanding with every passing year. Crowds grew. Activities increased. People had a great time. Jake worked at the store but took every opportunity to be with Arlene. They rode the Ferris wheel and roller coaster and just enjoyed being together. Jake liked being seen with Arlene. Arlene had similar thoughts strolling through the crowd. She was going to be a sophomore and her *"man"* was going to be a senior, all very impressive.

Friday night, Jeff and Anita walked through the midway, talking with people along the way. They played a little bingo, got a Maid-Rite. They didn't care much for the rides but went on the Merry-go-round if their kids weren't around to embarrass.

Ernie's Pool Hall was hopping. Kids and families enjoyed the carnival but those who didn't fit into either category got together at Ernie's. Ernie hired extra help to take care of all his customers.

The Franklin brothers walked over to the midway from their *"shack"* a couple blocks from the action. They stopped to get a sandwich and talked with some of the carnies. They watched kids playing the crane machines, and then spent enough money to buy whatever they couldn't grab with the claws. They looked at the machines as if they were Vegas slot machines. Getting discouraged, they moved on, heading for Ernie's. Two things happened.

First, they see Bud Cross walking towards them. He came up out of the shadows. They hadn't seen him in a long time and weren't sure if they were glad to see him now. They could do without him being around. He made them nervous. But he had a big smile and greeted them, *"How's it going, guys?"*

He takes them by surprise. They don't answer him right away, not knowing the mood he might be in. He walked between them putting his hands on their shoulders. They all headed to Ernie's.

They passed the bank and post office when they see someone pushed out the front door of Ernie's. He comes out fast, falling to the sidewalk and followed by another guy. A fist-fight is in progress, unusual for Emerald. These guys aren't local but knew each other and were really getting into it. Punches were thrown, and it was getting bloody. Bud, Darrell and Pete stand back to watch. A crowd gathers around; no one tries to stop them.

The second thing was Liz Jackson. She sees what is happening and picks up the pace to put an end to this scuffle. She identifies herself and told them to break it up. The two guys ignore her as they beat on one another. Punches are solid, and it hurts to watch what is happening.

Liz repeats the command which they again ignore.

Bud remembered looking at her thinking she was a joke. That night he found new respect for her. Dressed in full uniform, Liz approached the first one from behind, and with one swift move, laid him flat on the ground. He came down with a *"thud"* totally stunned. Hitting the ground his eyes got big. She turned him over, straddled him to cuff him when the other guy saw what happened and laid into Liz. Are these two guys now on the same team? Big mistake! The minute he grabbed her, she responded. In no time he was on the ground next to his partner/opponent. Laying there all he did was groan. He wasn't expecting Liz to take him down. Alcohol supplies a person with lots of false confidence. It wasn't long before both were handcuffed.

Ernie's cleared out, patrons wanted to witness all the excitement. This never happened in Emerald! And no one had any idea of what Liz was capable of. Tonight, the citizens of Emerald would see what a top-notch law enforcement officer they had.

When both were cuffed, Liz got up to receive a round of applause from the spectators. She took down both these *"bozos"* without breaking a sweat. Some hair fell over her eyes, but she brushed it back with a serious look on her face, at first.

Standing up, she gave a smile of appreciation to the crowd and said in an official, yet amusing way, *"Just doing my job. Nothing to see here folks, just move along."* These guys would spend the night in the town jail. Bud's view of a female *"Barney Fife"* was gone!

The excitement over, it was time for Ernie's customers to return to discuss and embellish what took place. This would be the topic of conversation for months to come.

# Chapter 106

Pete, Darrell and Bud stood there with mouths agape. This little brunette single-handedly took down two guys trying to *"beat the hell"* out of one another. Bud had a new appreciation for Liz and had second thoughts pulling anything when she was around. The trio spent the rest of the night drinking beer and eating pizza... and, most of all, behaving themselves.

Fred and Ginger had fun with their girls. Emily enjoyed tagging along. They looked up to her and she soaked it all in. They all met up with Jeff and Anita around 10:00 p.m. and decided to call it a night. Emily and the triplets were a little sad, but their drooping eyelids indicated they weren't going to last much longer.

Jake walked Arlene home for the very first time that night. Arlene didn't live far from all the excitement. They walked through the darkness talking and enjoying the evening. The moon was full and the sky, clear. Away from the carnival lights the stars were more visible. Casually swinging their arms, their hands brushed against one another. The first time by accident, the second was intentional and they were holding hands. Another milestone has been met. Isn't young-love great!

Bud, Darrell and Pete are the last to leave Ernie's. Bud wondered where they could get more beer. Pete took care of that problem, *"We got a couple twelve packs at home."* They staggered toward the Franklin's home, talking about the evening events.

Sitting on the lawn they drank and talked. They lived in the bad part of town, where houses looked abandoned although still inhabited. No one ever took care of them. They all needed paint. Porches needed repair and shutters barely hanging on. Somehow the tornado of 1986 missed this section of town.

*"You guys know anything about this gal I met ... the one with the money?"* Bud asked plopping down in a chair and opening a beer. He looked at Darrell first who was kind of in a stupor. Then he looked at Pete who wasn't as bad. Pete was always more talkative.

*"Who you talkin' about?"* Pete asked.

*"That broad I met in Alcoa."*

*"Oh, you mean Bernie..."* and then Pete caught himself. *"Uh... No, come to think of it, don't know who it could have been."*

*"You said her name was Bernie?"*

*"No, I was thinking of someone else."* Pete tried to cover his tracks, sorry he let it slip.

*"Well, Bernie or whoever, she has someone else she wants me to kill."* Bud wanted to see the reaction that the brothers might have. He wasn't disappointed.

*"Really?"* Both brothers were surprised. They couldn't imagine who it might be. Killing someone was serious business. And it was really out of their comfort zone. They didn't mind getting involved in some shenanigans but taking a person's life—that wasn't for them.

*"Yeah, but she never said who. She just said this person was really bad."* The brothers were relieved. At least whoever Bernie had in mind was not a good person. At the same time, they couldn't imagine who it would be. Who was so bad Bernie would want them killed?

They had been drinking but this line of questioning sobered them up enough to keep their mouths shut. The next morning, none of them remembered much about the night except for Liz taking down those two brawlers. All three woke up in the front yard as the sun shined in their eyes. Beer cans and bottles were strewn all over.

Unattended weeds hid most of the mess.

No one ever walked by their place, so few saw the pitiful condition. People avoided this neighborhood. There were a couple of cars that did drive by. One was a cop car. Liz pointed her spotlight at them passed out in their chairs. Didn't faze them. The alcohol wiped them out. The other car was Bernie's. Her plans for Bud's next victim were taking shape.

Bernie's plan would be poetic justice. The anniversary of Gloria's murder was coming up on the Fourth of July. If everything went according to schedule, Emerald would lose another leading citizen this Fourth if Bud agreed and she was willing to pay the price. He did, and she would.

## Chapter 107

"*And so we meet again."* Bernie was anxious to tie up the loose ends and be done with face to face encounters with Bud. This *"cloak and dagger"* activity left her uneasy.

*"Yeah, I've been thinking about what you want. How much you willing to pay?"* Bud felt he was in control looking at her with a cocky attitude. The amount better be good if he was going to do the job.

Licking her lips, she proceeded, *"I will give you $10,000 now and another $10,000 when the job is done."* There was no indication it was negotiable.

Bud was taken back at the amount. *"This must really be someone bad!"* He couldn't imagine having that much money!

*"It is, you interested?"* Bernie was getting impatient. She wanted this deal sealed.

*"I guess."*

Bud received a picture of the *"would be"* victim, and instructions on when and where it was to take place. Looking at the picture he had second thoughts. This person didn't look mean or bad or anything like he was told. *"You want me to kill …? You must be crazy."*

He always tried to justify his actions. It eased his conscience. At least it was that way up until Gloria. Even there, he justified what he did to make himself feel better. If she had just done what he told her to do, she would be serving drinks to this day. She made that fatal move. It wasn't his fault. It was hers.

Seeing the picture Bud wanted to think about it. He needed

time. He felt uneasy. Bernie advised him not to take too long. She wanted the job done on the Fourth, just a few weeks away. If he wouldn't do it, she would find someone else.

*"Uh, I'll get back to you."* That is where it ended.

He went to see the Franklin brothers. He needed to process this request. He wasn't planning on telling them anything more about what he was asked to do. The fewer people who knew, the better. The brothers were sitting on the front lawn in old lawn chairs missing a few straps. They each held a beer ... not their first.

Bud drove on the lawn close to the brothers. Pete gave him the *"stink-eye."* Pete was still hurting from getting shot. He would have a scar the rest of his life courtesy of Bud. Because of that scar the cops kept a suspicious eye on both brothers.

Without asking, Bud took the dilapidated steps up to the porch and into the house to get a beer. They heard the fridge slamming shut. He stood on the porch looking at the neighborhood. Opening his beer, he walked down the steps. He pulled up a chair and lit a cigarette blowing the smoke in Pete's direction. He sat down next to Darrell. He got along better with him than with Pete. It was quiet for a long time. The three just sat there. Bud was thinking, mulling everything over. Darrell sat with one leg over the other. Pete was bothered by mosquitoes more than the other two.

Three beers later, the conversation picks up. But the beer is gone, and they are still thirsty. Pete is designated to make a beer run. Bud wants to talk to Darrell alone.

*"Well, she, or whoever, wants me to do another job."* Bud is anxious to talk after Pete leaves. He doesn't waste any time.

*"What kind of job?"* Darrell really doesn't remember the other night.

# Chapter 108

Bud gets closer to Darrell. *"There is someone else I'm supposed to kill. Don't you remember? I told you about it the other night."*

Darrell is shocked, but Bernie seems to be capable of anything. Nothing was really going to surprise him. Darrell pretends to remember. *"Oh, yeah, yeah, I remember now. Who is it this time?"* trying to fake it.

*"Don't know the name. I feel kind of funny killing this person. Something just doesn't add up. What do you think?"*

Darrell asked, *"Well, how do you know who the target is?"*

*"Got a picture."* Bud pulled the picture out of his pocket sharing it with Darrell.

*"No way! You can't do it! You just can't! Tell ... tell Bernie to go to hell!"* Darrell was so upset that he used Bernie's name. Darrell knew the target, and this was going too far.

Bud was surprised by Darrell's response but had to admit he felt the same way. Still, the money looked good. And this would be the last time he would ever do anything like this. Little did he know, according to Bernie's plan, it would be the last time Bud did anything. Bernie planned on killing him after he did the job. It would look like an accident. But no one would know anything more.

Darrell shook his head, telling Bud again and again he couldn't do it. Bud told him to keep it to himself. He didn't want anyone else to know. Just then Pete returned.

The night ended shortly after that. The three managed to put down about seven beers between them before Bud left. Pete was sleeping in his chair and would wake up there in the morning. Darrell was still putting things together. *"Would Bud do the job?"* He hoped not.

The week of the Fourth is busy at the store. The sweet corn is not quite ready, but watermelons are popular and in good supply. The weather is cooperating. Few clouds in the sky and the threat of rain is nowhere in the forecast. The Fourth was on a Thursday this year so everyone got a day off in the middle of the week.

# Chapter 109

Fred gassed up the pontoon Wednesday afternoon. He knew there would be a long line the next day. This Fourth was going to be like most others. Fred, Ginger, Jeff and Anita would spend much of the day on the lake. The guys would do a lot of snacking. Anita and Ginger, clad in bathing suits, would talk and sunbathe. Ginger, absorbing all the sun she could—Anita being very careful not to burn. Towards evening they would come ashore to pick up the kids to enjoy the fireworks sitting on the lake.

This year one extra would join the group. Jake invited Arlene to see it all from the middle of the lake. Arlene would soon be turning 15, one step closer to dating. But there was one problem as far as Jake was concerned, guys were starting to notice her, and he didn't like that much. He didn't appreciate competition.

The fireworks were spectacular. Bernie watches from the lounge. She has been there since 8:00 p.m. She parked her car across the road a little ways from *The Dock*. It was the perfect spot to *"accidently"* pull out and run Bud down after the job was completed. She is nursing a Manhattan to provide the courage she will need. She has never done anything like this before.

The fireworks come to an end and people begin to leave. An instant crowd tries to exit all at once. Bernie bides her time, no rush at this point. The action she wants to see is yet to happen. Seeing Fred's pontoon come to shore, she leaves for her car.

*"I hope Bud is careful,"* Bernie thought. *"He better follow my directions to the letter. If he does... it won't be long, now."* She mixes in with those leaving, trying not to draw attention.

Fred has his own parking space and reserves the space next to his for the Emeralds. Both families call it a night. Before they get in their vehicles, Ginger and Anita head for the restroom as they always do. It is on the outside of the restaurant. Bernie counts on that. In just minutes Gloria's death will be avenged. Life will be a little sweeter... for Bernie.

The traffic is lighter now. Most people are home or on their way. Bernie sits in her car observing Bud making his way toward the restrooms. He tries not to arouse suspicion. Wearing what she told him, his right hand in his pocket holding onto a loaded pistol. He is about to make the full $20,000 promised. He rounds the corner and is out of Bernie's line of sight. She is a little nervous about that aspect, but it couldn't be helped.

An exhausting day, Anita and Ginger are tired. It was fun, as usual, but tiring. One last stop and then off for Emerald.

*"Arlene and Jake make such a cute couple."* Ginger comments entering the restroom.

*"I know, and I am so happy for him. He is really coming out of his shell. He says he is looking forward to school starting. He will be able to spend more time with Arlene."* Anita talks to Ginger openly after having to be quiet for so long since Arlene and Jake were on the boat.

The conversation continues. *"He has really opened up to you."*

*"Yeah, I never expected that to happen. But there are times when he still gets very quiet."* Anita confessed.

*"Ready to go?"* They head for the restroom door. They have no idea of what awaits them outside.

Bud took his time. No one is around to witness his actions. His breathing is heavy as he puts his hand on the door. Still, he hesitates, preparing to enter the restroom. He hears something and is spooked but decides he is just a little jumpy. *"Let's get this over with,"* he thinks. Gun drawn he proceeds.

# Chapter 110

Bud had to talk himself into it. It wasn't easy, but, he was committed. He parked Pete's Harley between rows of corn in the field close to the Alcoa turnoff. It is somewhat hidden. Bernie told him to borrow it to make his getaway easier and faster. Bud didn't know that if the plan worked out, there would be no getaway for him. He would be the victim of a fatal accident. A motorist would hit him as he ran across the road. Bernie would be that motorist.

And so, Bud waits. He waits for the fireworks to end. Cars leave and at first there is a long line. Cars creep along, spectators making their way home. This is the closest thing to a traffic jam most of these people will ever see. It takes a while for people to exit the state park. For those on the lake, it is perfect timing when they finally dock. Fred pulls up to his private entry to tie up his boat. Everyone begins to disembark.

The traffic is lighter now. Bud watches to catch an opportunity when Anita is alone. He sees her, and another woman go around the corner. This doesn't complicate things. He will take Ginger out as well if he must. That is probably what will happen. He has no qualms about that. He makes his way across the road. Grasping his pistol, he gets close to the restroom door and can hear them talking inside. He looks around. He presses against the door.

Hearing the hand dryer, he knows where they are in the restroom. He removes the gun as he gets ready to take his fourth—maybe fifth life. No one is around. No one will see him. He is hoping that his hood stays in place. His hands are sweaty. Another $10,000 is coming his way! He is about to enter the restroom. What he does will be done behind the door—perfect. This might be easier than he thought. Could be that their bodies won't be discovered for a while. His getaway will be even more successful. He feels good with these new thoughts.

Then he hears the words, *"DROP YOUR WEAPON!"* It is not a whisper. It is a command he isn't expecting. He stops dead in his tracts. He doesn't move. Where is that voice coming from? Who is there? He recognizes the voice but can't remember where he heard it. It is female. He gets a stupid puzzled look on his face.

Again, the command is repeated but with added authority, *"POLICE! DROP YOUR WEAPON ... NOW!"* Bud must decide. What will he do? Should he drop his gun and put his hands up? He doesn't know for sure who is giving the command. Who is it? He decides he has come this far; he is not going to back down. And besides, it is a female's voice. There wasn't any female he couldn't handle. He was sure of that.

Liz Jackson has been patrolling the lake area. She remembers what happened last year at this time. Gloria Pearson's murder hadn't been solved. She didn't want a repeat, so she kept an eye on everything and anyone looking suspicious. Bud fit into that category.

Earlier she noticed Bud out at the lake. She was surprised to see him by himself. She first noticed him going into *The Dock*. She hung around but then moved on. Closer to evening she noticed him again. He was still alone making him look more suspicious. He was up to something. She kept a close eye on his movements.

She parked her car down from *The Dock* and staying in the shadows spotted Bud crossing the road. She wondered what was going on. As he was looking around he pulled something out of his pocket. She followed him. As he went around the corner of *The Dock* he was out of sight for a moment. She moved quickly not wanting to lose him. Bernie would have seen Liz following Bud had not a car's headlights blinded her as two cars met, and drivers talked for a moment.

Three shots are fired ...two at first... then a third... and finally a fourth. Bernie hears them and wonders, *"Why did it take four shots? One would have done it at such close range. Well, at least she is good and dead. Maybe Ginger is also. So what!"* Now it was her turn to get her hands dirty. She tensed up. She turned the key in the ignition and waited for Bud to dart out onto the highway. She had to do it. This was the plan. *"Come on Bud. What the hell is taking you so long?!"*

Bud turned around too quickly. He goes for it. Nothing is going to stop him. His plan is to take *"whoever"* is giving him orders, completely by surprise. He turns and then remembers where he heard that voice. It is Liz Jackson's voice. He is committed and doesn't have time to stop. While she might be good at martial arts he has his gun ready to fire. With his gun drawn, Liz's L.A. training tells her to fire. And she does. She fires two shots hitting Bud in the chest. He winces holding on to where the shots have entered. But he also fires off a shot before Liz fires another shot that drops him. He is still alive but very weak.

Hearing the *"pops,"* Fred and Jeff stop everything and look at one another. They have no idea of what transpired but are concerned as their wives are not with them. They are familiar with the sound of a weapon being fired. It wasn't fireworks they heard, something else. They tell everyone else to stay where they are while they run to see what has happened.

# Chapter 111

As Anita and Ginger were about to leave the restroom they hear voices outside the door. Someone is giving commands. They look at one another and listen trying to hear what is being said. Then for a split second it is quiet. Two pops go off. Both get a surprised and intense look on their faces. What is going on? Then, a third pop. And with that pop Anita cries out, *"Ouch."* She puts her hand to the place where she felt a sting.

Ginger asks, *"What happened?"* She looks over at Anita who has a surprised look on her face.

*"I don't know, I just felt this sharp pain."* Anita explains holding her side.

Ginger is puzzled as she asks, *"Where?"*

*"Right... here."* Revealing where the pain came from, Anita removes her hand. There is blood on it. Ginger looks at Anita's blouse to see more blood flowing.

*"Oh my gosh, Anita, you're bleeding."* And then Anita falls to the floor, passing out. Ginger screams, *"Anita! Anita!"* She doesn't realize Anita has been shot! Ginger pulls up Anita's blouse to see what has happened.

Liz has Bud Cross on the ground. He is still alive but fading. She throws his gun to the side and calls the Highway Patrol for backup, requesting an ambulance. She hears panic in the restroom as Ginger screamed. Liz makes sure Bud is secured and then proceeds into the restroom. She fails to notice a bullet hole in the door. She will discover it later.

Entering she sees Anita on the floor, blood streaming from her side—Ginger right next to her. *"Is she alright?"*

Anita is alive, but her condition is uncertain. Ginger goes into *"nurse"* mode putting pressure on the wound, trying to stop the bleeding. But the blood flows regardless.

Fred and Jeff come around the corner to see the activity. Bud is on the ground. They smell gun powder in the air. They see Liz kneeling by someone as the door is propped open. Coming to the door, Jeff sees Anita unconscious on the floor, blood all over the place. The confused look on his face is only a minute part of the feeling in his gut. What has happened?!?!?!

Ginger becomes very professional at this point. She may be holding the life of her dearest friend in her hands. She yells at her husband, *"You and Jeff need to get out of here, NOW!"* She surprises herself at giving the command. *"Now—GET OUT OF HERE!"* Knowing Ginger is serious they leave. Liz backs up the command Ginger gave.

Bernie sits in her BMW across the road wondering what has happened. She can't see anything. She is waiting for Bud to come out, so she can run him down and be done with both him and Anita for good. But Bud doesn't show. Did he find another way of escape? She starts to look around to see if he might have come out some other way. She is baffled. But she is not going to leave until she has done what she needs to do. Tonight, Bud must die. That is her plan. The car is running. *"Where are you Bud?"*

The terrain is flat around the lake. The main highway is visible for miles. When emergency vehicles arrive, it is no surprise. Bernie sees flashing lights but can't tell if it is the Highway Patrol, an ambulance or what? Before long three patrol cars are at the scene along with an ambulance.

Bernie is nervous. She turns off the engine. Curiosity is getting the better of her. She wants to know what happened. She wants to know who the ambulance is for. Is someone only injured? Did Bud mess up this simple job? The paramedics get out removing the gurney from the back. Bernie stays in her vehicle straining to see and not miss a thing.

Bernie isn't going anywhere even if she wants to. The Highway Patrol blocks the road. This is now a crime scene. Bernie might even have to explain her presence. For right now, she crouches in her car, watching the activity. It is killing her not knowing.

Another ambulance arrives. *"Now what is going on? What has happened? Why two ambulances?"* Bernie's mind is clicking along, working through every possible facet of what might have taken place. She can't come up with anything...for certain.

One of the gurneys is wheeled out. She can't tell who is on it. There is an oxygen mask over the face of the victim. Everything moves too fast. *"Get out of the way so I can see!"* Bernie thinks. Too many people in the way. Patrolmen along with Liz Jackson are milling around. Doors are closed. The ambulance takes off.

A second gurney is brought out much slower. Lights aren't flashing as this one leaves. This person is in a body-bag. *"Who is it?"* Bernie is dying to know. Does it contain the body of the woman she hates; she despises? Does it hold the body of Anita? Maybe Ginger? It couldn't be Bud. Who is inside?

# Chapter 112

Bernie couldn't see Jeff getting into the first ambulance with Anita. They take off Anita on the gurney unconscious. Paramedics watch her vitals and treat her accordingly. The bleeding hasn't stopped but her breathing isn't impaired. Ginger wanted to go along but seeing Anita in good hands, Ginger knew she was needed in taking care of Jeff and Anita's children.

Entering through *"emergency"* they waste no time rolling Anita into surgery. Jeff watches her go through the double doors. He stands alone in a daze. Hands on his head he wonders what has happened and why? What was going on? All he knows is that his beautiful bride has been shot and once again her life is in danger.

Bud Cross lays on the ground, still conscious but it doesn't look good. Liz questions him on why he was there and what he was going to do. Nothing made sense at this point. Was he stalking someone? And if so, who was it and why? Surely, it wasn't either of the two women in the restroom. Why would he be interested in them? Why was Bud there?

Bud can feel that *"life"* is leaving him. He isn't in much pain but knows he isn't going to live much longer. He can feel it. Liz tries to find out as much as she can. Bud wants to cooperate. He wants to end his life in as positive a way which even surprises him. He tries to talk. She senses his minutes, if not seconds, are numbered. *"Bud, why were you out here? What were you up to?"*

His answer is slow and deliberate. *"I was... hired to ... kill...."*

*"Kill who?"*

*"The... blonde."*

*"The blonde? Anita? Why would he want to kill Anita? Did he want to kill Anita?"* Nothing made sense. *"Why would Anita have any enemies at all? Especially someone who would want her dead?"* Liz will keep asking questions as long as Bud can respond. *"Who hired you to kill her?"*

Bud opens his eyes and starts to move his lips but can hardly speak. He puts his lips together and says, *"Ber...."* Empty eyes indicated he was gone.

*"Ber? What was he trying to say?"* Liz doesn't have any answers, but she has a feeling who might. Time to pay a visit on the Franklin brothers. She feels that if anybody knows something, it will be these two jerks.

They opened the road after the second ambulance took off. When Bernie got the opportunity to leave she took it. This evening didn't turn out the way she thought. She didn't know what to do. But her curiosity was getting the best of her. Should she go to Alcoa and find out who was alive and who was dead? How would she do it? She wasn't sure. She decided she had to find out and drove in that direction.

As the area around the shooting is vacated, Liz heads back to Emerald. Her first stop: The Franklin brothers. They are sitting in the front yard. Liz approaches them in a very professional manner.

Seeing Liz walk over they straighten up in their chairs, not sure what they have done or why she is there. They always feel guilty. Pretty late in the day to get a visit from the cops. *"What can we do for you officer?"* Pete is the first to say anything. He doesn't know a thing about what happened.

*"Got some bad news for you boys. Your friend died tonight out at the lake. It looks like he was trying to kill someone. You know*

*anything about that?"* Liz questioned.

*"Our friend?"* Pete looked alarmed and confused. Darrell was the one who loaned Bud Pete's bike. Pete didn't even know it was gone.

Darrell added, *"Who would that be?"* trying to act cocky.

*"Bud Cross."* Liz looked straight at Darrell to see any reaction.

Darrell gets a surprised look. *"Bud's dead? How did that happen?"*

*"He pulled a gun on me. I told him to drop his weapon and he turned and aimed it at me."*

*"You shot him?"*

*"Yeah, he left me no choice. Before he died he said he was hired to kill someone. He tried to let me know who hired him but couldn't tell me who. You guys got any idea who would hire him to do such a thing?"* Liz knew that one or both probably knew something. She wanted to find out what it was. She didn't want another unsolved crime on her hands.

Neither of them said a word. Then Pete gave Darrell a questioning look and Liz knew something was up. *" What is going on guys? You know something. What is it?"* Still, neither said a thing.

Pete looked really scared but didn't say a word. He looked at Darrell again and then looked down at the ground.

*"You know, there was someone else that was shot tonight, looks like it was a stray bullet that hit her. They took her to the hospital. We don't know what her condition is."*

*"Who was it?"*

*"Anita Emerald."*

*"Oh, no!"*

Liz could tell both brothers were bothered by this but now they were stone silent. *"You sure you don't know anything about this?"* The brothers sat there looking stunned. *"If you decide you know something, let me know."* Liz got back in her patrol car and sat there for a moment looking at them and hoping that one of them would come over and talk but neither did. She left.

# Chapter 113

The area around *"Emergency"* has a number of vehicles in it. Ambulances are empty. Their passengers are inside. Some are receiving minimal treatment, waiting their turn. Others, like Anita, are rushed into surgery. Bernie pulls into the parking lot still wondering what she should do. Sitting in her BMW she weighs her options. She thinks it through. She has to make the right comments, ask the right questions. She finalizes her plan and heads for the entrance.

*"Excuse me. I think a friend of mine was in an accident earlier this evening and this might be the place where he was brought. I was wondering if you could tell me."* The receptionist is a man and Bernie put on the charm along with a concerned look. She is used to wrapping men around her finger. She sees this guy as being a pushover.

*"What was the person's name?"* The receptionist gives a look of concern.

*"Name?"* She should have expected that question. She had but it still startled her. She would be admitting she knew him. Of course, she knew him. After all, she said he was a *"friend." "His name is Bud Cross."*

The receptionist knew immediately what to do. If anyone came in asking about Bud, he was to contact the Highway Patrol. But he didn't want to arouse suspicion. *"Let me call to find out who was admitted and what their condition is."* He made the call. What Bernie didn't know was that the call was received in the emergency area by Officer Michaels, Iowa Highway Patrol.

Bernie stood by the receptionist's desk. *"Someone will be out to give you his condition in just a minute. Would you like to have a seat?"*

*"No, thank you. I think I will just stand."*

Bernie didn't have to stand very long. She paced the floor until Officer Michaels came around the corner. She wasn't expecting him. She was expecting a doctor or someone who worked in the hospital—not a police officer. She lost a little color in her face.

*"Are you the one asking about Bud Cross?"* Officer Michaels was very solemn, not knowing what to expect. Bernie could be a relative for all he knew.

She couldn't lie about it. The receptionist, not far away, heard the request and knew why she was there.

*"Yes, how is he doing?"* Bernie gave a look of concern.

*"Are you related to Mr. Cross?"* Officer Michaels starts to ask questions.

*"No. Uh ... I'm just a...um...just a friend."* Bernie had a difficult time finding the right words.

*"Might I ask, 'How do you know him?'"*

Again with more questions! This isn't as easy as Bernie thought it would be! *"Actually...well...I would see him in the bar every once and awhile. And...uh...well, I saw him tonight out at Jewel Lake for a while and then I was looking for him again and I heard there was some kind of accident and wondered, you know...well, is he here by any chance?"* She wanted to get this over with. She was very uncomfortable. *"Just give me an answer,"* she thought.

He responded, *"I'm afraid he died, ma'am. I'm sorry."*

*"Oh. No! How did it happen?"* Bernie tried to reveal some emotion but wasn't sure what kind to show. She needed more details.

Did Bud say anything before he died? Did he say anything that would incriminate her? And then, what about Anita. She was dying to know what, if anything, happened to her. Was she alive or did Bud come through with his part of the bargain?

# Chapter 114

Officer Michaels was a 25-year veteran and could tell by her body language and responses Bernie was more involved in what happened than she was letting on.

*"Ma'am let's go over and have a seat."* They both went to a secluded area. *"He was shot by a police officer. He had a gun and it appeared he was about to use it to commit some kind of crime, possibly hurt someone else."*

*"Oh, my!"* Bernie tried to act surprised. It didn't work with Officer Michaels.

*"Do you have any idea about why he would want do such a thing?"*

*"Oh, absolutely not! I wouldn't think Bud would ever want to do such a thing or hurt anyone. He was such a nice man as far as I know."* But she couldn't leave it there. She had to go on. *"Did he end up hurting anyone, you know, shooting somebody? I can't believe he would ever do something like that. He didn't seem like that kind of a guy."*

*"Yes, he did. Actually, it seemed like a stray bullet got her."*

*"Her?"* For the first time there was a glimmer of hope for Bernie. Maybe Anita had been shot. Maybe Bud had done the job.

*"Yes, a woman by the name of 'Anita Emerald,' happened to be in the restroom and she was hit with what appears to be a stray bullet."*

*"Oh, dear, Anita was shot? How is she?"*

*"You know her?"*

Oh, this was just too good. Bernie thought she could show some sorrow to reflect how sad it was that Anita was shot. And she could do it in front of some law enforcement official. He could testify she was filled with grief and totally surprised as well. *"She was a classmate of mine; we went to school together...how is she? Tell me she is okay!"*

*"She is in the operating room right now."*

Well, Bernie's questions had been answered and now she wanted to get out of there as soon as she could. She didn't appreciate all the questions asked and Officer Michaels was making her nervous.

*"How was it you knew Mr. Cross again?"* Officer Michaels asked the same questions to see if answers ever changed.

Bernie appeared to be upset about Anita and waterworks started as she cried. *"I'm sorry. I can't talk anymore. Poor Anita."*

*"That's okay. If I need to talk to you anymore where can I reach you?"* Bernie gave her phone number and address. Officer Michaels gave her his card, if she should remember anything important. Bernie was out of there like a shot!

# Chapter 115

The minutes ticked by. Jeff sat in the waiting room, his head in his hands. Then he got up and walked around. He watched the clock. He watched the door. He never got far from the door. His beloved had been shot—*been in the wrong place at the wrong time*—that was his summation. He had no idea she was fortunate, just to be alive! She had been the target! It could have ended differently. Instead of the operating waiting room he could be home thinking about a funeral. That still might be next!

The night drags on, the operation continues. Anita has lost a lot of blood. The bullet has been removed. She is lucky the bullet went through the door before hitting her. The velocity was reduced, and it was a lucky, or unlucky, shot, depending on how you looked at it. He just pulled the trigger and that was it.

The bullet had done some damage and stopping the bleeding was proving more difficult than expected. The entry hole was so small. If Anita lived through the operation she wouldn't have much of any scar… *IF* she lived. The surgical team was doing its best but there were no guarantees.

Officer Michaels contacted Liz Jackson to let her know about one *"Bernadette Carlson"* that had visited the hospital asking about the deceased Bud Cross. He gave her the details of the conversation and Liz had someone else to interview. This was the second Fourth of July where a shooting had taken place. Was this just a coincidence? Maybe. But it was highly suspicious.

Fred and Ginger didn't get any sleep that night. They spent the night at the Emerald's home. Their triplets didn't mind sleeping in Emily's room with her. The kids didn't know the full extent of what happened. Fred and Ginger tried to figure it all out themselves. Nothing made sense. They were waiting to hear from Jeff, waiting to hear if Anita was okay. But Ginger could only think about all the blood she saw. Ginger knew it was serious.

This was the second time Jeff was in the hospital finding himself in prayer concerning Anita. *"Why was it taking so long? How bad could it be?"* Jeff feared the worst. He started thinking of what life would be like without her. Ginger knew it was serious. She wouldn't have yelled if it weren't bad.

In the operating room no time is being wasted. Anita's condition worsens as they try to stop that stupid bleeding. Then the frightening words, *"We're losing her!"* The surgeon looks up. *"Blood pressure is dropping!"*

Jeff stared at the door waiting for someone to come and tell him how Anita was. And then the door opened, and he wondered if he wanted to find out. *"Please let it be good news. Please!"* he prayed.

What if his wife had died? He didn't want to hear that news. He didn't want to have to deal with his wife being killed.

Two people came through the door. One was the hospital Chaplin who just came from a family that had lost a teenager in a tragic accident. The Chaplin meant to be with Jeff much earlier but couldn't get away. He happened to meet the surgeon leaving the operating room and they walked out together. It didn't look at all positive to Jeff. The surgeon looked tired. He gave a blank expression squeezing his eyes at the bridge of his nose. He pulled off his skull cap. There was blood, Anita's blood, on his surgical gown. He didn't say anything right away. The Chaplin introduced himself and put his hand on Jeff's shoulder. Again, not a good sign.

The room was empty except for Jeff. *"Are you Mr. Emerald?"*

*"Yes, how is my wife?"*

The surgeon lifted his eyebrows and gave a sigh. Both Jeff and the Chaplin were waiting for his answer.

# Chapter 116

Bud showed the picture of Anita to Darrell that night. Darrell knew Bernie hated Anita and was almost *"psycho"* about getting rid of her. He never thought she would go this far. And he wasn't sure what Bud would do. This just wasn't right. The next night, after a few beers, he told his brother, Pete, and Pete got very nervous. He hated Bud and wasn't going to let Bud or Bernie get away with it.

*"I got something to tell you, okay?"* Pete finds himself where he never thought he would. He is looking down, hands in his pockets. He looks very nervous.

*"What is it Pete?"* Liz asks.

Pete stares at Liz wondering what she will do when she hears the news. *"I think I know what happened."*

*"What happened? What do you mean? You mean with Bud?"* Liz needs a little clarification.

*"Yeah, with Bud. I didn't think he would do it. I thought … I mean if I thought he would do it I would have told you."* Pete acts nervous and shakes a little. He feels guilty and scared about what he has started to say.

*"Told me what?"*

*"Oh, boy. This is bad. I'm not in trouble, am I?"*

*"Tell me what you know, and I will tell you if you're in trouble or not."* Liz is getting frustrated.

He started to spill his guts, but then suddenly shut-up before he said too much. He thought he might need a lawyer. *(Good call idiot!)*

When the lawyer arrived he and Pete talked for around 30 minutes. Liz then continued to question Pete who was very cooperative. Of course, there was going to be immunity if he shared everything. It became interesting when Bernie's name was mentioned. Pete explained how Bernie hated Anita and had it in for her after Bud shot Gloria.

*"Bud Cross shot Gloria?"* This was the first Liz heard of that although she suspected it for a long time.

*"Oh, yeah... he did. I was right there and saw the whole thing."* Pete got caught and didn't know what else to say. He decided to just let it all out and it felt good to come clean.

With this information Liz decided to contact Officer Michaels and share with him the information she received. The two of them talked and decided to pay a visit on Bernadette Carlson. Liz and Officer Michaels, each driving their own vehicles, pull into Carlson Estates.

They drive up to the address Bernie gave and ring the doorbell. No answer. They look in the windows and don't see any lights on. They walk around the side of the house and see nothing. No one is around. They ring the doorbell again. They pound on the door. No answer. Bernie isn't there.

Officer Michaels put out an APB. If anyone caught her license plate, he would be notified immediately.

Bernie decided it was time for her to *"get out of Dodge."* After her visit to the hospital she went home, packed a few things and took off. She wasn't sure where to go but knew she couldn't stick around. She thought she might look too suspicious. But what really looked suspicious was her leaving. Her first stop would be Minneapolis. She still had her penthouse apartment there. She went there to get away to think. That is what she told herself.

She needed to contact her lawyers. She wanted them to know what might be coming, at least give them a heads up someone might be looking for her.

Her next stop would be her sister's. She called her first to find out if it would be okay. No problem. Bernie was going to disappear for a while. It might have worked if she wasn't such a high profile. The owner of Carlson Industries couldn't just disappear. The corporate headquarters and Bernie's Minneapolis apartment were of great interest.

The Minneapolis PD put both under surveillance. On Bernie's way to the airport to fly to her sister's she was stopped. She got no further.

# Part 6

# The Future

# Chapter 117

Bernie Carlson would ultimately be charged with the murder of her husband. Her trial would take place in Hennepin County, Minnesota, where the murder occurred. It hit the papers big time including *The Emerald Examiner*. George Plummer was having a field-day getting the story out.

The little town of Emerald had a lot of activity, with reporters coming and going. Bernie's picture was seen on local news. But the hoopla didn't last long.

It would be a while before the trial would begin. Evidence would be collected. Both of her henchmen, Pete and Darrell, would be questioned, take the witness stand. Pete, of course would be immune from prosecution.

But an interesting twist surfaced. The new assistant District Attorney for Hennepin County would do the prosecuting. New in town this would be his first case. He had been working in Manhattan but longed to return to the Midwest where he grew up. His roots were in Emerald as well. And he knew the accused a little better than he wanted. He wondered if he should recuse himself or not. If he didn't and lost, it wouldn't look good. But he decided to go forth regardless. Seeing the evidence and knowing the person accused he was confident of a conviction.

And the news hit the papers. The prosecutor in the case of the state of Minnesota versus Bernadette Becker Carlson just had a nameplate affixed to his office door. It read *"Charleston David Becker,"* Bernie's estranged brother.

Back in Alcoa it was still a waiting game. Jeff sat hunched over in his chair, elbows on his knees holding his head in his hands. He couldn't believe how his life had changed in the last 24 hours. The Fourth of July was a beautiful day spent with family and friends. Life was good for the Emerald family and then everything fell apart. They did what they had done so many times in the past. What happened? And why did it happen. Now his future was so uncertain. His mind was going in a hundred different directions. What was he going to do? How would he continue without Anita?

And then he hears movement. He looks up to see two blue eyes barely opening and the heaviness of his heart is lightened. He has new hope thinking he won't have to continue without Anita. She tries to readjust herself in the bed and then cries, *"Ouch!"* She has pulled at the area where the surgeon had been working hours before. Then she notices the IV. She looks at it and then at Jeff once again and with dry lips she struggles to say, *"What happened?"* before falling asleep again.

Filled with renewed hope Jeff sits at his wife's bedside certain in his heart she is going to make it.

And so, the little Iowa town of Emerald will not lose any more of its population... today. And Jeff and Anita Emerald will move forward with their beautiful family. But on the horizon, a couple new teachers will be arriving in Emerald and both will have an impact on the Emerald's. One, especially will have an attraction to Anita. But that is all part of another story, ***Diamond.***

# About the Author

Rev. Larry L. Hintz is a retired Lutheran pastor living in Grand Chute, Wisconsin. Growing up in a small town in Iowa, his desire through the Iowa Gem Series, of which Emerald is the first novel, is to paint a picture of a small rural town and its people and situations which is different from the way most communities in the Midwest have gone.

Made in the USA
Monee, IL
19 January 2021

56095661R00187